M.E. Ellington and Steven Ellington

The Bradbury Farm: Thirstonfield Halt Book Two

www.mess-flicks.com

Paperback ISBN: 9798656328159

Proofreading by Melanie Lonsdale. Layout, Formatting & Cover by Martyn Ellington. Editing by Martyn Ellington & Steven Ellington.

www.martynellington.com

www.stevenellingtonspiritualistmedium.com

DEDICATIONS

M.E. Ellington.

To the readers who continue to crave new adventures, new journeys of discovery, and new literary heroes and villains - I thank you.

Steven Ellington.

To all those who dare to seek, investigate, study, chase, and search for all that is above and beyond the widely accepted, assumed, confirmed, and established conventional reality of this world. God bless you all.

<u>ACKNOWLEDGMENTS</u>

We wish to express our sincere thanks to Mel, Ollie, Andy, and Sharon. Our eclectic group of readers for helping with this novel.

M.E. Ellington:

I would also like to thank someone who I will never name or thank personally for giving me an insight into what made these two titles work and to the guy who cut me up at the lights in the black Audi. You sir, are a douche!

Also, I'd like to thank my children, without whom this book would have been completed much earlier…

Steven Ellington:

To all those who have impacted my life in a positive way, thank you. You have inspired me, enlightened me, motivated me, and above all else, blessed me with intense light faith and optimism.

I would also like to thank all those who have impacted my life in a negative way, thank you also. You have forever reminded me not to be like you, and your dislike has done nothing but tempered my sword of determination to attain life fulfilment.

Prologue.
The Bradbury Farm.

The Bradbury farm was much like every other farm found in the beautiful and remote, North Yorkshire Moors. Nestled in a shallow valley near the small village of Thirstonfield between the industrial town of Middlesbrough and the achingly picturesque fishing port of Whitby, the farm had been in the Bradbury family for one previous generation before Thomas Bradbury and his wife Anne – who were now into their late forties - had taken it over following Thomas's father's death after his mother had died a few years previously. Over the years they had built a life and a family on the farm, with their only child and son George. Whilst farms seldom made people rich the Bradbury farm did enjoy the additional income from, British Railways who rented the land that held Thirstonfield Station, as well as the land on which the line ran. The station itself had begun its life as a lowly Halt - a small service stop, for the people who worked and lived in the local area, including the farmers and people of Thirstonfield Village and the Thirstonfield Estate workers. Demand for the Halt had grown with the increasing numbers of people who travelled to the coast for their holidays as well as the need to transport goods, equipment, and personnel during the war. With the demand growing and the Halt itself expanding into a fully-fledged station, the rental income had also grown. Something the

Bradburys' had welcomed.

The Bradburys' themselves were much as you would expect them to be. Modest hardworking Yorkshire folk – country bumkins as the locals would describe themselves. Thomas had made some changes to the farm since taking it over, such as an internal bathroom, something of a luxury to some, but Anne had deemed it a necessity. Thomas had also extended the electricity supply to include external yard lighting and lights inside the barn, workshop, and farmhouse, replacing the oil lamps his father had insisted were used. Whilst some modernisation had been brought in, for the most part the farm was very much how anyone would picture an early twentieth century farm. Thomas had an older brother who had taken on a farm of his own with his wife a few years back. Found on the other side of the valley - closer to the market town of Stokesley. Thomas had a good, albeit often intermittent relationship with him. For the most part life was simple and rewarding.

That was until Thomas had found Jack Bright laying in the field on that summer day. After that, nothing – it seemed – could take them back to how things were before that chance encounter.

November 1946.
The Bradbury Farm, North Yorkshire.

The storm was hitting hard. The high winds and strong driving rain meant that no work could be carried out on the farm. In the distance thunder could be heard rumbling across the moors. By late afternoon - as the sun began to retreat - Jack found himself in his bunk. The sound of the thunder, wind and rain lashing the side of the barn brought with it the flashbacks that haunted his dreams. The sounds of the storm took him back to the war - to Holland and the foxhole he'd hidden in. He curled up on the bed, grinding his teeth and banging his fists against his head – trying in vain to alleviate the pressure which built inside his mind.

The door opened. It was Anne. Seeing his torment, she ran to the bed and sat beside him. She grabbed his wrists, restraining him while calmly speaking his name over and over. As Anne cradled him, she wasn't to know that Jack had mistaken the kindness she'd shown him since his return from the war as affection, and that in Jack's mind at least, these attempts to calm him, along with the physical caresses were clear signals of sexual attraction and craving. Nor was she to know what Jack had done to his mother, Doris, or that the red mist had returned and had control of him. As she comforted him, he struggled to keep from giving in to the same impulses which had taken over him that night. He fought those desires for as long as he was able to. But as the soft light illuminated Anne's form through her wet clinging dress, he lost what little control he had. Jack sat-up and took hold of her arms. Standing, he spun Anne around and pushed her down onto the bed. With one large hand holding her down, he unfastened his trousers. Anne pleaded with him, begging him to stop, but Jack tore her clothes from her. She yelled for Thomas, who was only yards away in their farmhouse, but the storm drowned out her cries. As the rain battered the side of the old barn Jack spun her around. With her cries now muffled by the bed sheets, he entered her. With his lust for the feel of a woman around him unsatisfied since that night he'd violated Doris, he let go what little restraint he still had. Moments later, and as lightning lit the foreboding night sky and thunder vibrated through the air Jack ejaculated, and in his euphoric state he let go of her. Anne scrambled from the bed. Distraught - her clothes shredded – she ran through the storm and back to the farmhouse.

Moments later Thomas burst into the bunk house, his shotgun pointing at Jack. As another crack of thunder split the air Thomas fired. The buckshot exploded from the gun, but Jack had already moved, and he was only grazed. He fired again – and missed again – his hands trembling with the emotions of what had happened and the struggle in his mind of taking someone's life, regardless of the heinous crime they had committed.

Jack saw his chance to escape. He pushed past Thomas, thrusting the shotgun barrel up as he did. Another volley split the air. The roof of the barn exploded in shards of splintered wood. As Thomas loaded another shell Jack made his escape.

With one shell loaded Thomas turned, his hands clasped tightly around the gun. He fired blindly into the darkness, only guessing where Jack may be. The shotgun illuminated the darkened doorway as another flash of lightning illuminated the farmyard for the briefest of moments. But Jack was gone. Thomas let the gun slip from his hands, dropping it onto the wet floor, its barrels smoking. As the sound of the rain began to fill the air, replacing the sound of the shotgun, he turned back to Anne and held her. As thunder rumbled in the distance, they both looked out into the darkness. They knew Jack was out there, but they didn't know where, or if he'd return.

Chapter 1.

I

Two weeks had passed since the storm, and since the night Jack had fled into it after committing the worst crime a man could against anyone and especially a woman who trusted him and believed him to be a friend. Anne had not spoken of it since that night even though Thomas had tried to reassure her - as best he could - that everything would be fine. He'd told her Jack had fled and would not come back. Yet Anne would not leave the house after dark and insisted that the shotgun remained loaded and by the door. She had withdrawn into herself and spent the days staring out across the farmyard whilst Thomas carried on with the duties demanded by the farm, and his love for Anne. In part at least, he blamed himself for taking Jack in, and for trusting him. He wondered – when time allowed – just what the events had been throughout both of their lives for them to meet when they did. Why his farm? For this reason, while Anne retreated Thomas threw himself more into his work than ever before. At least this way time seldom allowed his mind to wonder. Afterall, talking about it to friends and family would be almost as bad as the act itself. Anne would be blamed, and Thomas too. These were different times, and the way to deal with this was to bury it, and deny it even happened. Overtime he thought, no he believed – he had to, things would go back to normal. It was for these same reasons they wouldn't report the attack to the police. The only other person who knew what happened that night would surely never speak of it. Would he?

The days and weeks immediately after were difficult ones. Apart from blaming themselves they also blamed each other. Thomas questioned whether Anne had secretly harboured feelings of attraction and lust toward Jack, and that perhaps on that night she'd initiated it, only for it turn violent. He hated himself for these thoughts which often fleeted across his mind while he was alone on the farm. He never spoke to Anne about them, how could he? He knew deep down these were just ugly notions his mind pushed forward. A vent for the frustration and anger he felt toward himself for hiring Jack, and then for missing him when he'd pointed the shotgun at him. Thomas wasn't a violent, jealous, or angry man and that perversely made it much worse - in his mind at least. Perhaps if he had been Anne would not have been so close to Jack and then maybe this wouldn't have happened. Maybe if Jack had seen Thomas lose his temper once in a while then possibly Jack would have feared Thomas and wouldn't have dared to violate their trust in him. He was back to blaming himself and that sat better with Thomas than blaming his beloved wife.

Anne too had conflicting thoughts of anger and of guilt. Anger toward the two men she blamed directly. Thomas for hiring Jack, and Jack for the act itself. Why had Thomas missed from a point-blank range? Was it on purpose she wondered? How could it have been, was always the answer when she reconciled these thoughts. She'd fallen in love with Thomas partly because he was so peaceful, unlike the other men who always seemed to think beating their chests and telling her tales of some *fighting* triumph would impress her - they didn't. But she wondered, if Thomas had been a chest beater, a man with a certain demeanour about him, would Jack of dared to do what he did? But then, is this what she wanted now? A man of anger who would fly into a jealous rage. Why had she trusted Jack so much? How could she have been so naïve? Thomas had warned her not to get too close with Jack both emotionally and physically. But Anne only saw the good in people. She believed that after taking him in and treating him as part of their family he would never hurt any of them. When she had seen him that night, terrified of the storm, curled up on his bunk trying with all his might to shield himself from the noise she only felt a mother's protective love for him. All she wanted was to calm him and reassure him that the storm could not hurt him, and that the German guns of war had long since fallen silent. Not in her wildest nightmares had Anne thought Jack capable of what he did. Her overriding thought of that night kept pushing through. If she hadn't gone to that barn, if she hadn't cradled him. If she'd have been just a little less naïve then maybe, just maybe this wouldn't have happened. And like Thomas, Anne was back to blaming herself.

She would never trust anyone again. Even when long-known friends had visited them since that night Anne had told Thomas prior to their visit that he was not to leave her alone with them. Thomas of course agreed unreservedly with this request and never did.

As another four weeks passed, and Christmas came around Anne began to feel differently. She had known as early as that night that there was change within her. How, she couldn't say. She knew medically there was no way she could feel, let alone know of any changes, but she did know, and she had denied it to herself, even questioning her own sanity. But as the symptoms became more regular and her period stopped, she knew she could no longer deny her own truth. She was pregnant with Jack's bastard child. Anne knew telling Thomas would be as a big a blow to him as what took place that night. She would have to watch him take another hit, which she blamed herself for.

The first signs had begun a week before Christmas - six weeks after that night. Anne had kept them secret. The morning sickness was easy to hide. George, their seven-year-old son and only other child, was oblivious to such things and was spending the first week of the school holidays sleeping until around midday. Thomas – as usual – was up and out on the farm before the need to vomit washed over her. Before the morning sickness Anne had noticed a swelling in her breasts and as it had when she carried George the need to urinate had increased. These were her confirmations after her period had not begun when it should have. The morning sickness was just underlining what she already knew.

It was another week before Anne eventually summoned up the courage to tell Thomas. She wanted to wait until Christmas had come and gone, and the new year had been ushered in. It was also because of what happened the night before George returned to school. That night she climbed the stairs to bed around 9.30. George had long been in bed, but not before protesting that the Christmas holidays were too short. Thomas had fallen asleep in the large worn-out wingback by the fire in the living room. Anne turned off the lamp before she left the room leaving Thomas in a red glow, as the fire he snored deeply in front of, slowly died down. Outside it was a cold night, and Anne knew that once the last embers had extinguished and the room became cold Thomas would wake just enough to climb the stairs after her. Anne had gone to bed knowing the time to tell Thomas was here. She ran the scenario around her in mind as she lay staring up at the once white ceiling. It was then she heard it. A heartbeat inside her. She held her breath, listening. There is was again Anne gasped and sat bolt upright. She held her abdomen tightly. The doctor had told her when she fell with George that the foetus' heart would be developed by this stage and would be beating but she knew it was too small and weak to be able to hear it. Yet there it was. An internal sound, but nonetheless audible to her and louder than her own heart which was now beating considerably quicker than it usually would.

Then silence. Nothing but the sound of her rapid breathing. Was the foetus dead? She wondered. Had that heartbeat been so loud because it was the last-gasp efforts of a dying heart to keep going? She wanted to call for Thomas, but she couldn't, not yet, she hadn't told him. She lay down and slowly pulled the covers over her body, suddenly remembering just how cold this night was. Eventually, though she can't remember when, she fell asleep. Her mind spiralling with the thoughts of that sound and whether she'd imagined it, or not.

The following morning Anne waited until George began his walk to school. He'd called goodbye as he pulled the heavy farmhouse door closed behind him. Anne, as always, shouted back after him, "Goodbye George, love you." Thomas had been out tending to the cattle sheds since around six. He used George's departure for school, at around eight-fifteen, as his first break point of the day. A breakfast of bacon, eggs, black-pudding, and fried bread. All washed down with a strong, sweet cup of tea. He waved to George as he passed him across the darkened farmyard. January, in this part of the world was still somewhat dark at this time of the day, but there was enough ambient light for George to make his way across the yard without stepping into anything he'd rather not trudge through the school. George, as always, waved back to his father and smiled. Neither said anything. The smile and wave were enough to convey their *manly* love and admiration of each other.

Thomas entered the farmhouse, taking off his boots as he did. Stepping into the kitchen he smiled at both the warmth he felt and the sight of Anne who was – as always – preparing his breakfast. He sat at the table and poured a cup of what Anne called *builders tea* into the large green tin mug George had got him for Christmas. Adding a little milk and sugar, he took a gulp and sat back, warming his hands close to the open fire. Anne plated up his breakfast and brought it over to the large wooden table. She placed it in front of him, sitting opposite him as she did. She watched for a moment as Thomas cut into the cooked breakfast before taking a bite. Then she spoke. "I've summat to say Thomas," she said nervously but resolutely. "It's about that night." Thomas placed his knife and fork on the table. A look of worry came over his face. Anne hadn't brought it up directly for some weeks. It was referred to of course, and some of their routines and habits had changed. But Thomas knew if Anne was bringing it up directly, it wouldn't be good. He took another gulp of the tea, washing down the mulch that had been his breakfast. "Go on, wife."

"Well, there's no way of saying this easily, so I'll not beat about the bush. I'm pregnant. And that's that. Nowt we can do other than get on with it." Anne's shaking voice betrayed the confidence and sternness her words tried to convey.

Thomas sat back in the chair, placing the mug on the table. "You're sure?"

"Aye, I am." Anne replied directly.

"And you're sure it's..." Thomas stuttered. He was having difficulty saying Jack's name. He took a deep breath, "You're sure it's his - Jacks?"

Anne reached across the table and squeezed Thomas's hand. "I am Thomas," A tear formed in the corner of her right eye. Anne sat up straight, wiping it clear and taking a deep breath. "But it'll not be *his* child. It will be ours, just as George is."

Thomas squeezed her hand in return and smiled. "Aye, it will wife. As far as folk know, we've been blessed with another child to carry on the farm. It'll never know I'm not its real Da."

"That's the point Thomas, you're its real father." Anne's smile slipped away as her hand did from Thomas's. Then standing she turned back to the range and began moving the greasy heavy pans into a large sink of hot soapy water. Thomas returned to his breakfast.

II

Over the course of the next few weeks as January gave way to February, and the sound of the heartbeat returned. Anne knew by this and how she felt that night she'd first heard it, it was not the sound of a heart in the last throws of death. Rather, it seemed it was getting stronger and louder. By now Anne and Thomas had told their close friends and what remained of their respective families, but she hadn't told any of them of the heartbeat she could hear some nights, or the movement she'd began to feel as February came in. She knew they would dismiss this, and it could draw unwanted attention. That in turn could somehow unravel the whole chain of events and they would find out it wasn't Thomas's baby she was carrying, but that of a farm hand who'd now left. Of course, her closest friends and family would believe what happened, but her fair-weather friends and the village gossips would put two-and-two together and get five, as usual. There would be whispers of an affair gone wrong, of poor Thomas being cuckolded and that would lead back to school, and to George. Anne had long since decided that no matter what unusual symptoms presented, she would keep them to herself, and that included Thomas. He'd been through enough. If he felt she was in danger he may panic and tell the midwives, or insist they travel to the hospital in Middlesbrough. A place Anne didn't like. It was far too busy, she didn't much care for the locals and nor was she keen on the journey.

The winter months, as always, gave way to March and the weather began to change for the warmer lighter days of Spring. They'd be somewhat lucky. The loss of livestock they always endured during the harshest of winters had not happened this time, even though this winter would be recorded as one of the harshest. Thomas had planned well ahead, mitigating the worst of the affects. For the most part life had returned to normal. They'd told George he was to have a baby brother, or sister. George of course wanted a brother. The thought of sharing a bedroom with a girl repulsed him. He wanted a brother he could play with. Football, cowboys and

Indians, and hide and seek were all top of his list once his sibling was old enough. The farm was a huge adventure playground for George and now he would have someone to share it with. He prayed nightly for a brother, and insisted his mam only ever drank tea and not that awful smelling coffee. His friend Sam had told him that drinking tea was sure to give him a brother. This must be true, Sam's dad had told him that's why he was born a boy, and Sam's dad knew everything!

Anne's weight gain had begun in February, and her bump was now quite noticeable. She had become less withdrawn as the lighter and warmer days came in. The dark brooding skies of the winter had made Anne feel that Jack could be hiding in one of the many darkened corners the farmyard offered but as the weather warmed and the routine of lighting fires in the house was replaced by the opening of the windows and doors allowing the stale dank air of winter to be substituted by the fresh warm air of Spring Anne felt a renewed sense of optimism. So far, the pregnancy was textbook. Other than the heart beats, there was nothing she felt the need to be concerned over. As for the heartbeats, Anne had now pretty much convinced herself that they were just tricks of the mind. And given the situation, and how the pregnancy had come about, surely, she was entitled to some sort of an episode – wasn't she?

As April rolled in and Anne entered the second trimester the lambing season was well under way, which as usual took up most of Thomas's time on the farm. After the experience with Jack, both Anne and Thomas had agreed that they would not hire any help again. The trust they'd once had towards strangers and casual help had been stripped away from them by his repulsive act. This perhaps was one of the biggest legacies of that night, apart from of course what had taken place, and the impending birth. During her visits to the midwives, they had taken guesses at what sex the child would be. So far it was split seventy-thirty between a boy and girl. Whilst Anne believed silently that she was carrying another boy. With the lack of hired help, George was drafted in, though he protested frequently while explaining to his parents that "At 7-years of age, I shouldn't be working, it's no fair!"

April the 28th had been a normal Monday. George had welcomed school that morning after working for much of the weekend on the farm, helping his dad with the new-born pigs. They'd eaten tea – shepherd's pie – and then retired to the living room while outside the last of the April showers freshened the evening air. Around eight George had gone to bed and as was normal, Thomas settled in the large wingback with his paper. The country was still in the early stages of recovering from the war. Money was tight and rationing was still very much a part of everyday life. Earlier that day Anne had made the trip to Thirstonfield Village after George had left for school and had been lucky enough to get the rations, she needed for their tea from the local butchers; Harry and Lucy. This was partly because Thomas supplied them with meat from the farm and because George was friends with their daughter, Mavis. At around half-nine Anne was too fatigued to stay up any longer. At this stage in her pregnancy – around halfway through – the demands of the baby inside of her were increasing daily, and her blood supply had increased to satisfy this demand. She could feel the baby move around and her *bump* was becoming *very* visible. She remembers climbing into bed, but she wasn't sure what time she'd fallen asleep, or what time Thomas had come to bed - she only remembers waking to find him next to her asleep.

As Anne lay in the dark, a pain came on suddenly. A sharp piercing pain which drove through her. She screamed in agony, clutching the bedsheets as her hands made fists. Then she felt a warmth between her legs. Her right hand scrambled for the bedside lamp. Pulling the chord, the bedroom illuminated. By now Thomas had heard her screams and was awake. Anne pushed her right hand between her legs and brought it back. It was saturated in her blood. "Get me to the hospital!" Anne mumbled through the excruciating pain which now radiated around her body. Thomas lept from the bed and pulled on the trousers and a jumper he'd discarded over a chair when he'd come to bed in a sleepy haze a few hours earlier. As he helped his stricken wife from their bed George burst into the bedroom, his mam's screams had woken him too. "What's wrong, Ma?" He asked, his voice allowing his fear and concern to radiate through his words. "I'm fine son," Anne tried to reassure him. But George could see his mam clearly wasn't fine. As Thomas lifted her from the bed George could see the dark red stain soaking into the white bedsheets, and the dripping red liquid which left a trail across the floor as Thomas carried

Anne through the house and to their truck. George stood in the kitchen, terrified and with no idea what he should do.

Thomas turned to him as he made the door. "Clean up the mess son. Don't want your Ma' to see that when we get back, we'll be home soon." George nodded, "Will do, Da." With that, his mother and father disappeared into the night outside. George watched as the door slowly closed behind them, the small metal strike clinking as the latch secured it. Then he heard the truck engine, and the whine of the gearbox as they drove away. In the silence, and with his mind still scrambling over the last few minutes, George turned and made his way to the washroom to retrieve the bucket and mop.

III

In the passenger seat of the truck Anne held her stomach tightly. She'd felt no movement since the pain had started. She put her hand between her legs, and it seemed, much to her relief, that the blood had stopped coming. Thomas wrestled the old Bedford truck along the winding country lanes which would eventually lead him to Middlesbrough and to the General Hospital, located in the village of Linthorpe. "Hold on Anne, we'll be there in no time," Thomas reassured her. He smiled as best he could at her whilst saying the only words of encouragement his bewildered mind could assimilate into a coherent sentence. Anne grimaced at the continuing throbbing nature of the pain. Though time seemed to have stood still from the moment this began Thomas was pulling the old truck into the hospital car park before she was aware of her surroundings. He rushed around to her side, shouting for help as he did. Flinging the suicide door open, he helped Anne out of the truck as a nurse and orderly appeared with a wheelchair. "It's my wife, she's expecting, and she's began t' bleed," Thomas barked at them frantically. They helped Anne into the chair and then sped her into the hospital where the nurse stopped Thomas's ingress any further. "You stay here sir; we'll call you when we know what's happened." She said, firmly, yet softly. Thomas - disarmed by her composure and obvious authority, nodded as he watched the orderly, over the nurse's shoulder, disappear with Anne into a side room.

Thomas sat on one of the many chairs in the waiting area. His elbows resting firmly on his knees while his hands cradled his head. He looked up at the large clock which seemed to tick louder now he was focused on it. 01.35. am. He sighed and stood. The need to get rid of the *pins & needles* in his legs urging his exhausted body to move. A thousand thoughts ran around his mind. Not least of which was his need to be back at the farm. The lambing season was not yet over, and he couldn't afford to risk losing any of them. *I should have told George not to go to school today,* he thought as he paced along the dark corridor. Their decision to not hire help this year was taken for obvious reasons. But he knew it could put them on the back foot. They could lose animals, crops, and then orders from the butchers and shops they supplied. Not to mention their own family demands. Once that happened it would be impossible to catch back up without hired help, and he knew Anne - at the moment anyway - would not entertain such a thought. A voice brought him back to the hospital. "Mr. Bradbury?" A nurse, younger than the previous was calling him. "Are you Mr. Bradbury?" She asked.

"Aye. How is she? How is Anne?" He answered impatiently.

"Your wife is fine; you can go in if you please."

Thomas nodded and smiled as he walked past her and into the small side room. Inside he found Anne laying in a single bed. Crisp white sheets were pulled up to her shoulders. She looked beat, but otherwise better than he'd expected. He sat next to the bed taking hold of her hand. "What did they say?" Thomas asked, removing his flat cap, crumpling it into his coat pocket.

"They don't know what it was. The doctor's examined me, and checked, the baby is fine."

"You had me scared for a while there, wife." Thomas dared a moment of levity and even a smile.

"Aye, had ma-self scared too tha knows," She smiled back. But Thomas could tell it was a tired smile, and one which had taken some considerable effort. Anne continued, "You should get back to the farm – and George. No need you staying here, nowt you can do."

Thomas knew she was right. He would only be in the way, and he had to get back to the lambs, and George. "Ok, I'll be back later when George is home from school." He stood and kissed her on her forehead. "I'll see tha later." Anne let go of his hand and nodded before closing her eyes. He watched for a moment as she drifted off to sleep. Then, as quietly as he could, he left the room and made the drive back to the farm.

Daylight had broken by the time Thomas pulled the truck into its usual resting spot. He entered the farmhouse to find George asleep at the dining table, and the blood stains cleaned from the stone floor. Even the blood-stained bedsheets were soaking in the wash bucket next to the sink. Thomas smiled to himself and then woke George from his slumber. Groggy, and wiping his eyes clear of sleep he smiled at his father, and then noticed his mam was not with him. The smile disappeared. Thomas recognised George's confusion.

"She's fine lad. Just resting at the hospital for the day. We'll go pick her up later. You go catch some sleep, ya can stay off school today. Help me around t' farm." George nodded and hugged his dad before heading upstairs.

The day moved along without further incident. Though George sometimes wished he'd gone to school given the tasks he'd been given. The lambs were doing well, and the cattle all seemed fit and strong after the winter. Thomas dared to believe that things may now be *on-the-up*. Before it seemed reasonable that a day had come and gone, it was time to visit Anne. George was keen to go get his mam from the hospital, but not before Thomas insisted that he and George changed out of their dirty clothes. "I'm not taking you looking like that," Thomas had shouted at George as he climbed the stairs to change. Adding "You're like some waif." George hadn't argued the point; he was too eager to make the visit to Middlesbrough and see his mother. The old Bedford truck wasn't really built for three even though it did have a bench seat, so it wasn't often George was included in trips to the big town. Once he was judged old enough to remain at the farm, he was usually left behind.

Thomas closed the kitchen door behind him and climbed into the truck to find George waiting excitedly. "C'mon then lad, let's go get your mother," Thomas said, as he started the truck.

When they arrived in the room where Thomas had last seen Anne, she was sat up - smiling as they entered. George rushed over to her and hugged her.

"How ya feeling?" Thomas asked, pulling George back a little.

"Aye, much better. The baby's moving and the doc's checked the heartbeat which he says is strong."

"So, you can come home?" Thomas asked, smiling with relief.

"Aye, seems so," Anne answered, adding "But I've to take it easy. So, you'll need to help mummy," Anne said looking directly at George, who smiled back nodding enthusiastically.

The doctor entered the room, dressed in the familiar and somewhat reassuring white coat – complete with stethoscope hanging around his neck. He turned to face Thomas directly, "I've checked your wife over Mr. Bradbury and can find no signs of anything amiss. I'd say she is clear to go home, but she's to take it steady."

Thomas nodded and stretched out a hand, which the doctor shook firmly. "I'll see she gets the rest she needs doctor," Thomas replied, with the respect a doctor would normally receive.

For George at least the ride home wasn't as comfortable as the ride to the hospital. With Anne somewhat larger than she was the last time all three were in the truck together, George was relegated to the back. His travelling companions were largely made up of empty sacks and wooden crates, as well as the remnants of everything else Thomas had carried in the back of the truck since they'd managed to buy it. Once home, Thomas insisted that Anne take the large wingback next to the fire. Though the fire wasn't lit, this chair was the most comfortable and supportive. He switched on the wireless and made her a large, sweet brew.

Chapter 2.

I

Anne was now in her third trimester and the physical changes to her body which she saw every day, along with the vivid dreams which seemed to now come with increasing regularity reminded her of that night, and of Jack. Thomas hadn't made any references to the night for as long as she could remember. He'd promised her when the pregnancy became known that he wouldn't. Internally however, he did continue to battle with the thoughts which sometimes became dark. His memory and imagination seemed to gang up on him. He saw fleeting glimpses in his minds-eye of Jack and Anne fucking consensually. His large hands gripping her hips from behind her. But these were always replaced quickly by the thought of what took place. The consensual sex replaced by Anne's screams for help, while the looks of pleasure on her face were replaced with looks of fear and revulsion. Thomas didn't know how long these thoughts and images would stay with him. He had no one he could ask, and nowhere he go for comfort and council. He knew Anne was the victim and he felt positive that whatever he felt, she felt it worse by a magnitude he couldn't possibly fathom. And yet, he couldn't talk to her either. Perhaps, once the baby is born these thoughts and images would disappear.

As the summer rolled through and the workload on the farm increased. *Making hay while the sun shines* wasn't just a saying in these parts - it was a way of life and survival. The village of Thirstonfield depended on the local farms for their produce all year. Food was, back then, very seasonal - the way nature had intended it to be. Summer fruits and crops had a short life span, and Thomas had already begun to plan for the autumnal crops which would hopefully see them through the coming winter. But as the season ran through, he was falling ever further behind. He hadn't the desire to bring this up with Anne because the only way to arrest it was to hire help, and that question had been asked and answered passionately. He worried not only about their own winter food stores but also what long-term economic effects it would have on the farm.

But even taking this on board, he knew Anne still wouldn't bear the thought of strangers on the land, especially if they had returned from the war like Jack. So, it was for this season at least, largely Thomas and when he could convince them, their known friends and family. Though his reasons why they weren't hiring extra help with the coming harvest were becoming ever more tenuous each time he was asked. His go-to was always costs and money, but even that was starting to raise questions. "I'll need to tell them summit wife," He once complained to Anne, secretly worried about their future as well as the farm, but she wouldn't hear of it. "Ya can't tell the truth Thomas. Ya just can't!" she'd replied, shouting him down. Thomas knew she was right, of course. They were too far in now to announce what had happened. And nothing about the outcome of telling the truth had changed. In fact, it would now be much worse. And so, Thomas continued to lie and bluster his way through the continual questioning of his farm management. But he knew that the farm would continue fall further behind unless he could convince Anne to let him hire the additional help he would need to secure the food stores for the winter, especially as there would now be another mouth to feed. Perhaps he would try again closer to the birth of their child. Anne, or more accurately the baby, was due August 11th according to the doctor's and the date Anne had given them of the night the baby was conceived. Since the scare back in April the pregnancy had largely gone smoothly.

As July rolled to an end Thomas decided to let the beef herd go, though he would keep a couple of dairy cows and one bull. He simply no longer had the hours in the day to tend to them, and because of this they were becoming a drain on the rest of the farm's finances. He wouldn't tell Anne of his decision until she asked, and by then they would be gone. Besides, the sale income would see them through the winter when added to the quarterly income from the railways he would receive at the end of October. After that there would be no further income again until the spring. Even with the harsh winter last year their coal store was still around half full, and that at least meant that now Thomas was turning his attention to the coming winter their outlay wasn't going to be high as usual. The sale of the herd also meant that the last of the baby supplies would now be affordable. Though he had a suspicion that would outweigh any savings on the coal they didn't need to buy.

At around two-thirty in the morning Anne woke to the baby kicking. The pain her body had blanked out after George had been born returned sharply, and with it the memories of what happened next. It was August 10th, 1947. "Thomas, it's coming, the baby, it's coming!" Anne shouted as she roused Thomas from an exhausted sleep.

"Ok, I'll get dressed." Came the half-asleep reply.

"I don't think there's time for a journey to the hospital Thomas," As Anne spoke her waters broke.

Thomas jumped from the bed. "I'll get towels." Thomas left the bedroom and headed for the airing cupboard. As he did, he shouted George to get his arse out of bed. When Thomas came back into the bedroom, he found Anne on her back, her legs raised and open and the bed sheets kicked onto the floor. She was breathing hard, beads of sweat formed on her head. Thomas placed the towels as delicately as he could between her legs, ready to catch the new-born when it made its entrance. George entered the room, entirely unprepared for the sight which would meet him. Thomas turned to him, "Get to Doc Brown's. Tell him ya Ma' has gone into labour, and be quick on your toes lad," George scurried out of the bedroom.

Small villages like Thirstonfield all had their own

local doctor. He was normally a man of age and had delivered and buried someone from every family in these small communities. When a new, younger doctor came along, he would always and without exception work alongside the trusted and prevailing doctor. Not because the new *doc* wasn't qualified. It was simply because the community had to get to know and trust the newcomer.

Anne felt the need to push. She gritted her teeth and bore down. Thomas doused her head and tried as best he could to keep her calm, though his expertise was with livestock. But even Thomas, a hardened Yorkshire farmer, knew to change his bedside manner. Doc Brown arrived a little after four. George and Thomas were then ceremoniously barred from the room, much to George's relief. He'd helped with the lambing and that in itself had given him reason enough to chuck-up his breakfast on more than one occasion. The thought of seeing his mother go through it wasn't worth thinking about. Thomas paced nervously in the small parlour which was located directly under their bedroom. The screams and mumbles of pain were both audible and nerve-wracking.

In the bedroom Doc Brown was fighting to save both Anne, and the baby. The baby was in breech, and though the caesarean section had recently become a recognised procedure Doc Brown, as well as the rest of the medical fraternity, hadn't adopted it as the model when the baby was in breech. And besides, the risk of attempting such a tricky operation in a dimly lit bedroom would increase the risk beyond what it already was. He instructed Anne to turn over and to get onto all fours. Grimacing through the pain Anne did as she was instructed.

Downstairs in the parlour Thomas had heard the difference in Anne's cries. The sound of the pain had also become a sound of fear. Thomas instructed George to wait in the kitchen. Then he climbed the steep stairs. At the top he grabbed hold of the door handle and then stopped. His instinct to burst in was now in conflict with the Doc Brown's orders for him to stay out. But after that night, he couldn't simply ignore the cries which now reverberated around the small farmhouse. Anne cried again. It was enough for Thomas to be jerked into action. With no further thought he twisted the doorknob and entered the bedroom. The sight which met him shook him. Anne was on all fours with Doc Brown behind her, his hands covered in blood which ran down her legs and onto the bed. Doc Brown turned around. "Thomas get out, I need to concentrate." He barked.

"What's wrong, doc?" Thomas returned.

"The baby is in breech. Now out and close the door behind you!"

Thomas backed out of the room, shaken by what he'd seen and what he now knew. He'd lost more breech births with the livestock than he'd saved. He knew how risky this was to both the baby and the mother. Slowly, he made his way downstairs and back to George. All he could do now was wait.

After what seemed a lifetime of waiting, he heard

Anne scream and then become silent. Moments later a baby made itself known. Thomas rushed up the stairs before Doc Brown had the chance to call for him. He entered to see Anne sitting upright, holding their new son. "Congrats to you both, he's a fine strong lad." Doc Brown said, as he cleaned down and packed up his bag. "What are you going to call him?" He continued.

Thomas was about to tell Doc Brown they hadn't decided on a name when Anne cut across him.

"He's to be called Arthur, Doctor."

"A fine name. I'll write it in the birth certificate when I get back to the surgery, along with his weight," He checked a piece of paper, "Nine pounds -four." With that Doc Brown left. "I'll see myself out." He shouted as he made his way down the steep stairs.

"I didn't know we'd settled on a name," Thomas said, as he sat beside Anne and his new son.

"It just *feels* right. He looks like an Arthur. Anyway, that's his name now." Anne replied.

Thomas knew not to push this. And besides, he wasn't too bothered Arthur was a good strong Yorkshire name. George appeared in the doorway. "Is it clear, can I see it?" He asked. Anne smiled, and gestured for George to come in. "Aye, come meet ya new brother George. This is Arthur," George gently took hold of the baby's hand a shook it. "Nice to meet you Arthur. I'm your big brother George."

II

October rolled in and with it the darkening nights. Arthur was now a few weeks old and placing all the demands on his parents any child of that age does. George, for the most part, had lost interest in his new brother. The novelty had worn thin - George was impatient for the days when he could play with him. For now, he was nothing more than a small annoying, noisy thing which had taken away his mother's affection and what little time his father had for him.

Following the birth Anne had become more distant. Thomas had noticed a change in her. When George was born Anne had immediately bonded with him. Her love was instant and unwavering. More than that she seemed to have boundless energy to care for his demands regardless of the time of day - or night. But it was different with Arthur. Thomas had on more than one occasions returned to the farmhouse to find Arthur screaming in his crib while Anne just sat and stared at him. Eventually of course, she would nurse him, or change him but not with the love and care she had with George. Thomas worried that Anne didn't love this child because he was, biologically speaking Jacks bastard, but that was not the infant's fault – was it? His intuition was to be around more to help Anne with her duties. Not only to help her but for his piece of mind too. But he couldn't. The demands of the farm were simply too much. For now, he'd have to believe that Anne would not cause Arthur any harm and that eventually, her mothering instincts would come through.

Thomas knew this was always a possibility. That night last November had left its mark on them all but none more so than Anne herself. Perhaps if she hadn't fallen pregnant as a result of Jacks attack then maybe, just maybe, things would now be back to normal. But how could he really expect them to be when every time Arthur made himself known Anne was instantly brought back to that night on November 13th. As he wondered about this while finishing up for the day – which as always meant hustling what livestock they had left back into the barn – he wondered just how Anne would be when that date finally came around. With the last animal inside Thomas turned to leave, but then stopped. In the lowering light he looked to the rear of the barn and the door which led to the bunk Jack had used. Pushing his way through the animals as they bedded down, he pulled open the door and stepped inside. It was exactly as it had been the night he'd sent Jack running. The door on the adjacent wall which allowed access outside without the need to go through the barn was closed tight. He looked to the bed where Jack had attacked Anne and the small table next to it which still had a couple of Jack's personal items placed on it next to the small oil lamp, including a picture of Doris Jack's mother. Thomas pulled on the door, making sure it was still locked – it was – then he turned. Jack's clothes were still neatly folded on the end of the bed. On the opposite wall Anne had placed an old tall-boy for Jack to use and on top of it was jug and basin. Next to it was a child's spinning top. Around the edges were the words "See-saw Margery Daw," Thomas hadn't seen this before, maybe he hadn't taken much notice of anything that night. He looked up to the small hole in the roof where the shotgun had exploded through it. Sighing he pulled a large brass key from his pocket and stepped back into the barn pulling the door shut behind him and locking it. He would decide what to do with all the crap later. Right now, he needed to head in and get cleaned up for tea. With each passing year he noticed the cold nights made his aches and pains worse and come on sooner. A hot bath would soon remedy that.

A half hour later Thomas made is way down the narrow stairs and into the kitchen. Bathed and changed he could smell that his dinner was almost ready. Passing by the living room he noticed George sat listening to the radio and reading a *Beano*. Thomas smiled to himself as he made his way into the kitchen and sat at the large table. "By, tea smells good wife," George said pulling his chair closer to the table, its legs scraping on the flag-stone floor.

"It had better," She answered turning from the stove "Used the last of the minced lamb, doubt I'll get more meat until next week now. We're almost out of tats as well."

Thomas could hear the change in her voice. She sounded tired, almost defeated. "I'll check the stores in the mornin'. See what's what." He tried to reassure her. But her demeanour didn't change. She placed his dinner in front of him and managed only the slightest of smiles.

"I'll go check on Arthur; he's been asleep for a while." She said through a sigh as she left the kitchen.

Thomas finished his dinner and placed the used pots in the large sink which Anne had filled with hot soapy water. He'd not heard from her since she'd left to see to Arthur. Curious, he made his way into the living room. The fire crackled as it gave of its heat and a gentle red glow which softly illuminated the room in the places the small lamp couldn't reach. Outside, the weather had closed in and a thick fog now engulfed the farm. Thomas moved over to the windows and pulled the curtains together. He turned to see George, who was asleep, cuddled up to Anne on the sofa who was also asleep while the radio played in the background. Arthur was in his crib, awake and lying almost perfectly still. Thomas leant over and smiled at him, cooing as he did. Arthur did not respond at all to his father's presence. He just gazed directly at him. Thomas felt a cold shiver run down his back. It felt as though Arthur was staring directly into him. Thomas smiled down at him, pulling his blanket a little further up. Arthur's gaze did not move, and Thomas noticed that all the time he'd be bent over his crib, the infant hadn't once blinked.

Unsettled Thomas made his way back through to the kitchen and cleaned down from his dinner. This, of course, was normally Anne's responsibility but he couldn't wake her just to wash a few pots. Once he'd checked the door was locked, he made his way back into the living room. Switching off the radio, he woke George and Anne and stoked the dying fire down to its last embers. Without saying a word George heaved himself up the stairs and into his bed. Anne gathered up Arthur and carried the now asleep infant up to their bedroom before placing him in the cot. By the time Thomas had made his way up the stairs Anne was in bed and was seemingly asleep. He hadn't heard her speak to Arthur as she carried him up. She hadn't said *Goodnight,* as she always had done with George. Thomas said it for her to the sleeping infant. "Goodnight, son. Sleep well. Everything will be fine in the days ahead lad. You'll see."

As Thomas climbed into bed and pulled the blankets over him, a single tear rolled from Anne's open eyes.

Thomas was woken by the sound of Arthur crying. As his eyes adjusted to the darkness of the small hours he sat up. He looked over to Anne who was sat with back to him at the end of the bed - bending over Arthur's cot. "What's up with him?" Thomas asked wiping his eyes and yawning. Anne didn't answer. Thomas moved toward her, her dark featureless figure in the dim light of the bedside lamp remained motionless. Thomas moved up behind her and placed a hand on her shoulder, still she didn't respond and still Arthur cried. "Wife, what's going on?" Thomas's voice raised a level. This time he tugged on her shoulder. She spun around. As soon as she did Arthur stopped crying.

"He's evil, this one," She said staring at Thomas. Her face full of anger.

"What?" Thomas backed away slightly and climbed out of the bed, standing at the side of the cot. "What do you mean, evil? He's just a bairn," Thomas snapped back.

Anne didn't respond. Climbing back under the sheets she turned her back on Thomas and Arthur.

Thomas looked down into the cot. Arthur was uncovered, naked and clearly cold. His clothes and blankets were on the floor next to cot. Thomas looked back to Anne. As he dressed Arthur and swaddled him in the cot, he wondered if Anne could deliberately hurt their little boy.

The following day Thomas was up and out on the farm before Anne Arthur and George woke-up. As usual Thomas used George going to school as his first break time. He waved as George passed by on his way to school and made his way back into the farmhouse. As he entered, he found Anne nursing Arthur. "How's Arthur this morning?" Thomas Asked.

"He's hungry enough, I'll give him that," Anne replied

"That's a good sign, means he's in good fettle."

"Your breakfast will be done soon enough." Anne announced as she stood and laid Arthur down in his crib.

"That's fine, wife. I've to clean up yet."

Thomas made is way to the sink and cleaned his hands of this morning's farmyard. Then he made his way back to the table and sat waiting patiently for Anne to finish. "So, what was up last night?" Thomas asked as delicately as he could.

Anne turned and brought his cooked breakfast over. "Up with what?" She asked, placing it down.

"I woke to Arthur crying, and you were sat over him. He was naked, no sheets on him,"

Anne looked a little confused. "Are you sure, think you may have dreamt it Thomas. I wouldn't do such a thing." Her response was polite enough, but also forceful enough for Thomas to know he should accept that maybe he had dreamt it. To push it anymore seemed pointless now. He watched as Anne picked Arthur from his crib.

"Time to get this little man cleaned and settled." She said, smiling down at the infant.

Thomas smiled at them both as they passed by. Everything seems fine, he thought to himself, taking another gulp of tea.

III

October 1949.

Arthur was now a boy of two. Things on the farm had returned to as much normality as could be expected given what had happened and the fact that the country - as a whole - was still recovering from fighting the world war. Financially, on the farm at least, things had struck an even keel. Thomas had managed to find a balance that allowed them to keep some livestock for meat and dairy as well as a few agricultural fields. The rental income from British Railways who operated and ran Thirstonfield Halt was a large part of their income, and that too had risen during the war as the station was expanded to accommodate the increased military demands as well as the increase in civilian demand.

Though still mostly housebound – mainly for his own safety – Arthur was now running around freely. George had found a new interest in his baby brother now he was more than a noisy lump constrained to the cot. His dreams of playing with him around the farm now seemed to be coming much closer. He was already able to play some gentler games indoors with him. It seemed Anne too had accepted Arthur. Thomas didn't know exactly when that happened, other than he just kind of noticed it one day. No longer had she been leaving him to cry because he was wet, or had soiled himself, or was hungry. Maybe it was when Arthur began to talk and move around that something clicked, maybe it was before that, he couldn't rightly tell, but for Thomas it was enough that things were at last calmer. And that was good enough for him.

Unfortunately, this calm didn't last long enough. Thomas wasn't sure what time it was exactly when he watched the small police car bounce up the rutted farm track before pulling up outside of the farmhouse. George was in school and that was the first thing that came to Thomas's mind. He stepped out of the pen which held the few pigs they had and made his way over to the police car just as the local officer, who Thomas knew well enough - PC William Dowding - climbed out. Putting on his police helmet as he did. Anne too had seen the approaching car and came outside with Arthur cradled in her arms. PC Dowding greeted them both as they approached, before gesturing that they all go inside. Once inside Anne placed Arthur down and sat next to Thomas at the kitchen table. They could both tell by PC Dowding's expression that this wasn't going to be a pleasant visit. He sighed and then removed his helmet.

"I've come as the bearer of bad news, I'm afraid," PC Dowding announced. "We found the body of your niece, Mary just on the fields between your brothers farm and the pub in Thirstonfield Village."

Thomas gripped Anne's hand tightly. Mary was his only niece to his brother. She was slender, happy girl, loved by everyone who knew her. His mind scrambled to think who would do such a thing. "Do you know who done it?" Thomas stuttered the question out.

"We haven't found him yet, but we have a description."

"What is it? The description," Anne asked.

PC Dowding checked his pocket notebook. "A few people in the pub saw a large man wearing a long coat and hat follow Mary out when she left. Some said the hat was tilted slightly, as if to hide his face."

A cold bolt of lightning struck Thomas. It was Jack. He would recognise that description anywhere. He gulped back his emotions. "His name," Thomas began "Is Jack Bright. He worked here as a farm hand before and after the war." His voice shook as he said his name.

"Do you know where he might be?" PC Dowding asked.

"The last I knew he had a house in Middlesbrough. He would catch the train from the station," Thomas wiped the tears from his face as he spoke.

"You said he used to work for you. Why'd he leave?"

This time it was Anne who spoke up. "He just did.

Said he'd had enough of farm work. Always knew he was a good for nothing lout." Unlike Thomas, Anne's voice carried anger.

PC Dowding stood and replaced his helmet. "Thank you," He paused before he left. "I am sorry for your loss. She was a lovely lass."

Once PC Dowding had left Thomas turned to Anne. "What did I do?"

"Whatever do you mean Thomas?" Anne asked, puzzled by his statement.

"If I hadn't missed that night. If I'd shot the bastard, then, Mary…" Thomas struggled to finish his sentence. He stood wiping the tears from his face, and then continued. "George will be in from school shortly. I best get finished up."

Anne watched as Thomas left the kitchen. She turned back to Arthur who had sat quietly while PC Dowding had visited. She leant forward and picked him up, sitting him on her knee. She sang quietly to him. *"Seesaw Margery Daw, Johnny shall have a new master,"* Arthur smiled.

Later that evening George and Arthur were in bed. Dinner was cleaned away and Thomas and Anne were in the living room listening to the radio. Thomas, as usual, was falling asleep in front of the fire. A mist had rolled in from Whitby on the North East coast. It had rolled across the moors bringing with it drizzling rain, a chilling stiff breeze, and the sound of the passing steam trains. Anne had often commented that on nights like these, when the air was cold and dense and the wind blew in just the right direction, she could hear the huffing of the steam trains, and the train they could hear just now was the last train that ran from Whitby to Middlesbrough, calling at Thirstonfield Halt Station. Between his snoozes Thomas looked to the clock which hung above the mantle and checked it against his own pocket watch. It seemed he was a few minutes out. He pulled out the pin and turned the hands to read nine-thirty, ready for when the mantle clock would chime.

At precisely nine-thirty pm, it chimed, and as soon as it did every clock in the house, including Thomas' pocket watch stopped dead. Thomas looked across to Anne who stared blankly back at him. He stood and made his way into the hallway to check the grandfather clock which had once belonged to his father. It too had stopped at nine-thirty. Suddenly Arthur began screaming, shortly followed by George. Thomas and Anne bolted up the steep narrow staircase and burst into the boys' room. Arthur was sat upright in bed holding his head. George who had screamed in nothing more than a primaeval response to his brothers cries of anguish was now silently watching his brother.

Anne picked up Arthur, "What's wrong son?" Her concern almost tangible.

Arthur began hitting the side of his head. "Head hurts, head hurts," He repeated over and over. Thomas grabbed George and took him downstairs.

Once in the living room he settled George on the sofa and pulled a large woollen blanket over him, "He'll be ok son, just a headache." Thomas reassured him.

A few moments later all was silent once again. As Thomas examined the clock in the hallway Anne came down the stairs. "Is he settled?" Thomas asked.

"Aye, he is. Just woke up with a thumpin' headache is all," Anne turned her attention to Thomas's examination of the clock. "What's happened?"

"Every damn clock has stopped," Thomas felt a chill run down his back making him shake and hunch his shoulders.

"Someone walk over your grave?" Anne asked.

"Aye wife, I think someone has," Thomas replied pushing his watch back into his pocket. "They've all stopped at the same time too. What do you make of such a thing?"

Anne didn't answer. She turned and headed back into the living room. Thomas followed part-way in. "I'm going to check the clock in the workshop, see if that's stopped." Anne nodded as she picked up George, "I'll get this one back to bed."

Thomas pulled on his boots and coat and opened the kitchen door. Outside, the farmyard was engulfed in the mist. The soft yellowish glow of the farmyard lights could barely be seen through the murk which now swirled around. What light could be seen seemed to be diluted by the swirling fog that surrounded it. Thomas reached down and picked up the shotgun they kept by the door and stepped out of the farmhouse, pulling the heavy door closed behind him. The air was thick and silent, save for the distant clanging from the station. Even the animals in the adjacent barn were now huddled together for warmth, sleeping their way through this dank cold night. As Thomas breathed in, his lungs filled with the abnormally cold and damp air and it seemed to him to penetrate every recess. He coughed the damp air out. As he exhaled the thick clouds of his breath seemed to hang in front of him before being absorbed back into the night. He gathered himself together and made his way to the workshop where he kept the modest farm machinery he had and his Bedford truck. Sliding the think wooden door across he entered and made his way through the dark wooden shack which was illuminated by only a single overhead lamp. Navigation was possible, but detailed examination of the shadows and enclaves was not. Thomas wasn't a man with much of an imagination. He had no need for fantasy or thoughts outside of his immediate concerns. But on this night, and after the news that had been brought to him earlier that day it seemed his imagination was making up for lost time. In every darkened corner Thomas imagined that Jack would rise, overpower him, and then slay his family as he now believed beyond doubt, he had Mary. Eventually, Thomas reached the small office at the back of the workshop. He entered and checked the only other clock they had. It too had stopped at nine-thirty. This clock in particular struck a fear in Thomas he had not felt before. Not even on that night. No, on that night it was not fear that coursed around Thomas, it was anger and hatred.

Thomas turned and with his shotgun level and pointing ahead, he made his way out and back across the farmyard as quickly as he could. As he reached the door and the relative safety of the farmhouse, he felt with absolute certainty that just at the point of reaching for the handle he would be pulled back into the mist. Relief finally came when he slammed the kitchen door behind him, locking it and sliding across the thick bolts into their strikes. Gasping, he placed the shotgun down and pulled off his boots. The noise of the door slamming had Anne running into the kitchen to see what the commotion was. She found Thomas sat at the table, out of breath.

"What's up?" She asked, moving to the window, and looking out.

"Nothing wife, I'm fine, everything's fine," Thomas gasped out, and continued once his breath was steady. "No one is to go out there at night. No one!"

Anne nodded and backed away from the window, pulling the curtains across and shutting out the mist as it rolled up against the panes.

Anne watched while Thomas lifted himself from the table and marched through the house, along the hallway and to the front door - they never used. He pulled on it and pushed the already fastened bolts further across. He turned and smiled as reassuringly as he could, but Anne knew Thomas well and the only other time she had seen this way was the last time Jack had been on the farm. "Everything alright Thomas?" She asked, concern growing inside of her.

"Aye wife. Just checking is all. Nowt to be afraid of. I think tomorrow I'll walk George up to the school bus. Give me a chance to talk to him."

Anne nodded and smiled. "Is it bedtime?" She asked, trying to bring some normality back.

"Reckon it is, the day's done. I'll see to the fire. You get yourself up."

Anne began climbing the stairs while Thomas made his way into the living room. There he peered once more through the curtains before stoking the embers of the fire and turning off the lamp. After checking both doors once more, he made his way to George and Arthur's bedroom. Both boys were asleep. Thomas pulled their door closed and then climbed into bed next to Anne.

"Thomas," Anne whispered.

"Aye, wife."

"I haven't heard the train leave, have you?" Anne asked, half asleep.

Thomas paused. He'd heard the usual faint noises

from the station when he'd gone outside, but he couldn't remember hearing the usual heavy huffing of the train pulling out of the station. "Reckon we just missed it. Nothing to worry about," He reassured Anne.

Anne turned over, pulling the thick blankets up to her neck before closing her eyes. "That's probably it." She replied, almost asleep.

Lying awake until he could keep sleep away no more, his mind continued to scramble about the clocks. Especially the workshop clock.

IV

The following morning, the mist had dispersed, and the air had been left clear and sweet. As if it had been cleansed. Thomas walked George as far as the main road, where he met up with his friends to complete the rest of the walk to school. He didn't mention the clocks or Mary to him. The Bradbury's weren't an especially close family. Some factions hadn't spoken in some time, and while Mary's murder at the hands of Jack had hit Thomas and Anne hard, George was only a boy of two years when he'd last seen her. At some point he would of course tell him. He'd have to because there would be a funeral to attend, but for the time being Thomas figured it best to keep from mentioning it.

It also meant that Thomas would need to go and see William, or as he called him Bill - his older brother. This he worried about more than telling George. Not because he and Bill didn't get on, quite the contrary, it was because Thomas and Bill weren't what you would call open and comfortable with their personal feelings. Life on the North Yorkshire moors was a beautiful and almost idyllic one, but it was also a hard one. There was little time to explore your feelings and thoughts. It was simply a skill they hadn't the time or need to develop growing up. Still, once he had the farm *started,* as Thomas titled it, he would make the journey to Bill's small farm on the other side of Thirstonfield Village.

It was a little after eleven when Thomas watched the small police car pull up. Thomas was in the workshop working on his truck. The damp air last night had gotten into the ignition system preventing it from starting. Thomas, as always, had lit a small fire under the sump to warm through the oil and engine block, while the HT leads and coil, he'd removed, dried out and warmed up on top of the small paraffin heater he kept especially for this task. He put down the oily rag after wiping his hands as best he could and made his over. "Hi," Thomas shouted, making his presence known. It was, PC Dowding again. This time however Thomas noticed he had a bandage and dressing across his nose and cheek.

PC Dowding turned toward the voice and waved. Thomas stretched out an oily hand, which, PC

Dowding took and shook before realising just how dirty it was.

"What happened to you?" Thomas asked, pointing to the medical dressing.

PC Dowding rubbed it. "Can we talk inside, it's about Jack Bright," He asked as he pointed toward the farmhouse.

"Aye, if we must." Thomas turned and led the way.

Entering the kitchen Thomas found Anne at the table feeding Arthur a mixture of boiled vegetables. He smiled to her as he gestured for, PC Dowding to sit at the table.

"PC Dowding says he's info on Jack," Thomas announced. Aware that he'd caught Anne by surprise.

Anne took Arthur from the table and set him down on the floor. Then, she moved over to the stove and placed the kettle back over it. "It's just boiled," She said, nerves clear in her voice. "I'll make us a cup of tea first."

"I'm ok, thanks." PC Dowding replied.

"No, we'll have a cuppa and that's it settled." Anne replied, sternly.

Neither PC Dowding nor Thomas responded. Rather, they sat patiently until Anne poured the re-boiled water into the tea pot before setting it down on the table with three mugs, a jug of milk and a small caddy of white sugar with a single small spoon stuck firmly in the middle. "Just let that mash, while I see to Arthur," Anne ordered, placing a tea-cosy over the pot. Turning, she picked up Arthur and put him into his playpen. Immediately Arthur sat and began playing with an assortment of toys. Without saying anything else Anne then poured the now strongly brewed tea into the three mugs before adding just enough milk to make it drinkable. "Sugar?" She asked, PC Dowding.

"No, thank you." He answered.

Anne placed the green tin mug in front of Thomas before adding what sugar they could spare. Serving herself last, she sat opposite the police constable and took a deep sip of her tea. "Go on then, what have you got to tell of him."

"Before I tell you what I've come here for, I need to ask more about him," PC Dowding said, pulling out his notebook. "I need to know as much as you can remember about him."

Thomas and Anne looked at each other - it didn't go unnoticed by PC Dowding. Thomas took a deep breath.

"I first spotted Jack lying in one of our fields, before the war. I knew he was running from summat, but I never asked what. We were shorthanded, you see, and I could tell by his build he'd be a good worker. So, we offered him a place to stay and a job on the farm." Thomas took another sip and continued.

"Everything was fine. He began to open up about his home life, and he mentioned his mother worked in the station at Middlesbrough.,"

"Doris?" PC Dowding asked, checking his notes.

"Aye, that's her. Anyway, when war broke out, I promised Jack I wouldn't report him - that he could stay on the farm. Didn't see the harm. Everyone reckoned we'd beat Hitler by Christmas, so I thought what's the point of Jack going. By the time he signed up and got over there, it'd all be over. Besides, farm workers were excused from the call-up."

PC Dowding continued to scribble in his notebook. "Go on," He said, without looking away from his writing.

Thomas took a deep breath. "One day I'd been to tha village. While I was there someone told me that the station in Middlesbrough had been bombed. I knew I had to tell Jack what had happened. Of course, when I did, he left. He wanted to make sure his mother… Doris, was ok."

"What happened next?" PC Dowding looked up from his notebook.

"Doris was killed in the bombing. Jack was so angry he joined the war effort. It was clear it wasn't going to be a quick victory like they'd said. I think he wanted revenge for the death of his mother. I thought we'd not see him again. I was sure he'd be killed over there."

"So, he came back here?"

"Aye, he turned up after the war. He had a terrible scar across his face. He didn't talk about the war, ever. I tried to bring it up with him, but he wouldn't talk. He just walked away whenever I did." Thomas finished his tea. Tipping the tin mug back as far as he could, draining the last drop.

"Why did he leave?" PC Dowding asked.

Anne looked at Thomas, shaking her head.

"Why do you want to know all this? You said you'd come to tell us summat?" Thomas said, firmer than he normally would.

PC Dowding closed his notebook and pushed it and his pencil back into his pocket. "We found Jack last night, at the station. When we tried to arrest him, Jack killed himself. But not before breaking my nose." PC Dowding rubbed his face once again.

Thomas felt relief. He shouldn't, he knew that. Afterall someone is dead, but there was a side of him that couldn't be denied, and that side was glad Jack was dead. He wrestled for a few seconds with his thoughts before Anne interrupted him.

"Good riddance to bad rubbish, is all I'll say on the matter." Anne's voice was full of bitterness.

PC Dowding looked toward Anne in puzzlement. "Why do you say that?"

Thomas, now at peace with being glad Jack was

dead answered. "As I've said, when he came back from the war, he was a changed man. He was a troublemaker, and a bloody thug, and I didn't want him around my family. That's why he left. Because I sacked him before he caused any trouble."

PC Dowding nodded. "That's all I needed to know. I guess you won't need to worry about him coming back."

"GOOD!" Anne half-shouted.

PC Dowding stood and made for the door. Just as he was about to leave Thomas stopped him.

"What time did he, you know, kill himself?"

PC Dowding looked directly at Thomas. "It was nine-thirty. Threw himself in front of the last train. Anyway, I'm off to see William. Thanks for your help. I don't expect you'll hear from me again."

After PC Dowding had left Thomas turned to Anne. "The same time all the clocks and watches stopped. And the same exact time Arthur woke up screaming. But there's summat else, wife."

"What do you mean?" Anne asked, already chilled by what Thomas had just confirmed.

"The old clock in the workshop, it also showed nine-thirty too."

"So?" Anne scoffed.

"That clock hasn't worked for years, but the last

time I was in there, I happened to look at it - see if I could fix it but I couldn't, it's too busted up," Thomas paused "Thing is, it'd stopped at two-thirteen. But last night when I went to check on it, it was reading nine-thirty, just like the rest."

"What does that mean?" Anne asked.

"I've no idea wife."

Chapter 3.

1953.

I

It was spring. Arthur was now a boy of five, and since the night Jack Bright had killed himself Arthur had changed. He'd become withdrawn – a loner who refused to play with George and insisted on carrying around the rusting old spinning top which was left in the room Jack once lived in, even taking it with him when he began to attend the local primary school. He'd come across the spinning top while shadowing Thomas. Whilst in the barn Thomas had laid his keys on top of an old metal table. Arthur, who had paid the door at the end of barn no mind previously had suddenly and unexplainedly been drawn to it and what was on the other side. While Thomas had his back turned Arthur had taken the keys and unlocked the door, slowly pushing it open. Jack's room met his gaze exactly as it had been left. Arthur, without taking any notice of the photograph or clothes had made directly for the spinning top, pulling it off the tall-boy on tip toes.

Maybe it was because Anne used to sing the nursery rhyme to him as a child, or maybe it was because the spinning top still played it through the rust and decay, but he had become obsessed with the *See-saw* song as he called it. His presence was often predicated on Anne and Thomas hearing Arthur singing the song before he entered the room. Sometimes it was nothing more than a whisper. Other times, it was a full virtuoso performance which would crescendo until either of them would shout Arthur to stop. Even then Arthur did not stop entirely. Rather, he would begin again in a mournful whisper. "*See-saw Margery Daw...*" On one occasion, as Arthur walked past Thomas singing as he sat at the kitchen table Thomas convinced himself that Arthur had changed the words, "*See-saw Margery Daw Jack shall have a new master.*" Though he wasn't sure, he brought it up with Anne later that night. Anne dismissed this as nothing but Thomas's hearing playing tricks on him. Still, it unnerved Thomas. Arthur, as far as Thomas knew, had never heard the name Jack mentioned except for the couple of times PC Dowding had come around. But that was a few years back, surely Arthur could not remember the name from that far back and those few mentions. He decided that Anne was right. All the years around loud machinery and animals had definitely dulled his hearing. It was a constant source of frustration with Anne that there were times when Thomas didn't hear her requests or questions. Sometimes Anne wondered if his hearing problems were more selective than physiological.

Another thing had changed on the farm. The day after PC Dowding had informed them of Jack's suicide, Thomas had once again found all the clocks stopped at nine-thirty, the time of his death. On more than one occasion he'd had them looked at to see if there was something mechanically wrong, but each time they were given a clean bill of health. And yet, every night at nine-thirty each clock and watched stopped and every morning Thomas had reset them. Eventually, and beginning to suspect something he would never have previously considered, he'd destroyed them all, except for the old grandfather clock passed onto him by his father. As much as Thomas wanted to, he couldn't bring himself to do it. At one point he'd found himself standing over it with an axe raised above his head, but he simply couldn't bring it down. Instead he'd wrapped the old clock up in a thick tarp and tucked it away in a distant corner of the workshop behind an old plough which had long seen its working days. He knew it would remain there long past the days Thomas and Anne had left on the farm. At some point he would tell George of its whereabouts. Until then it would remain hidden. In addition to this Thomas had now barred anymore timepieces on the farm. When asked he'd refused to explain why. The irrational thoughts that it was somehow Jack reaching them and taunting them from beyond the grave were not something he would share with anyone – even Anne. Nor would he share his admission of being scared of these thoughts.

Anne was becoming more concerned about Arthur. His teachers had risen disquiets themselves when she had collected him from school. He remained isolated in his class, not wanting to mix or even talk with the other children. On one occasion when another child had attempted to play with Arthur, he'd pushed him away before swinging the spinning top at him. When Mrs. Bates, the teacher, had intervened Arthur had swung it at her too, snarling as he did. This time it made contact and the rusty edge had scratched her arm. Arthur had been immediately marched to the headmaster's office, yet still, he clung to the spinning top. He was on his final warning. Anne had been told without any uncertainty that should another incident like this occur, Arthur would be banned from the school. Anne had sought to discipline Arthur by taking away his other toys, but this seemed to have no deterring effect on him. When Anne had brought this to Thomas's attention, he'd taken away the spinning top. Upon doing so Arthur had begun hitting and clawing at himself on the side of his head and screaming the nursery rhyme at the top of his lungs. When Thomas had tried to restrain him, Arthur had bitten him hard enough to draw blood. After witnessing the violence towards himself and his father, George asked if he could sleep with Thomas and Anne. Though George was the older of the brothers, Arthur had grown disproportionately both in size and strength compared to George who was now becoming afraid of him. Anne allowed this for one or two nights, but their bed wasn't a big bed, and Thomas needed his sleep. And so, after a couple of nights of relatively restful sleep, at least for George, he was back in the room he shared with Arthur.

It was on the second night of George being back in

his own bed when he'd been woken by the sounds of Arthur's bed creaking, followed by the floorboards in their bedroom. George, slowly opened one eye, allowing in just enough light to make out where Arthur was. As his slightly open eye adjusted to the dark, he found Arthur standing over him, looking down on him. George pulled his eye closed and held his breath, he was sure Arthur was about to attack him. In the absolute blackness of his closed eyes George could sense Arthur leaning closer to him. He could hear and feel the warm exhales of Arthurs breath on his cheek. The warmth moved up his face. Each exhale allowed George to map in his mind's eye where Arthur was relative to his facial features. Then the breathing stopped. George could not hold his own breath any longer. Slowly he exhaled into his bed sheets, hoping that they would mask the sound of his escaping air. George didn't dare move his head to draw fresh breath, he had no choice but to draw in the warm fetid air he'd just respired, hoping to a least draw some fresher air in through his bed sheets. As he did, the warm breath on his face came again. This time it swirled around his eye. George could sense Arthur leaning ever closer to him. Suddenly he felt Arthurs lips press on his closed eye lid. They seemed to linger for a long time before completing a soft kiss which was followed by a small moist tongue which gently licked his eye lash. The pressure lifted, leaving behind warm spittle which tracked along the eye lash, penetrating in behind his lid.

With his eyes still closed, and the spittle now

behind his eye lid George heard the breathing of Arthur move slightly followed by the floorboards creaking. George wiped his eye dry before daring to peek again. Arthur was leaving their room. George expected him to turn right, toward their parents' room but he didn't, he turned left toward the stairs. George could hear his footsteps and the odd creak as he made his way down. A few moments later he heard the kitchen door open, and then close. Certain that Arthur was out of the house George got out of bed and made his way to the small landing and window which overlooked the farmyard. Under the moonlight and yard lamps he watched Arthur enter the barn. It was a few seconds before the commotion began. The animals sounded scared, then silence. A shaft of light broke the darkened yard as Arthur emerged from the barn. Immediately, George scurried back to bed, pulling the blanket over his head, and closing his eyes as he tried as best he could to calm his own breathing.

After what seemed like far more time than it should be, he heard the kitchen door open then close, and then the footsteps as they made their way back up the stairs. The door to their bedroom opened and then George counted the steps across the room. Once again, he could hear Arthur's breathing. Then Arthur spoke and George realised he was once again standing over him. "Tell Thomas and Anne I went out, and I'll hurt you in your sleep," Arthur whispered this so close that George could once again feel the heat of his breath through his blanket. George didn't answer, he didn't dare confirm to Arthur that he was awake. Rather, he hoped if he feigned sleep then Arthur would believe it and his threat wouldn't count.

The following morning George made his way down for breakfast after he had washed and dressed. He ate it silence. When George felt he could, without being noticed, he took a quick glimpse over to where Arthur sat eating his bowl of porridge as he played with the spinning top. As Anne made breakfast for Thomas, his dad entered the kitchen. "Did any of you hear owt last night?" He asked, pulling off his boots before sitting at the table.

"No Da, I heard nothing," George replied, looking across to Arthur.

"What about you Arthur?" Thomas asked.

Arthur stopped eating and looked up, the spoon still in his mouth. He shook his head a few times and then looked back down to his bowl.

"Why'd you ask?" Anne said, placing his breakfast in front of him.

"It's the strangest thing. I went to the barn this morning and there's blood on the floor, and one of the chucks has gone. I'm wondering if a fox got in."

"How could a fox get in, the barn's closed up - isn't it?"

"Aye, it is. I'll keep an eye out."

George wanted to tell them about last night. He'd almost summoned the courage to do so when Arthur spoke. "Can George walk me to school today? I'd like to spend time with him."

George felt sick. The last thing he wanted to do was spend any time at all with him. Especially when that meant they'd be alone before they made the main road where his friends would be waiting.

"Sounds lovely, doesn't it George," Anne said, smiling. "Isn't it lovely Thomas, he wants to spend time with his brother."

Thomas looked up and winked at Arthur and then George. Arthur smiled at both Thomas and Anne before standing and making his way to the door. "Let's get going George. We don't want to be late."

Out maneuvered, George stood and picked up his school bag. "See you both later," He smiled as he addressed his parents.

While Arthur stood in the farmyard waiting, George pulled the kitchen door closed behind him looking through the ever-decreasing crack as he did until he could no longer see inside the kitchen, and the relative safety it offered him. With the solid *clank* of the door's strike finding the latch George turned and headed out of the farmyard. He walked past Arthur without speaking to him. With his head down and walking as quickly as he could - without he thought being too obvious - George hoped to keep Arthur behind him so he wouldn't engage with him. His plan unfortunately didn't

succeed. Within half the length of the yard Arthur
was alongside him.

"Should have told Da you'd seen a fox, George."
Arthur softly said as he kept pace.

"Thought I was ta say nowt?" George retaliated.

"Best you do, brother."

George pushed his hands deeper into his pockets
and dropped his head as far as he could. Arthur
didn't speak anymore as they trudged up the track.
George was thankful when they reached the top of
the track and joined the main road. *Finally* - he
thought to himself - his friends would soon be
along. At least now until the end of the school day
he'd be free of Arthur. "Right Arthur, off ya go.
You can walk alone from here; my friends will be
here soon."

Arthur looked along the long road each way.
"Can't see any friends," He sneered.

George checked for himself. The two-lane country
road was nestled between a steep bank on one side
and a grassy drop off which eventually led down to
the grazing fields of their farm. The track they had
walked up met the road at a somewhat sharp
angle, which meant Thomas craning his neck when
he wanted to turn right out of the farm to head
toward Thirstonfield Village. Typical of a country
road, the tarmac had long been laid and had over
the many winters and summers turned to a mottled

light grey. The intermediate white lines which marked the centre of the road, had for the most part faded and cracked, leaving only sporadic dots of faded white paint.

"They'll be here soon." George complained.

"Says you!" Arthur snapped back

George knew he couldn't wait much longer. If they didn't make the bus stop, they'd miss it and if that happened it's almost an hour walk to school with Arthur to keep him company. "Okay, let's go." George said, resigned to his fate.

As the two boys turned, they heard a shout. Looking back George smiled when he saw his friends coming around the bend – a few yards behind them. "Hold up," Harry shouted again as they ran toward them. George turned to Arthur, "See, told ya they'd be here."

Once Harry, James and Frank had caught up to George and Arthur, they began walking toward the bus stop, Arthur tagging along behind them.

"Guess what?" Frank said excitedly as the group of boys continued.

"What?" Answered Harry.

"We're getting a puppy. Ma' talked dad into allowing one for the house."

"What kind?" Asked James.

"Well, I wanted an Alsatian, but Da won't have one in the house, so we're getting a Labrador,"

The boys continued to compare notes on dog breeds and why they agreed with Franks father that getting an Alsatian was not such a good idea so soon after the war. Though Frank still disagreed with them, and his father. They reached the bus stop just in time to see the old bus come around the corner, its green and cream paint long faded, and the bright chrome of the bumpers and light fittings now pitted and rusting. With a squealing protest of the breaks it pulled alongside the sign which indicated the official stopping place. The boys climbed aboard and made their way to their usual seats. Arthur at this point split from his brother and friends and headed for the rear of the bus, and the single seat which was located by the emergency exit. No one but Arthur would choose to sit here. It indicated to all the school that you were alone and that you have no friends. But for Arthur it was ideal. He wanted the solitude and was not in the slightest interested in making or maintaining any friendships. With a jolt the bus set off. Arthur watched the countryside pass by. The background din of the many conversations was soon blanked out as Arthur's mind began to drift away. The nursery rhyme once again played over in his head. As it did, Arthur mouthed the words, singing softly enough to not be heard over the sound of the bus and chit-chats. Lately, as Arthur had sung the nursery rhyme in his head a distant voice had somehow joined in with him. It had begun so subtly that Arthur had not previously noticed it, but over the last few weeks the voice, which was that of a grown man, had become ever so slightly more audible to the point that Arthur had looked around to see if anyone was standing with him, singing it, but there never was. Today the man's voice was not present, and Arthur continued to murmur as he travelled to school, "*See Saw Margery Daw...*" The bus snaked along the winding roads, eventually passing the entrance to the station before reaching Thirstonfield Village and the small village school.

II

Thomas had finished his breakfast and made his way out into the farmyard, hoping to figure out how the fox had managed to get into the barn and then drag away one of the chickens without either the normal commotion or the usual tracks and clues. Inside the farmhouse Anne continued to clear up after breakfast. She had paid no further mind to the chicken going missing. This happened, it was part of living in the country. She would often tell Thomas that the foxes have to eat too, and while Thomas agreed that *nature would be nature*, he still felt aggrieved when they took one of the farm animals. As Thomas checked the barns integrity, he heard a car pull up outside. Sighing that he never seemed to be able to get anything done without interruptions, he made his way outside, already guessing who the caller may be. He was wrong on every guess. The car was marked with, *British Railways*. He watched the two suited men climb out of the Rover P4. Thomas knew these two men had some importance within British Railways to drive this type of car. One step down from senior management types who themselves would drive a Jag and not a Rover, Thomas thought to himself as he walked over, holding out a hand to greet them. Neither of the men reciprocated. Rather, they smiled and tipped their bowler hats while being careful where they stood.

"Mr. Bradbury?" The younger man asked.

Thomas studied the two men for a second. The older man was clearly in charge, as was usually the case, and this younger man – who Thomas guessed was his subordinate - was no doubt brought along to help ease whatever news had to be delivered and possibly for some sort of backup, just in case. Whatever their reason for them being here Thomas doubted it would be good news. Snapping back Thomas replied, "Aye."

"Can we go inside to talk? please."

Thomas pushed the thick rag he'd tried to clean his hands with deep into the back pocket of his overalls and sighed. "This way then," as he led the way into the farmhouse.

As they entered Anne appeared from the hallway. Thomas spoke before Anne, hoping to deflect any direct interrogating brought on by the shock of their sudden appearance. "These gentlemen are from the railway," Thomas announced with a concerned look on his face.

"Take a seat, gentlemen." Anne pointed to the kitchen table. "I'll make some tea."

"No, we're fine, thank you Mrs. Bradbury, we won't take much of your time." The older man responded.

"Well, I'll have one all the same. I think we'll need it, won't we?" Anne replied, already putting the kettle over the lit flame.

"I'm Kenneth, and this is Raymond, we're from British Railways, but you've no doubt guessed that." The older man said as he removed his hat, placing it on the table.

"Is this about the station?" Thomas asked. Dread rising inside him.

"I'm afraid it is," Kenneth answered, glumly. Thing is, Mr. Bradbury, the takings are down. Hardly anyone is using the station anymore; it's costing more to keep it going than it's making. We'd hoped folks would have got back into their routine after the war, but it's not the case. Most people are staying at home, no longer travelling to the coast and we can't turn it back into a Halt just for the locals as it once was. And of course, the M.O.D no longer need it," He stopped to draw a breath. His shirt clung tightly to his fat neck.

Anne cut across him. "So, what does that mean?" She asked as she transferred the now boiling water into the tea pot.

"To put it bluntly Mrs. Bradbury we're closing it. We no longer need it, so we won't be renewing the lease."

Thomas felt like he'd been kicked in the stomach by a horse. Losing the income from the station would be a huge blow to the farm. "When?" He asked.

"It'll be the end of January – next year. When the last of the Christmas travellers are done and the kids are back at school, but we'll begin cutting back services after this summer." Kenneth answered. "Then we'll need access to the land to remove our equipment and such."

"When will you stop paying us?" Anne asked, pouring the mashed tea into Thomas's green tin mug, followed by a splash of fresh milk and a little sugar.

"The final payment will be at the end of January, when we normally pay the quarterly rent. But it will include a severance to cover us finishing the lease early and to cover us returning. As I say, we'll need to remove equipment. Things which aren't safe to leave behind and such."

"And when do you think that will be?" Anne asked.

"We'll get the important stuff out before the winter sets in. The rest will be in early spring. I reckon we'll be done and out by May," Kenneth answered.

"What about the buildings?" Thomas asked.

"No point in us taking them down, it'll cost too much, and we have no use for them. Feel free to use them once we're out of your way."

"So just what will you be taking?" Anne asked.

"Anything we can lift up and transport by train, Mrs. Bradbury. We'll take the tracks up too; we can use them farther along the line." Kenneth stopped and looked between them. "Look, I know things are tight and this is the last thing you wanted - or needed. But we simply can't keep a station running that's losing as much money as Thirstonfield. Once we're gone you could sell the station house and shed or rent them out. There are Plenty of people still looking for properties after the war. They'd be glad to get out of those prefabs the government knocked up."

"Aye, well if you'd have left it well enough alone as a Halt this wouldn't have happened. It was you lot that had delusions of grandeur, making it too big. And now it's us that has to take the brunt, as always. And I'll have no strangers renting on my land. That station served the community. What's people living there going to do?"

This time, Raymond spoke. "It won't take much once we've gone to make the station house into a nice home. You could leave this old place, move in there," He said, looking around the farmhouse. His face unable to hide what he thought of the old place.

"And what's that supposed to mean?" Anne snapped at him.

Kenneth stepped back in. "It doesn't mean anything. Anyway, Mr. and Mrs. Bradbury, we've taken enough of your time. We'll be on our way. Good luck for the future."

Anne stood and headed for the hallway. "Good riddance!"

Thomas followed the two men out to their car. Kenneth held out his hand, which Thomas shook. "I am sorry about this Mr. Bradbury." He said, with a sincere and apologetic smile crossing his face.

Thomas didn't reply verbally; he simply reciprocated the smile and nodded a little. He watched them climb into the car and continued to watch them until it disappeared at the top of the track where it met the main road. Thomas then looked around the old farm and scratched his head. He had no idea yet how he would replace the lost income come January. He turned and headed back inside where he found Anne sat at the kitchen table. She had the same look on her face. It was one of concern. Thomas sat next to her and held her hand. "We'll find a way wife,"

"Aye, how's that then?" Anne replied quietly.

"I've no idea yet. But we'll figure summat. We

always do."

"Aye, happen we will. Stay there, I'll make us a butty." Anne said, pulling her hand away and standing.

"Ta."

III

The old school bus pulled up alongside the farm track. As usual Arthur was sat in the single seat next to the emergency exit, the spinning Top on his lap - spinning slowly. George stood from his seat and looked back to where Arthur was sat. He was tempted to leave Arthur in whatever world he was in while he mouthed the words to the nursery rhyme once again, but he knew he couldn't do that. As George watched him spinning the Top and mouthing the nursery rhyme, he felt sorry for him. He was after all his younger brother, someone that George should look after. Since the moment he found out that his mother was pregnant George wanted a brother to play with. A brother to play those games that the other boys played with their brothers. But there was something different about Arthur. George had felt it from a young age, but he'd been reluctant to talk to his mother and father about it for fear of being told he was jealous of his younger brother. His mother had already spent much more time with Arthur than she had with him. George had felt some resentment towards him and towards his mother for that, but as Arthur had grown and George himself had become older and a little wiser, he understood that the demands of a baby would always take precedent over his own.

There had been an upside to his mother's attention turning almost solely to his brother, he had spent much more time with his father working on the farm. This had made George feel more grown up than when he'd been the single child on the farm. Yet for all of the responsibilities his father had given him, he still yearned for his mother's attention, he still needed those hugs on a night when he wasn't feeling well, and he still needed to be told that he was her special boy. These internal contradictions were part of George's confusion and conflict towards his brother, but after the night when Arthur had snuck out of the house and had confessed to George what he done to the chicken, he now felt unsafe in his own home and yet he couldn't take this information or how he felt to his parents for fear of the retribution Arthur had promised.

Eventually, George walked up to Arthur and gently kicked the bottom of his left foot. "C'mon Arthur, we're home." Startled Arthur hastily pushed the spinning Top into his school bag and followed George off the bus. As the boys began the slow walk down the track towards the farmhouse, the bus pulled away. George looked back to see his friends waving from the windows. He smiled and returned the wave as the bus disappeared behind the hedgerow which skirted the road. They walked past the pile of mulching wood and George thought about Arthur's confession, but as he had that morning, he decided against confronting him. As they neared the barn Arthur handed George his school bag.

"Take this in for me, tell Anne I'm in the barn." Arthur ordered.

"You're… you're not going to hurt anything again, are you?" George asked

Arthur smiled, shaking his head.

Reluctantly George took Arthur's bag and watched him as he entered the barn. Then, as quickly as he could George ran for the farmhouse and entered to find his mother preparing their dinner. She turned and smiled and then stopped. "Where's Arthur?" She asked.

George dropped the bags by the door, "He's in the barn. Said I was to tell you."

"He needs to be in, and gettin' ready for his tea, never mind the barn." Anne protested.

"I tried to tell him Ma, but he'll not listen to me." George said, as convincingly as he could.

"Stay inside and get yourself washed up for tea George." Anne directed as she headed for the door.

George smiled at the thought of Arthur being

chastised and headed up the narrow staircase.

Anne entered the barn. Inside it was laid out with stalls on along the right side for their pigs. Since Thomas had sold most of their livestock only two of the six stalls were in use. At the end of these stalls was the chicken coop. Along the opposite wall sat Thomas's work bench and tools. At the far end was the door which led to what was Jack's bunk room. Anne noticed the door was open and the large brass key was still in the lock. Quietly, she walked along the length of the barn and towards the open door hoping the livestock wouldn't give her away. Other than a few complaints from the oldest and largest pig they remained quiet enough that her silent approach wasn't compromised. As she reached the door, she heard Arthur talking. It seemed to Anne that he was having a full conversation with someone in the room. She pressed as far as she could without disturbing them.

"Do you live here?" She heard Arthur ask, but she heard no reply to his question. "What do you mean, you used to?" Arthur asked. A cold shiver ran through her. She wanted to enter the room but decided to wait. She wanted to hear who, if anyone, was in the room with her son, or was he simply talking to himself. "My name is Arthur, what's yours?" Anne could feel her adrenaline rising. "Can I call you that? Ok, I will. And will you be my friend?" Arthur's words were clear, yet Anne could still not hear a reply. "I took it, I hope that's ok, I like the sound it makes and the tune."

Anne scrambled to think what Arthur could be referring to. Then he began to sing, *"See Saw Margery Daw…"* Anne felt sick to her stomach. That damn rusting spinning top, she would throw it out when he left for school tomorrow, she decided. The conversation continued. "So, where are you now if you're not here?" A pause and then Arthur continued. "I… I don't understand. How can you be here and not here, but just be inside me?" Anne's instinct told her to run into the room and confront whoever was in there taunting and playing with her son. But she needed more of the conversation. "How can you be my father, my Da is alive, you're not." Anne held her hand to her mouth. Arthur's conversation continued. "No, you're wrong, my father's name is Thomas, it's not you, you're not Thomas! You told me your name is Jack."

Anne burst into the room. All her fears and memories of that night came flooding back to her as she entered. She didn't know what to expect. A thousand thoughts engulfed her in the seconds it took to be in the room behind Arthur. Once inside she froze. Only Arthur was in the room, sitting on the bed where Jack had taken her by force. Before she had time, Arthur spoke. "This is my friend Jack." Arthur pointed to his left and to the spot directly adjacent to Anne. Her body ran cold as she felt the hairs on her neck stand to attention. Without looking to where Arthur was pointing Anne grabbed her son by his arm and pulled him from the bed and out of the room. Slamming the door behind her, she turned the brass key and then turned to Arthur. She knelt, glaring at him. "You are never-ever to go into that room, or this barn again! Do you understand?" Arthur could tell his mum was shaken. "Yes mummy. Should I go inside for tea now?" He said calmly and with no emotion reflected in either his eyes or expression. Anne let go of his arm. Arthur walked slowly out of the barn singing. *"See Saw Margery Daw, Anne shall have a new master…"* Anne turned back to the door and removed the brass key, slipping it into the pocket on her apron.

Chapter 4.

I

Anne entered the kitchen shortly after Arthur. What she had just witnessed had shaken her. Anne was not predisposed to believe in anything which she couldn't feel or touch except of course for God. She would simply not contemplate that Arthur could somehow be talking with Jack Bright. Such flights of fancy and nonsense had no place in their lives. And yet, she struggled to reconcile the conversation she'd just heard with any rational explanation. George was still upstairs while Arthur was only now sauntering his way towards the staircase, allowing the spinning top to flay by his sides. The cheap tin clanked every time it hit his thigh, while Arthur muttered the nursery rhyme. She had no idea where that damned spinning top had come from. She had first seen it in Jack's bunk when he'd returned from the war - though she had never thought to question him about it directly. She had brought it up with Thomas, who'd told her to not be such a *busy body*. It's his business, he'd said, not ours.

Thomas was in Thirstonfield Village picking up a few supplies. Anne felt alone and vulnerable. She knew he'd be another hour because he wanted to call at the station on his way back through. They'd never visited, they had no need to – or the time, so they weren't sure what developments and additions had taken place. After the visit by the railway men earlier that day, Thomas had felt it necessary to visit the station to see exactly what was going to be left behind and what state the land around it was in. He also wanted to look over the buildings. Though Anne had dismissed the notion of renting or selling the station house, for the same reason she had not allowed more help to be hired, Thomas believed it may be necessary to keep the farm financially viable. Though this is a conversation he would have with Anne another time.

Moving to the bottom of the staircase Anne stood and listened, holding her breath, hoping not to hear another conversation between Arthur and Jack. Did she really just think that, she questioned herself. There are no such things as ghosts, and yet as much she had tried in the short time it had been, she still couldn't explain where Arthur could have gotten the information he'd relayed. Silence - to her relief there didn't seem to be any further conversations. The only discussion seemed to be between Arthur and George who were discussing school, and just how bloody awful it was. Sighing with some relief Anne returned to the kitchen. When their meal was ready, she plated Thomas's and put it in the warmer where it would wait for his return. The rest she placed out on the table and then called for George and Arthur to join her. The two boys made their way down and sat at the table. "Where's Da?" George asked, tucking into the homemade pie and veg. "He's down the village George. Won't be long, just eat up - there's a good lad." Anne replied, hoping for Thomas's quick return.

Arthur did not speak during the meal. The spinning top, as always, was beside him on the table. Anne looked at it with antipathy. She had never hated an inanimate object this much and this quickly. Every now and again he would push down on the spindle and the rusting top would spin away, and the tune would begin. Anne wanted nothing more than to reach across the table, grab it and then crush it. But she resisted the urge to do so. She wondered why she had sung this to him as a baby, even before she had discovered the toy. It wasn't a tune she had sang to George, nor was it one she remembers from her own childhood. For some reason she just seemed to hum it one day while comforting and Arthur picked it up. As they finished their meals, they heard the old Bedford truck pull up outside. Anne's heart lifted – something it had not done on Thomas's arrival since their courting days, or at least shortly after they were married. Though she was always pleased to see him, the *giddy as a schoolgirl* feeling when they saw each other had long since left. This lifting feeling was entirely down to the trepidation she felt for both herself and George after witnessing Arthur in Jack's bunk.

Moments later Thomas entered. When he did George left the table to hug his father, "Hi Da," he said excitedly. Arthur simply looked up, his right hand still pushing ever so slightly on the spindle.

Thomas hugged George, "Hi son," then he turned to Arthur, "No hugs from my other son?" Anne's heart sank. What if Arthur repeated what she'd heard earlier – that Thomas was not his father, that Jack was? Before Arthur could reply, Anne cut across their conversation. "Well, what's the news from that station?" She asked, clearing away their dinner plates. Arthur looked across to her, and then stood and left the kitchen – the spinning top tucked under his arm. George followed behind him, with Anne shouting after them. "Get yourselves ready for bed now. Then you can read for a while, do ya hear?" No response came but Anne didn't follow it up. She needed to let Thomas know what had happened, but that could wait until they were in bed and when she felt Arthur would surely be asleep. First, she needed to know about Thirstonfield Station.

"Well, tell me then. What's tha news?" She asked, placing the hot plate of dinner in front of him.

"They've added a lot since the last time we went, wife." Thomas answered as he blew on a fork full of hot pie.

"Like what?"

"There's an engine shed. They weren't sure about leaving it, but they've decided to leave it. Said the glass roof would be too costly to take down."

"What about the station house?" Anne asked, washing the pots already used.

"That's much the same, a bit of fancy stuff around it, but it hasn't changed much. The station master has made it look nice." Thomas replied chewing the food he'd taken off the fork.

"Well, what's the fancy stuff?" Anne pushed.

Thomas swallowed another bite before plunging his fork back into the pie, "There's benches and such, flower beds and a grand clock hanging from the wall. Leaving it all they've said. Only taking what they can use elsewhere and the railway equipment - tools, spare parts, and such. There's an old train in the shed they said they're going to tow back to the yard at Middlesbrough. They said it's done-for, but they can use it for parts."

Thomas cleared his plate with the last slice of bread and butter before standing. "I'm off to get changed. That were nice, wife."

Anne smiled and placed the last of the pots into the sink. Once washed and cleared away, she headed for the boy's bedroom. Inside she found George and Arthur laying on their beds, reading the comics they'd bought with their pocket money on their last visit to Thirstonfield Village. "C'mon you two, go brush your teeth, soon be bedtime." George and Arthur left the room, heading for the small bathroom. Anne turned back their sheets and fluffed up the pillows. A few moments later they returned, climbing into their beds. Anne leaned over George who yawned and gave her a hug. Anne moved over to Arthur's bed who had already turned to face the wall. She kissed her hand and placed it on his forehead. "Goodnight boys. Sleep tight." As she left the room, she flicked the light switch off, but left the bedroom door slightly open allowing a shaft of light to find its way in from the landing. Once downstairs she closed the living room door almost completely. Only leaving enough of a gap so that she could hear any commotion from upstairs. She sat opposite Thomas who was in his wingback chair by the fire, reading the local newspaper he'd picked up while in the village.

"I've summat to tell you Thomas," Anne began and continued. "Arthur got into that bunk room today while you were over at the village. The one Jack stayed in."

Thomas let the newspaper rest in his lap.

"I followed him in," She took a deep breath. "When I got close to the door, I heard him talking to someone."

"What? Someone was in there, with him?"

"No," Anne replied, "That's just it, there wasn't."

"He was talking to himself? That's harmless enough, wife. We all do that," Thomas smiled and winked.

"No, he was talking with…" Anne paused, she had no idea how to phrase this. "He was talking with Jack."

Thomas stared at Anne. She could see him trying to

make sense of what she'd just told him. He sighed heavily. "How can that be? Jack's dead. The bobby told us, he killed himself."

Anne shrugged. "I don't know, but when I listened, I heard him say Jack's name. Arthur doesn't know that name Thomas, we've never spoken it in front of him."

"We may have done - maybe slipped out, or he overheard us." Thomas argued.

"I heard him Thomas. I heard him say that you weren't his father, and that Jack was. We've never spoken of that to anyone, ever. Not even each other, not since we found out I was carrying him. He couldn't have overheard that."

"Has he mentioned it again?" Thomas asked.

"No, I went into the room and brought him out. While I was in there Arthur said Jack was standing next to me," Anne paused, the internal contradiction between what she firmly believed and yet couldn't explain once again pushing forward in her mind. "I felt summat in that room Thomas," Anne stopped, gathering herself. "I've locked it now and put the key up on top of the dresser in the kitchen, he's not to know where it is. I want that room clearing. And I want that damned spinning top destroying."

Thomas thought for a second. He didn't believe in ghosts and spirits. Like Anne, God was the only otherworldly belief they had. He convinced himself quickly that Arthur must have heard them talking one night. Maybe when they were in bed when they thought the boys were asleep. He wouldn't challenge Anne on this now, he could read how upset she was. For now, he'd go along with it. But he would do one thing. He'd get rid of that bloody spinning top. "Ok, wife. Let's see what he says over the next few days, there'll be a simple enough explanation for what you heard. I'll wait until he's asleep and then I'll go get that toy and crush it."

"See that you do, there's summat about that damned thing gives me the heebe jeebies." Anne replied, lifting her knitting from the bag which rested by the side of her own wingback.

A few hours later Thomas stirred to find Anne asleep opposite him, her knitting laying across her lap. The fire was almost out, and the house was in silence. As he came around to somewhere between asleep and full consciousness Thomas remembered his promise. He stood and made is way to the boys' bedroom. As quietly as he could he entered the room and made his way in, allowing the light from the landing to illuminate the room enough to navigate and find the spinning top. Squinting through the dim light he located it on the floor next to Arthurs bed. Picking it up he turned and made his way back down the stairs and into the kitchen. Anne, woken by Thomas's movement, followed him in, clearing her eyes of the dry sleep. "You got it then?" She whispered.

"Aye, I'm gonna take it to the workshop and sort it."

"I'm off to bed, see that you do a proper job on it."

Thomas nodded and headed out of the kitchen and across the yard to his workshop. Pulling the door open he made his way past his truck and the covered Grandfather clock and into the small office. He laid the spinning top on the bench and picked up a claw hammer. "Bloody thing" he muttered as he brought the hammer down on the thin tin.

II

As was more or less always the case, Anne woke before George and Arthur. Thomas, as always, would already be up and *starting the day* - another of his favourite sayings which simply meant seeing to the animals and checking the immediate area for signs of foxes as well as other problems and generally getting himself ready for the day's work ahead. She climbed out of bed and made her way down to the kitchen to begin breakfast. Once that was started, she made her way to the boys' bedroom to wake them and to get them ready for school. She entered to find George still asleep, his leg hanging out of the side of his blankets whilst Arthur was completely under his blankets. She could see he was hunched over by the shape of the small mountain scape the blankets made. Assuming Arthur was reading his comics Anne moved over to his bed and reached out a hand to pull the blankets back. As she got within reach, she stopped. From under the blanket she could hear it. It was faint, but she could make it out. It was that worn and out of tune spinning top and Arthur was singing along in a similarly out of tune whisper and his breathing seemed rapid. *"See Saw Margery Daw Jack shall have a new master,"* Anne heard the change in the words. There was that name again - Jack. Without hesitation this time Anne pulled the blankets back. Arthur was sat with his back to her, hunched over what she believed to be the spinning top, cradling it, and hiding it between his crossed legs. She could clearly see the motion of his right shoulder as his arm moved rapidly up and down which she imagined was pushing and pulling on the spindle, keeping the top playing the tune. Anne put her hand on his left shoulder and pulled him around on the bed, opening him up to expose the spinning top. As Arthur spun around on the sheets, tilting backwards - slightly off-balance Anne could not see the spinning top. She looked to where she thought it must be and saw that Arthur was masturbating frantically while he sung the nursery rhyme. Arthur looked up and met her gaze. He smiled at her before Anne had time to register what she was looking at and to avert her own gaze. "Morning mummy," Arthur said, still stroking himself. Repulsed, embarrassed and in utter shame she shouted at Arthur to immediately stop and to put himself away. Without any suggestion of his own embarrassment and without any concept he was doing anything wrong, he tucked himself back into the flap in his pyjama bottoms and climbed off the bed.

On hearing the commotion George had woken but not before Arthur had got out of his bed and was making his way down the stairs. "What's happened mum?" George asked, wearily and wiping sleep from his eyes. Still in shock at what she'd witnessed Anne turned away from George's gaze and made for the door. "Nothing George. Just get yourself up for breakfast." Anne paused at the top of the stairs. Should she go to find Thomas or wait until the boys had left for school. She was still standing there when George finally appeared, passing by her on his way to the bathroom. Anne half smiled at George and then without saying anything further she made her way down to the kitchen where she found Arthur sat waiting for his breakfast. He was sat with his back to the kitchen door. Anne hesitated before entering the kitchen. She didn't know how to handle this. What the hell was she supposed to do or say? Was she supposed to say anything? She knew the boys would do this one day, but not at this age, surely this wasn't normal – was it? She decided for now not to say anything. She would pretend like nothing had happened, and then talk to Thomas later, he could deal with this one – she decided. She walked into the kitchen and poured out a bowl of porridge from the pot which was simmering on the stove. She turned and placed it down in front of Arthur. As much as she tried, she couldn't bring herself to look him in the eye. Rather, she smiled while looking down at the bowl of steaming porridge and simply said. "There you go, now eat up."

As she turned to pour a bowl for George, Arthur answered her. "Thank you, mummy, "Arthur took a mouth full of porridge off the spoon, and then continued. "It's ok, Anne."

She stopped pouring George's porridge and turned to face Arthur. Thrown by the use of her name rather than, *mummy* Anne answered him "What's ok?"

Arthur took another mouthful. "To do what I was doing."

Anne felt sick to her stomach. "Why would you say that? It's wrong. God doesn't want you to." Anne was flustered and her reply of half scorn and half utter discomfiture gave it away. "Who told you it was ok? Was it an older boy at school? And my name is, Ma or mother. Not, mummy or Anne."

Arthur plunged his spoon back into the emptying bowl. "No, Jack told me it's fine to do it. All the soldiers did it, he said it makes me a man."

Anne pulled herself together, she needed to stop this quickly. "Aye, well it is wrong, and it's even more so to then say what you have. We'll have no more of it, or talking of it, or this Jack fellow. Do you hear me, my lad?"

"Sure Anne, I'm sorry." Arthur said, far too calmly for Anne's liking.

Anne turned back to the stove and finished pouring the porridge for George. As she did George entered. She turned and put the bowl down in front of him. Trying as hard as she could to keep herself together, she smiled at them both, "Now, you eat up and then finish getting ready for school. I just need to go see your dad for a minute."

Anne exited the farmhouse as calmly as she could. Inside she was still shaking with the adrenaline which continued to surge around her body. Her mind scrambled not only at Arthur's actions and what he was doing but by his absolute detachment from what his actions were. As soon as she heard the farmhouse door close behind her Anne let go of her restraint, which by now was hanging by the thinnest of threads. Hysterical and running as quickly as she could she made for the workshop. Inside she found Thomas working on the Bedford truck. She put her arms around him, crying. "What? What is it?" He asked.

"Arthur…" Anne muttered between the tears.

"Why, what's wrong with him, is he hurt?"

Anne pulled back a little, wiping her eyes dry and regaining her breath. "When I went to wake the boys this morning, I found Arthur…" She gulped another large breath, "I found him playing with himself."

Thomas smiled. "Ok, it's a little early but it's normal, wife. We knew that one day it'd happen."

"No, not yet, it's too young an age, and there's more to it than just that Thomas. When I found him, he wasn't bothered, he didn't try and hide it or put himself away, he just looked up at me and smiled while he was still at it." Anne steadied herself "He told me that Jack told him to, and that he'd enjoy it and it'd make him a man."

Thomas's smile slipped away. "This again."

"There's summat else Thomas. When I got close to him, before I pulled his blankets off, I thought I'd heard the spinning top."

"Impossible, wife. Follow me." Thomas turned and headed for the small office.

Anne followed him in. Thomas picked up the damaged spinning top, holding it in front of her. "See, can't have been. Has he noticed it gone yet?" Thomas asked.

"I don't think so. He's not said anything."

"Best get back, wife. I'll follow you over soon." Thomas said, dropping the broken toy onto the worktop.

Anne left the workshop and made her way back to the house. Once inside she found both boys had eaten their breakfast and had gone to finish getting ready for school. Anne picked up the bowls and placed them in the sink. As she turned to wipe the table clear of the dropped slops of the porridge Anne heard Arthur shout from upstairs. "Where is it, where's my *spinner*!"

A loud crash followed Arthur's demands to know where his toy had gone, followed by another. Anne ran up the stairs and into the bedroom. There she found Arthur's bed and bedside draws overturned. George was in the corner, trying as best he could to hide or at least keep out of Arthurs eyeline. "Stop it!" Demanded Anne. Arthur turned, his face full of hate and anger. "Tell me where it is you bitch," Already on edge after the events earlier, Anne slapped Arthur across the face. He stumbled but managed to stay on his feet. "Do not talk to me like that!" Anne bellowed at him. George began to cry, unused to this kind of confrontation, especially towards and from his mother. Arthur turned back towards her, a red hand-sized mark already forming across his face, the rage still very apparent. He screamed at her – his voice breaking as he did, then he charged, lashing out, his fists clenched. Anne reached out to grab him but instead his clenched fist caught her, knocking her arm across her body. Grabbing it Arthur sunk his teeth into her arm. Anne screamed in pain, trying to shake Arthur lose.

Thomas entered the kitchen, wiping his hands and removing his boots as he did. He expected to find Anne at the stove, preparing his cup of tea and cooked breakfast as she always had, but the kitchen was empty. Then he heard Anne's screams. He rushed up to find Arthur hanging onto her forearm, biting hard. Thomas grabbed him and pulled him off her, throwing the small boy across the room. Arthur landed heavily on the upturned bed, twisting his arm. He squealed out in pain.

"My arm, my arm, daddy my arm."

Anne reached over to George, guiding the sobbing boy from the room and back down to the kitchen. There she cleaned the deep wound inflicted by Arthur's teeth, wrapping a bandage around it. She heard the bedroom door slam, and then Thomas coming down the stairs, his heavy steps making every stair either creek or thud. He entered the kitchen. His eyes red, clearly, he'd been crying. He made his way over to Anne. "How's your arm?" He asked, looking over the dressed wound. "It's fine, where's Arthur?"

"He's in his room, for now." Thomas sniffled. "I think I broke his arm Anne. What the hell was I thinking."

Anne put an arm around him. Thomas rarely used her name; it was only ever when the worst things happened. The last time was at his father's funeral. "You did what you had to Thomas."

"Nonetheless, I need to take him over to see the doc." Thomas pinched the top of his nose, wiping away the last of the tears, then turned back towards the staircase.

Anne moved over to George and cradled him. "Don't worry son, this was a one off. He won't behave like that again. I'm sure of it. Now go on, get yourself off to school and don't worry about Arthur."

George, who had mostly calmed down gave his

mother a hug and then left to catch the school bus. After he'd left Thomas came down with Arthur, still cradling his arm and wincing in pain. Anne felt nothing for her son's pain as she watched him being led out the door by Thomas. Arthur looked over to her as he walked through the kitchen, but Anne turned her head. Once she heard the truck leave, she made her way back up the stairs. Regardless of how she felt about Arthur right at this moment, she knew she would have to tidy their bedroom. Standing in the doorway she sighed heavily and then entered. It didn't take her long to stand the bedside draws back against the wall and right the upturned single bed. She pulled the sheets off, cursing as she did "Disgusting boy, these'll need boil washing!" She made up the bed with clean sheets and wiped the drops of blood from the floor left by her injury. As she finished cleaning – and hour or so later – she heard the faint sound of the spinning top begin again. She closed her eyes and clenched her fists by her side. Taking a deep breath, she whispered to herself "It's not here, it's not here." The out-of-tune tinny music continued almost too softly to hear, but it was there, of that she was sure. She turned her head, trying to locate the source of the soft-almost distant sound. Then she remembered the top still being in the shed. Was it possible that the mechanism was still working even though Thomas had smashed it, she wondered? She stood and made her way back out across the farmyard and to the shed.

Anne pulled the heavy doors open and stepped inside the dank building. She made her way to the office at the back. The smashed toy lay exactly where Thomas had thrown it down, but no sound came from it. And yet, in the distance, she could still hear it. Trying to focus on the origin of the sound, Anne turned, tilting her head as she did. She moved through the

workshop and back outside. She turned again, trying to locate the source of the sound. Slowly, she moved over to the barn and then stopped. She was sure the sound was coming from within the barn, and yet is was no louder now than when she had been in the bedroom. Frustrated and now also incensed to find the answer Anne ran back to the house and pulled the brass key down from off the dresser. Determined to conclude this once and for all, she ran back to the barn and to the locked bunk room. Opening the door, she stepped inside. As she did the tune stopped. All was quiet - it was silent. Even the animals on the other side of the wooden wall made no sound. She stood and held her breath straining to hear the tune again. Then in her left ear, exactly where Arthur had said Jack had been standing, she felt a soft breeze across her ear, followed by a whisper.

"I'm back."

III

Thomas pulled the truck up outside the doctor's surgery. Arthur had winced and cried the entirety of the journey, while Thomas had remained silent. His mind was conflicted about what he'd done. He felt unimaginable guilt for hurting his son and yet an equal amount of anger for what he'd walked in on and for what Arthur was doing to Anne. The scene played over in his mind and each time he replayed it, something changed. Some versions portrayed Arthur as a small boy, flung through the air by himself- a towering goliath of a man. In this version Thomas was unequivocally the villain. A monster who should never be trusted with his children again. In other versions, the one's he used to try and justify his reaction Arthur seemed somehow bigger, more powerful and Thomas's actions were the only ones that could bring the attack on Anne to an end and potentially save George from harm.

Thomas turned the engine off and turned to Arthur who was still wincing and holding his arm. "Come on son. Let's go see the doc." Thomas climbed out of the truck, the guilt still with him and yet he felt unable to acknowledge it to Arthur. He Led his son into the waiting room of the small surgery located on the high street of Thirstonfield, opposite the village green. The receptionist watched Thomas enter, guiding Arthur in and sitting him down in one of the wooden chairs placed in a semi-circle along the back wall. Thomas approached the desk where the receptionist sat. A woman, who as far as Thomas could tell had been there as far back as he could remember, and yet she seemed to look exactly the same. Maybe she was just one of these people who always looked old and wore that type of glasses.

"We've had an accident on the farm, is Doctor Brown in?" Thomas asked, quietly. He looked back around the waiting room and at the other patients. Thomas wondered if they'd already decided what had happened to Arthur.

"He should be finishing up soon. I'll call you when he's free."

Thomas nodded, he understood the instructions and returned to Arthur. "How's your arm, son?"

Arthur wiped away the last of his drying tears. "It hurts, daddy. It hurts so badly."

Thomas sank back into his chair. A few minutes later the unaging receptionist called over to him. "The doctor will see you now, Room 3."

Thomas led Arthur through to a dark narrow corridor lined with doors. The top half had rippled glass with the room number and name of doctor written in green with gold outlining. They reached, Room 3. Thomas knocked. "Enter." Came the answer. Inside the room, Doc Brown sat behind a large wooden desk. On it were a few piles of patient files, a black Bakelite, and a table light. In the corner were placed a set of scales, and next to them an examination bed. A single light fitting with three bulbs illuminated the room. Thomas and Arthur sat in the two wooden chairs at the desk.

"What can we do for you today, Mr. Bradbury?"

"It's my son Arthur. We had an accident at the farm."

"What happened?" Doc Brown asked.

Thomas stuttered a little. "Ya know, boys will be boys."

Doctor Brown stood and made his way around to where Arthur was sat. "Let's have a look."

Arthur presented his arm. As Doc Brown leant in to examine him, Arthur moved closer to the doctor. Within inches of his head Arthur whispered. "Daddy hurt my arm on purpose. He's always belting me." Doc Brown pulled back a little in shock at what he'd just been told. He'd known the Bradburys' since moving to the village as a young doctor. He'd delivered both Thomas and his brother, as well as George and Arthur. He moved back around his desk and sat in the large old leather chair which creaked as it took his weight. Doc Brown pulled off his glasses and turned to Thomas. "How did this happen, exactly?"

"As I said, just an accident on the farm." Thomas stuttered his answer again.

"Yes, but how exactly. Where and on what?" The doctor pushed.

"Oh, I was in the barn. Anne came running out to say he'd fallen on the stairs." Thomas turned to Arthur. "That's right son, isn't it?"

"And the red mark on his face?" Doc Brown asked.

Arthur looked back at Thomas. The wistful look of an injured child he'd worn since it happened was now gone from his face. It was replaced by a surreptitious smile. Then turning back to Doc Brown Arthurs expression once again became melancholy "It was my Da, Doctor Brown. He did it this morning. He threw me across my bedroom. That's what hurt my arm, and my mummy slapped my face."

Thomas felt a heat rise inside him. A dread, an anger, an embarrassment. He looked firstly to Arthur whose expression had changed again. It was now full of mischief. A sardonic smile spread across his face before he turned back to face Doc Brown, wincing, and holding his arm once more.

"Well, Mr. Bradbury?" Doctor Brown asked.

Thomas didn't know how to respond. Before he'd thought through the best course of action, he found himself talking. "He was biting his mother, doc. I heard a noise up the stairs and ran up to find him biting her - he drew blood. All I did was pull him off her, I didn't mean to do it so hard. I panicked."

"Is this true Arthur?" Doc Brown asked.

Arthur glared at Thomas before turning back to Doctor Brown, wincing again. "She destroyed my favourite toy Doctor. I was angry. I am sorry."

"Was that when she slapped you Arthur?"

It was Arthur's turn to feel uncomfortable. But it was Thomas who spoke up first.

"No Doctor, she slapped him after he called her a bad name."

Doc Brown turned to Arthur. "Why did you call her a bad name?"

Arthur, now looking like a scolded child spoke quietly and without looking the doctor in his eyes. "Because she took away my spinning top."

"Is that also why you bit her?"

"Yes, Doctor, it was. I am sorry."

"Are you Foul minded or feeble minded?" Doc Brown asked Arthur directly. "Because these are the actions of a feeble mind, or a foul mind."

Arthur turned to Thomas. Instantly, any anger Thomas felt towards his son evaporated. All he could see before him was a lost, frightened little boy. Thomas now felt the need to defend him.

"No Doctor, he's not of a feeble or foul mind. It was nothing more than a temper tantrum and I pushed him a bit harder than I'd meant to. I'm sure things will be fine once we're home. I've brought him here to see if it's broken."

Doc Brown pulled off his glasses and sat back in his chair. It groaned again. "Aye, well as that may be, I'll have to let the family welfare workers know, they'll probably pay you a visit in a week or so. And no Thomas, it's not broken. Just badly sprained."

"Do what you have to do Doctor, but what should I do about his arm?" Thomas asked, standing firm, yet still not being disrespectful.

"Rest his arm. Put it in a sling while he's not using it. After a few weeks it'll heal fine."

Thomas thanked him and then guided Arthur out of the room. Thomas felt utterly confused regarding Arthur. He had seen Arthur change in that room from a hurt little boy, full of regret and fragility to a manipulative child who seemed to take pleasure in telling the doctor what had taken place. It was almost as if he was purposefully trying to get himself and Anne into trouble. Even now as Thomas led his son out of the office and back to their truck Arthur insisted on holding his hand, and of course Thomas reciprocated the gesture. It dawned on him that maybe Arthur had played him in the surgery and was again right now, but he dismissed this notion quickly on the grounds that he was too young to understand that kind of behaviour let alone how to do it, and that surely his own son wouldn't behave like that towards him. Would he?

They arrived home after the usual time it took to navigate the old truck along the country lanes back to the farm. Thomas pulled up outside of the farmhouse and instructed him to go inside while he pulled the truck into the workshop as he did every night. Arthur obliged his father's request without any hesitation. Thomas smiled at him as he climbed out and gave him a fatherly wink. Arthur smiled back before pushing the old door closed and heading off across the farmyard.

Inside Anne was preparing their tea. When Arthur walked in, his arm in a sling she felt the same emotion as Thomas. The anger and repugnance she had felt earlier that day evaporated the moment she saw him, just as it had with Thomas. Wiping her hands on her apron she took Arthur in her arms and pulled him in close. "I'm sorry, son. You just shocked me, that's all. But you know from now on you mustn't do that."

Arthur hugged her back. "Yes, mother I know, I won't."

She kissed him on his right cheek and let him go. "Get yourself changed; George will be home soon then we can have a nice tea."

Arthur smiled at her and turned, heading for the door which would lead him to the staircase. As Arthur walked out of the kitchen Thomas entered. Anne embraced him too. "How is he, did the doctor catch on?"

Thomas hugged her before sitting at the table. "He

didn't need to Arthur told him what we'd done."

Anne gasped. "What did Doctor Brown say?"

"He asked if it was true, and when I said it was, he wanted to know why."

"Then what?"

"I explained why it had happened and what Arthur had done. As soon as I did, the Doctor asked Arthur if he was feeble minded," Thomas pulled off his boots before continuing. "I told him he wasn't, that it was all a misunderstanding and that we'll be fine now."

"Did he agree?" Anne asked, a concerned tone clear in her voice.

"He said he'd have to inform family welfare, and that they may visit to see how things are."

Anne sat adjacent to Thomas, slumping in the chair. "What'll we do Thomas. What if they ask about things and the truth comes out?"

"It'll not, so long as we only tell em what they ask. Besides, if we try extra hard to make him feel..." Thomas struggled slightly to finish his thought.

"Feel what?" Anne pushed.

"Ya, know, feel a bit extra special. When they do come, all will be fine."

Anne thought. Perhaps Thomas was on to something. George was her perfect little man. He caused them no problems, he was doing well enough at school and was eager to carry on the farm with his dad. Maybe she could spare a bit of extra attention and praise on Arthur. Maybe this whole thing had been more her fault than his. What really was the problem with the spinning top anyway? She wondered to herself. Was it really doing him any harm? "Aye, you may be right about this Thomas. I mean, we did take his favourite toy away from him, maybe this is more our fault than his."

IV

Over the next few days, they tried to pull Arthur closer to them. They had noticed Arthur's tendency to be alone, and George had told them that he always sat by himself on the school bus. Yet it seemed their efforts were beginning to work. By the time August rolled around, and Arthurs birthday, it seemed they had become a tightknit family. Anne had stopped hearing the spinning top's distinctive out-of-tune rendition and even George had begun to play with Arthur the games he always imagined he would. The family welfare workers did pay them a visit as Doc Brown said they would. They looked around the farm and the house, and where Arthur and George slept. Anne had remarked to Thomas – as quietly as she was able - that this was stepping over the line. Thomas had hushed her and suggested she just smile and tell them what they needed to hear. Eventually, they concluded that Arthur had deserved the slap, "*Spare the rod, spoil the child.*" The senior looking woman had remarked and that the injury to his arm, which was now fully healed, was nothing more than a little over exertion on Thomas's part. "*A natural reaction of a loving and worried husband.*" She'd also surmised. They left by telling them they could see nothing wrong, and the case – as far as they were concerned – was now closed.

As a surprise for Arthur, Thomas and Anne decided to lay on a surprise birthday party for when he and George returned from school. It was a warm sunny day and Thomas's brother and his family had turned up, and George had planned for some of his friends to come home with them on the pretence that they were coming down for George. Anne had tried to find another spinning top, or at least one which was similar, but it was to no avail. Even when they had gone into Middlesbrough, the local toy shops were still somewhat bare. Toy manufacturing had begun again after the war, but it was a slow recovery. In the end they had decided to buy him a toy railway. It comprised of a small oval track, a steam locomotive – which was clockwork – and two carriages. It wasn't a cheap gift, but after the progress they had made with Arthur, they wanted to ensure that this newfound closeness would continue.

Arthur, George, and a couple of his friends entered the farmhouse to the sounds of "Surprise," and

"Happy Birthday Arthur." The celebration which consisted of jelly with ice cream, sandwiches for the grown-ups and of course a birthday cake with six candles on it seemed to be going well. Arthur had received his present with an equally large amount of delight and enthusiasm to set it up and see it working. Thomas and George soon set about the task. Anne decided they were just as eager to play with it as Arthur, though she kept that thought to herself. Once the train had ran around its small loop a few times, and the clockwork had ran itself down, Arthur retired with the comic book annual his uncle and aunt had bought him to the small settee which was largely unused and was placed in the kitchen/ diner simply because there was nowhere else it could live.

As Arthur sat reading, he heard a whisper. "Happy birthday, son." Arthur looked over his shoulder, fully expecting to see Thomas sat on the arm of the settee, but when he turned Thomas wasn't there. He was with his brother across the room. Arthur turned further, trying to see if someone was playing a trick on him. "Happy birthday Arthur." The voice came again. This time he recognised it. It was the same voice he'd heard that day in the bunk. It was the voice of Jack. The voice of a man who told him he was his real father, and the voice that told him he should pleasure himself to be a real man, just like the soldiers had. Arthur looked around. George and his friends were sat at the table, playing a game of cards. Anne was talking with his aunt, and Thomas was still with his brother. Arthur pushed his hands against his ears, but the voice still penetrated his mind. "Look at them, all happy while they ignore you." Jack's voice said. "These aren't your real family, they're pathetic. They're not like you. No, you're stronger than them, they couldn't possibly understand what strength you will have - what you'll be able to do when you grow."

Arthur looked around the group of people in the room. The feeling of *not belonging* began to creep back out of his subconscious. The voice continued "Thomas, the man who calls himself your father tried to kill me. He fired that shotgun at me, he hurt me son. But I was too quick for him." Arthur's gaze moved to the shotgun which still leant against the wall near the door.

He whispered in reply, desperate that the people around him would not hear him. "You're lying, my father wouldn't do that."

The voice responded. "Ah, but he did, he tried to shoot me because your mother wanted me, she wanted the feel of a real man inside her."

"What do you mean?" Arthur whispered, unsure of what Jack's references meant.

"Ah, I forget, you're still a boy, you don't yet understand what women really want, what they really crave. But one day you will, and like me you'll be able to oblige them, my son."

Arthur stood, gently placing his book on the settee and made his way to the door which led into the hallway. "Leave me alone," Arthur whispered again. "This is my family and my father wouldn't try to harm anyone."

The voice became angry. "But he's not your father, is he? I am, I planted the seed in your mother, I'm the one that brought about your life. You are nothing to these people. They've destroyed your favourite toy. A toy I brought back from the war, especially for you Arthur, because I knew one day, I would have a son to give it to, and what did they do? They smashed it. Would they do that to George?"

Arthur thought for a moment. "No, they wouldn't"

"It was Thomas who did it. He smashed it with a hammer, I know where it is. Would you like to know? Would you like to see what your so-called father did to your special toy? The one I brought especially for you?"

Arthur turned away from the kitchen, standing with his back to them all in the threshold of the doorway. "Yes."

The voice sounded pleased. "That's my son. Go to the workshop, go to the back and into the small room."

Arthur snuck out of the house and made his way to the workshop. Following the instructions from the voice, he made his way to the back of the building until he came upon the small office. Inside, exactly where the voice had told him it would be, Arthur found the smashed spinning top and lying next to it the hammer Thomas had used. Arthur felt the same rage build inside him the day the top had been taken away. The voice came back.

"See, my son. I told you, you're not one of them, you never will be, you'll always be second best to their precious George. They lied to you, told you that you lost this toy and yet here it lays, smashed by Thomas with that hammer."

Arthurs gaze moved to the hammer. He picked it up, gripping it tightly. The voice came again. "That's it. Let the anger out my son, it's the mark of a true man to seek retribution on those who have wronged you."

Arthur turned around looking for something on which to take out his anger. On the far end of the counter he noticed something covered in a sheet. Arthur moved over to it and pulled off the cover. It was an antique dolls house. He'd heard Anne talk about it. He remembered it was her mothers. "That's it, that's perfect, open it up and smash the inside. Strike it with all your might, my son." Arthur opened the small house and lifted the hammer as high as he was able. Then, with all of his might, he brought it down on the doll's house interior. Again, and again he struck the beautifully crafted house until it lay smashed. Pieces of exquisitely crafted miniature furniture lay scattered around the workshop. The dolls who had inhabited the house fared no better.

"Pick up the pieces and cover it over again. Let's

keep this our secret." The voice told Arthur.

Arthur did as he was instructed. Once the pieces were lay inside the house, he pulled the sheet over it, covering it so it looked exactly as it had before he'd attacked it. Placing the hammer back on the table, Arthur picked up the spinning top before leaving the workshop. As he left the workshop and walked across the yard and back towards the house, he sang. "See Saw Margery Daw, I shall be their new master."

Chapter 5.

I

As with every year, the seasons rolled by and autumn now began to make itself known. The days were drawing in and Thomas could feel the change in the air, especially in the morning air which seemed much crisper and sharper. In the cooler denser air, they could hear the sound of the clanking and machinery at the station, and the leaves were for the most part a glorious golden brown. That wonderful stage between the green of summer and the dark mottled brown they became after the life within them had come to end. Another change had happened on the farm. After learning of the imminent closure of the station Thomas and Anne decided to diversify their farm and bought a small herd of sheep, along with a collie dog pup, they decided to call, Shep. Sheep was a livestock Thomas had not farmed before, he'd always been a cattle and pig farmer, though he'd sold the cattle herd a while back, deciding instead to concentrate on the pigs. But with the loss of income once the station is closed, it seemed he would have no choice but to expand.

Following Arthurs birthday and despite their best efforts Arthur had continued to withdraw into himself, though they didn't know why. It seemed to them that they had made great strides in the lead up to his birthday, but something had changed that day. They'd noticed that Arthur had left the kitchen but simply assumed that he was tired from the celebration and had gone to his bedroom to lay down, after all that's where Thomas had found him when they realised that he wasn't with them. But as the days passed by it was obvious that Arthur was slipping back over. Once again, he was becoming a recluse in his own home. He would, more often than not, be found sitting near the bunk door singing the nursery rhyme. Both Thomas and Anne noticed that when he was in the barn the animals around him seemed to act differently, they became quiet and guarded, behaviour that prey animals exhibit when they sense a predator nearby. Shep, so playful with George wouldn't go near Arthur.

He'd also stopped playing with George, and no longer wanted to spend time with Thomas. He'd began to exhibit the same temper tantrums he had when his spinning top had been taken away. As far as Anne and Thomas were aware, Arthur still believed what they'd told him, that he had misplaced it. They had suggested to him that he could have left it on the school bus, or even at school and that someone had taken it. What they didn't know was that Arthur had it hidden under his bed, in the box which contained his toy train and that when the house was asleep, he would bring it out, and stroke the dented dome, while whispering the nursery rhyme. On one occasion Arthur had disturbed George while putting the box back under his bed. George was laying with his back to Arthur, yet he could hear him doing something followed by a silence. George wondered if Arthur knew he was awake, but quickly convinced himself he couldn't possibly know that. Apart from the fact it was pitch black and you were not able to see your hand in front of your face, George wasn't facing Arthur's bed. After the sound of Arthur's moving had stopped George began to slip back to sleep. Just as he felt himself going over, he heard Arthur say something. George held his breath. Was he talking to him, or was he talking to himself?

"What's it like, where you are?" He heard Arthur whisper.

There was a pause. "I don't understand." Another pause. "Stop telling me I'm just a kid, I'm smarter than you think." A shorter pause "Yes I am, dad."

George felt a wave of relief, he hadn't realised his dad was in the room. Perhaps he'd been asleep, perhaps that was the noise which had woken him, and it wasn't Arthur moving something. George turned over in bed to face Arthur's bed and switched on his bedside light. Thomas was not there. Only Arthur sitting upright and staring at the doorway. George looked to the closed door. No one was there. "Who you talking to Arthur?" George asked.

Arthur slowly turned his head to face George. In the dim light of the bedroom Arthur's face seemed somehow distorted. George wiped his eyes, trying to focus. "I'm talking with my dad, he's right there." Arthur pointed to the door.

George strained in the gloom, but again he could see no one. "Da isn't there, there's no one there." He looked back to Arthur. A cold chill ran down George's spine and the hairs on his arms stood erect. Arthur's face wasn't his own, and yet it was somehow familiar. Arthur smiled. The distortion deepened.

Arthur's smile widened further, and with it his face changed entirely to that of a man. A man with a scar which ran down the side of his face. George screamed in fear, pulling the blankets over himself. Trembling and unable to see anything but the soft light of his bedside lamp as it shone through the sheets. George heard Arthur get out of his bed and make his way over to his. A shadow cast over him, then the light extinguished, and George was in complete darkness. He felt a tug on his sheets. George held on to them as firmly as he could. Then, with more force than he could resist the sheet was pulled away from him. The face he'd seen replace Arthur's was now only inches from his own. George screamed again, "Ma, Da!" As he shouted his bladder emptied and George felt the hot sogginess of urine between his legs. Seconds later the door burst open and Thomas entered, flicking on the ceiling light. The room was instantly bathed in white light. George looked back to Arthur who was still standing over him. His face was normal.

"What's going on?" Thomas demanded to know.

George was still too frightened to talk. "I don't know," Arthur began. "He screamed and I got out of bed to make sure he was ok, then you came in."

Anne followed in a few moments later. George, embarrassed by his bed wetting, tried desperately to hide it. But Anne had already sat on the bed to comfort him. As she leaned over to him, she felt the urine soak through and onto her own nightwear. "C'mon son." She said, pulling back the sheets. Arthur looked across to see the dark damp patch in George's pyjamas. Sniggering to himself he climbed back into his own bed as Thomas, Anne and George left the room. "You'll have to sleep with us tonight, I'm not changing the bed at this time. Go get yourself cleaned up,"

"Goodnight," Thomas said to Arthur as he turned off the light. As Thomas pulled the door closed behind him Arthur mouthed, "Goodnight dad." The voice whispered in reply to him. Goodnight son."

George climbed into his parents' bed. Still unsure of what he'd seen. Thomas almost immediately fell asleep while Anne tried to reassure George. "It's alright you know; everyone has an accident from time to time." She said, snuggling George under the sheets.

It was Arthur. His face." George began.

"How do you mean?"

"His face wasn't his Ma; his face was different. Older, like a man's face."

Anne wasn't sure how to react. "What do you mean, George, his face wasn't his?"

"It was different somehow. Like it was only part of his face. It looked older and it had a scar down one side."

Anne felt a chill run through her. She would never forget the scar Jack returned with from the war. It was why he'd taken to wearing the hat, always tilted slightly to hide it. Perhaps her hearing the spinning top wasn't just some kind of memory of sound, or an episode of weak mindedness as her mother used to say about folk who imagined things. "What else?" Anne asked.

"I woke when I heard him moving. Then when I heard him talking, he said dad, so I turned around and put the light on, I thought Da was in the room," George sniffled a little. "But there was no one there. He pointed to the door and said he was standing by it. I hid under the covers, but he pulled them back and that's when I saw that face."

"But Arthur said he got out of bed when he heard you cry."

"He's lying Ma. I swear, honest, I'm not telling fibs." George struggled to keep his composure.

Anne pulled him in close. "It's ok son. We'll get to the bottom of it, I promise. Now get some sleep, lad."

"Night Ma." George said. But sleep wouldn't come easy to him. Every time he closed his eyes, that face was there to greet him.

The following morning George climbed out of his parents' bed and made his way to the bathroom. He'd decided to get dressed for school before breakfast. This would limit the chance of being upstairs and alone with Arthur. Outside it was a bright autumn day and the trees had lost the last of their summer dressing. The bare wooden branches heralding the coming winter. Since taking on a herd of sheep Thomas had begun his day much earlier than he used to. The only field suitable for them was a good thirty-minute walk from the farmyard. As usual he'd brought Shep along with him. At just under a year old there was more play in the young dog than there was hard graft, but Thomas was training him and so far, the dog showed promise. Anne was downstairs in the kitchen preparing the boys breakfast. George was the first to the table, followed a few minutes later by Arthur.

"What's this nonsense last night?" She asked Arthur as she placed down the boys' porridge.

Arthur could tell she was not in a good mood this morning. There had been none of the usual greetings and repetitive breakfast traditions. He didn't answer her. Rather, he slid his spoon into the porridge, and while looking directly into her eyes he took a large slurp of it. Some of the thick cereal spilled back out of his mouth.

Anne approached the table. "I asked you a question lad." She insisted upon him.

Arthur rolled his eyes and dropped the spoon into the bowl. A large plop of porridge spattered out. Sighing, Arthur answered. "What?"

Anne composed herself. "I asked what this nonsense was in your room last night. Were you talking to yourself again?"

"No, I was talking to my dad, Jack." Arthur said, defiantly.

"No, if anything my lad you're imagining such things, it's that feeble mind of yours again, there was no one there, there's no such things." Anne reprimanded him.

"Well, he was. He comes every night and we talk. So what?" Arthur ran his fingers through the spilt porridge and then ran them through his mouth.

"Aye, and I've told you to not mention his name again, haven't I? So that's the end of it! No more lad, do you hear me, no more!" Anne scolded him. Her voice raised and her face turning a dark scarlet.

"Aye, and if I don't stop, then what. You'll hit me again Anne? Thomas will break my arm this time?" Arthur stood and threw his spoon into the bowl, spilling a larger amount. Then he turned to George. "I told you not to say nowt, didn't I!"

Anne glared at Arthur. "You leave your brother out of this. Now go and get ready for school. And be quick about it."

Arthur smiled at Anne and then made his way out

of the kitchen. George didn't know how to react, or what to say. Silently and slowly he ate as much of his breakfast as he could, but the adrenaline which coursed around his body following Arthur's warning took away his appetite. Around a half hour later George and Arthur were heading out of the door on their way to school. Anne had hugged and kissed George, wishing him a good day. For Arthur she'd given nothing more than a cursory glance and half a smile. This hadn't bothered Arthur who was now convinced by the voice of Jack that these people he lived with were not and never would be his family. For now, he needed their home, he knew he couldn't survive the coming winter living rough, even if he made his way to the towns and cities and it would be safer for him here than in a shelter of some kind.

II

January 8th, 1954.

Winter had now fully replaced the bright crisp days of Autumn and the farm had transformed once again. Thomas had brought the sheep down from the grazing fields and into the building he'd used for the cattle herd. During the last days of summer and throughout the autumn he'd transformed it into a habitable holding shed for the sheep. The temperature now struggled to rise above zero and not for the first time this winter a thick covering of snow lay across the moors and the shallow valley. Travelling by truck was impossible and for the last week the boys had not been able to get into Thirstonfield Village to attend school. While George was quite happy with this Arthur was feeling more and more pent-up as each day passed by. The farmhouse was not a large house. It consisted of a 'cosy' single living room – or parlour – as Anne insisted it was, a narrow steep staircase, two bedrooms and a small, often cold, bathroom. The single largest room was the kitchen which also served as the dining room as well as the entrance. But even this wasn't a sizable room.

Another day had slowly drifted by and following dinner they were once again in the living room. Outside, night had already taken hold, the sun set quickly in these parts and at this time of year, around four in the afternoon. January was a cold dark and long month. The snow which had claimed the land continued to fall outside in the pitch darkness, only the odd snowflake was visible when it passed through the yard lights. Inside, the fire had been burning continuously for the last few weeks. Anne had only allowed the flame to die when she needed to clear out the grate. Thomas sat in his wingback, with Shep faithfully by his side. The collie was now over a year old and had become a fully-fledged sheep dog. Anne sat opposite him. George lay on the floor in front of the fire, reading one of his comics while Arthur sat on the small settee. Outside the wind had picked up. It whistled around the sharp corners of the farmhouse, ever so often a gust would blow down the chimney, causing the flames to flicker and dance before the hot air forced the freezing gust to retreat. Arthur looked between them. His disdain for them had increased over the last few days. He could no longer bear to be in this room with them. He stood and left, closing the door softly as he did. Making his way up the stairs he entered his room and pulled out the box from under his bed. Checking no one had followed him, he slid off the lid and pulled the spinning top out. Secretly, Arthur had been repairing the damage inflicted by Thomas. The hammer blows had dented the thin tin that was the outer skin, but the mechanism had largely been left intact. All Arthur had to do was reattach a spring and realign one of the barrels which held the notes. Once he'd figured this, he then set about pushing the dents back out from the inside. Tonight, was the final stage of the repair. Carefully, Arthur pushed the biggest dent out, using a sock tightly wrapped around his hand to give him the shape he needed. Then he slid the cover back over and using a knife he'd snuck upstairs he tightened the screw which held it all together. Arthur placed it on the ground and took a step back. Save for a few scratches and uneven ripples he couldn't remove; the spinning top was back to its former glory. Now all he had to do was take it back to the bunk house where he could keep it. He knew Anne would not go in the bunk house again and Thomas had no interest. Though she had put the key up on the dresser Arthur had found another way in for now. A small opening could be made by pushing the slats behind the bed apart. For now, Arthur could fit in between them and under the bed where the opening came out. But he knew before another year passed, he would be too large. He checked out of the window. The snow was still falling hard. From his vantage point he could see that it had built up against the side of the barn he needed to access the bunk. For now, the spinning top would have to remain a secret under his bed. He placed it carefully back in the box and then slid it under his bed. As he did the voice came back. "That's a fine repair son." The whispering voice said. Arthur smiled, switched off the light and climbed on to his bed. As he lay in the darkness, he pushed his hand inside his trousers.

When George was eventually sent to bed, he found Arthur asleep, curled up, dressed and on top of his blankets. George thought about leaving him like that but knew once the fire had gone out the house would soon become cold. Taking a clean blanket from the small cupboard in the corner, George covered his brother and then climbed into his own bed. Pulling the cord on his bedside light, he whispered "Goodnight brother."

After a few days, the snow cleared enough for the school bus to begin running again. George and Arthur made the walk along the track and up to the main road where George met up with his friends. As the bus pulled up Arthur backed away from it. "C'mon Arthur or you'll miss it." George said as he climbed up the step.

"Am not going to school no more, it's a waste of

time." Arthur replied, stepping further away.

"But you must, the teacher will ask where you are."
George replied, now in the doorway.

"Tell him to fuck off for all I'm concerned." Arthur
turned and walked away from the bus and towards
the station.

"Let's go!" The driver insisted.

George stepped in the bus and sat next to Frank.
"He's getting worse."

"Creeps me out George. I don't know how you live
with him." Frank replied as the bus set off.

"I've no choice, mate."

An hour or so later Arthur had made it to
Thirstonfield Station. British Railways had closed it
the second week of January. The station master and
other employees had all left and the station house
was now being used by the team who were
responsible for stripping out what they could reuse
or sell. Arthur pulled back at the security fence
which skirted the rear of the perimeter and slid
under it. Without worry of being caught he made
his way down amongst the hustle and bustle of the
workers and into the engine shed. He walked over
to the inspection pit. Over it was the steam shunter
he'd heard Thomas and Anne talk about. This
small train it seemed had a incurable fault and had
been laid up here. He'd also heard them say that
they were going to tow it back to the
Middlesbrough yard today. Arthur made his way

down the steps and under it. Looking up he could see the inner workings of the locomotive. The inspection pit was illuminated by small lights sunken into the walls, yet still it was dark and dank. The walls were stained with oil and grease. A few tools lay scattered around as well as a couple of hand rags. As Arthur kicked around the debris, he disturbed an oily towel. Under it something shiny caught his eye. Arthur bent over and pulled the towel to one side. Under it lay a curved knife. He could see clearly how sharp it was. He picked it up and ran his finger along the blade. It cut through his flesh with ease. Arthur gasped. As he did a voice shouted.

"Hey, you, lad. What the hell do you think you're doin' in here?" A large overweight balding man headed towards the pit. "I asked you a question. You're not meant to be in here, now hop-it."

Arthur didn't respond perhaps the way he expected him to. Rather Arthur wedged the knife into a crack between the wall and floor and kicked the towel over it.

"What are you doing under there?" The overweight man, who couldn't see what Arthur was doing asked.

Arthur Slowly made his way up the steps and out of the pit. "This is mine." Arthur replied with the man standing over him.

"What the hell are you talking about?"

"This is my parents land, I'm from the farm, the Bradbury Farm." Arthur announced.

"I don't care if you're old man Bradbury himself, you shouldn't be here, it's not safe. Especially for a young'un such as yourself. Now, get yourself home, there's a good lad."

Arthur didn't respond verbally, he simply turned and headed out of the shed and back onto the platform. Other men were removing items from the station masters house. Arthur followed them inside. The house was almost empty. Just a few pieces of furniture now remained. Arthur heard two men talking in the kitchen.

"What's left boss?" One man asked.

"Anything that's not bolted down or fastened to the walls and floors is to go. That's what they said." Another man answered.

Arthur couldn't see the men, but he didn't need to. He just wanted to listen for now.

"And upstairs?" The first man asked.

"No, that's all clear. Nothing left up there we can take or need."

Arthur heard what he'd been waiting for. He moved quickly across the hallway and up the stairs. There were three bedrooms and quite a large bathroom compared to what he'd been used to on the farm. Only the master bedroom had any furniture remaining - a large wardrobe in the corner. Arthur decided this would be his new hideout. The place he would come when he couldn't stand to be around the Bradburys'. Moving back down the stairs, indifferent to whether he would be seen Arthur made his way back outside. The station was a hive of activity. He watched as a larger steam engine pulled the smaller broken engine, he'd just been under, from out of the engine shed and onto the main line. "Oi, clear off, go on, git!" Another man began shouting at Arthur. This time Arthur ran back around the house and back through the fencing and up the shallow hill which surrounded the station. He watched the man stand on the other side of the fence waving him away. Arthur smiled at him and turned. He'd seen what he wanted.

George had arrived at school and made his way into the classroom. The teacher, a Mr. Ingledew called the register. There were a few kids missing, but none from the same family, so George couldn't use the weather as an excuse why Arthur wasn't in school. He would have to make up some other reason and hope that Arthur would not only come into school tomorrow but also validate why he wasn't here today, or they would both get into trouble. Eventually, the call came around the George. "Here sir." He replied.

"Arthur Bradbury?" Mr. Ingledew called. No answer came. "Arthur Bradbury?" Again, no answer. "George, why is your brother not in school?"

George could feel the heat of his embarrassment climb up his face. "He's not well. Got a cold, from the snow."

"No doubt running around in it was he?" Mr. Ingledew asked. His small glasses perched on his nose.

"Yes sir, that's it." George answered.

"Very well."

Frank turned to George and wiped his forehead while making a *phew* sound.

By the time Arthur returned to the bus stop at the top of their farm track the snow had stopped falling. Only a light fresh covering replaced the dirty melting *slush* which now covered the roads and pavements. He watched as the school bus trundled along the road towards him. Eventually, it stopped, and George got off. "Did they ask where I was today?" Arthur asked.

"Yes, I told them you had a cold from playing in the snow."

"Good, just keep that up." Arthur said, smiling at him.

George didn't reply. He shrugged and then headed down the track and home with Arthur following behind him.

As they walked Arthur could hear Jack's voice once again. You did good today, son. You don't need school, I didn't go that much, hated it anyway - waste of time." Arthur smiled as he tagged along behind George. He whispered his reply to the voice inside his head. "What excuse did you use for not going?"

The voice sniggered. "I didn't give an excuse; they couldn't make me go."

Arthur thought for a second. "Hey, George."

George turned around. "Wha?"

"I'm not going to school tomorrow. Don't give them a reason, just tell em I'm not coming back. Ever!"

George shrugged again and turned back to face the way he was walking.

As they entered Anne was setting the table for their dinner. The usual routines had begun again now the snow was abating and life could resume some normality. "How was school?" She asked as the boys came in, dropping their bags by the door.

"It was ok Ma." George answered, moving to the range to warm his hands.

"And you Arthur." Anne asked.

"I had a good day too." He smiled at George before making his way up the stairs.

III

Arthurs truancy continued for a week or so before Thomas and Anne were called into the school. George, has he'd promised, had not told Mr. Ingledew Arthur's whereabouts. All he would say at registration was that Arthur wasn't with him, and that he had no idea where he was. That at least was the truth. George had no interest in what Arthur was doing or where he was going, and he certainly didn't want to bring it up with him.

When Tomas and Anne arrived at the school Mr. Ingledew took them to see the headmaster, a Mr. Mason. He was a stern looking older man. Close to retirement and very much of his time his passion for shaping the young minds of the future had long since left him. Like all aging academics who now seemed to spend their time fulfilling administration duties, he counted down the days to retirement. Thomas and Anne sat opposite the headmaster.

"You know why you're here, yes?" Mr. Mason asked, sternly.

"Yes, and may I say we had no idea that Arthur was missing school." Anne replied.

"He has a brother here George, is that correct?" Mr. Mason asked. Ignoring Anne's initial plea.

"Aye, that's right." Thomas replied. Feeling slightly

like he used to when he was dragged before the headmaster as a boy.

"So how did you not know Arthur was missing School?"

"What's that supposed to mean?" Replied Anne.

Mr. Mason leaned forward slightly on his desk. "Why didn't George tell you Arthur was missing school Mrs. Bradbury."

Thomas and Anne looked at each other, They had no idea why George wouldn't tell them. "I don't know." Replied Anne.

Mr. Mason leaned back again. "Aye, well. Be that as it is, and what with the previous troubles Arthur has caused at this school, perhaps it's best if he's home schooled from now on."

"You're kicking him out?" Thomas asked.

"I think he's done that himself. But yes, I'll not have disruptions for the kids who come here to learn." Mr. Mason looked between Thomas and Anne. "If you want my advice, that lad needs some specialist help."

"He's just fine, thank you very much headmaster." Anne replied defiantly yet knowing within herself that Mr. Mason was probably right.

Thomas and Anne left the school and headed into the village centre to stock up on a few supplies, *it seems a wasted journey to be through here, and not get what we need*; Anne had told Thomas. Once loaded they headed back to the farm. As the truck trundled along the country lanes, only recently cleared of the last of the snow Anne turned to Thomas. "Do you think Arthur needs seeing to?"

Thomas thought for a moment. He'd been suspicious of Arthur's behaviour. Just little things he said or did and the way Thomas would catch him looking at Anne or George when he thought no one was watching him. But he'd swept these under the carpet. Partly because of how busy he was and because he didn't want the stress of having to deal with it. He figured it was a stage he was in, and that at some point Arthur would grow out of it. But he couldn't ignore these things. And nor could he ignore how Arthur was conceived, who his father was and the fact that Arthur believed his dead father was talking to him.

"Thomas!" Anne raised her voice to bring him back.

"Yes, wife. I was just thinking, that's all."

"Well, you haven't answered my question."

"I think we need to keep an eye on him. That's what I think for now." Thomas replied, weaving the truck off the road and down the farm track.

With the engine running Thomas and Anne removed the couple of bags of food. Anne took them into the farmhouse while Thomas pulled the truck into the workshop before switching off the engine and placing the oil tray under its sump. Closing the workshop door, he followed Anne into the Farmhouse. "Another thing, wife. We'll have to chat with George to see why he hasn't said anything."

"Could be he's a bit frightened of him?" Anne replied.

"Could be. But even so, he knows he should've said summat."

After dinner was cleared away Thomas and Anne called both George and Arthur into the kitchen. "Sit yourselves down." Thomas instructed them when they entered. Both boys sat next to each other. Anne and Thomas sat directly opposite them.

"We were called to see the headmaster today," Thomas began "Want to know why, or do you already know?"

George looked down at the floor. A trick he'd learnt when Mr. Ingledew would ask one of the students to volunteer for something odious, like reading out a piece of literature or their homework. Arthur however didn't. He was relishing the coming confrontation. "Well?" Thomas barked.

"Happen it's to do with me not going to the bloody school" Arthur said. He turned to George. "I bet it was you what told them!"

George instantly denied it. "No, I never said a word, honest." There was a palpable fear in George's voice.

"Aye, and you'd best not." Arthurs threat was real.

"And just what's that supposed to mean?" Anne asked Arthur directly. "We'll have no violence and threats in this house, or you'll be dealing with me. Do you understand, my lad?"

"Anyway, I'm not going back to that school. They're all Ninnyhammers, the bloody lot of 'em." Arthur avoided answering Anne.

"You don't need to worry about that, you've been as good as kicked out!" Thomas raised his voice. Something he rarely did.

"And my lad, there'll be no more swearing. Now go to your room and stay there. I don't want to see you 'till the morning." Anne scolded Arthur.

Arthur stood. His face showed no emotion as he left the room. As he climbed the stairs, he made sure they could hear each step. As he did, he whispered to himself *"See Saw Margery Daw, they all shall have a new master…"*

Thomas then turned to George. "Why didn't you tell us he was nicking off, son?"

George fumbled his words a little. "Because… because he's told me to say nothing Da. Or else…"

Anne reached across the table and clutched his hand. "Are you frightened of him? It's fine George, you can tell us."

A tear ran down George's face. "He's strange mam.

He talks to this Jack on a night. He thinks he's his dead father, and he thinks I'm asleep, but I'm not. And that night, his face did change, I swear it."

Anne squeezed his hands. "It's ok son. He won't dare hurt you, don't worry. Me and ya' father will keep an eye on him from now on."

At the top of the stairs Arthur listened to their conversation. He turned his head slightly, facing into the darkness of the bedroom behind him. "Aye dad you were right. They're not my family."

The next morning George was downstairs and ready for school. Picking up his bag by the door, he said goodbye to his mam and then left. As he passed his father, he shouted *bye* and continued up the track and to the main road to meet up with his friends. As usual he was at the make-shift bus stop before them. As Harry, Frank and James approached George could tell that Frank was upset.

"What's up?" George asked.

"It's his dog. It's gone missing." Harry said.

"When?" George asked.

"We don't know. Came down this morning to see to him, and the door was open."

"Wasn't he in the yard?" George asked.

"No, that's the thing, the gate were open too. My Ma would never leave the gate open, or the door." Frank replied. His voice quivering.

"His father thinks someone did it on purpose. He found summat in the yard. Tell 'em what it was Frank." James said.

"I've brought it into school, I'm gonna take it to the police after." Frank opened his bag and pulled out a pyjama top. "There's dried blood on it too. Here look." Frank turned the top around. A large patch of dried blood stained the front of the garment. "I hope Archie's ok."

George swallowed hard. "I'm sure it's nothing. He'll be home when you get in, you'll see."

At the farm Arthur sat at the kitchen table with a pile of books and a school exercise book in front of him which Mr. Mason had provided Thomas and Anne. Before beginning the days chores, Anne had sat Arthur at the table and given the mathematics book and instructed him to work through the first four pages.

Anne gathered the laundry. Lifting a pile from the boys' bedroom she began to sort them. "Arthur, where's your 'jama top?" Anne looked under his bed, waiting for a reply.

"Dunno, it was there his morning." Arthur shouted back up the stairs.

"Well it isn't here now, or I wouldn't be wasting my time asking you."

Anne pulled the box out from under the bed, trying to see if the top had slid down the back of the bed and against the wall. But it wasn't there. As she grabbed the box to slide it back under, she heard a metallic rattle. Anne craned her neck, looking up from her crouched position. Behind her, the bedroom doorway and top of the stairs were clear. Anne shouted "Arthur, you doin' your work?"

"Aye, I am." Came the reply from downstairs.

Slowly Anne pulled the box back from under the bed. She shook it gently. The metallic rattle came again. She thought for a moment. Then, carefully, she began to lift the lid. Halfway up the lid stuck fast. "Damn it!" She whispered. Anne maneuvered the box through ninety degrees and loosened the stuck side. Sitting upright with the box between her legs she began again to lift the lid. Just as the lid became free a shadow appeared over her. "Why are you opening that?" Arthur asked.

"I was looking for your top, son. And I heard something rattle in here. I wanted to make sure your train wasn't broken."

Arthur walked around to her front. He placed his foot on the box lid and pushed it down. "It's not. You're just hearing the tracks rattle - that's all."

Anne's fingers snagged in the lid, but Arthur kept pushing with his foot. "Arthur, my fingers are caught."

Arthur stopped pushing down but for a second or so, he didn't relieve the pressure. Once he did Anne pulled her hand free, cutting her finger on the sharp cardboard. "Ouch," Anne yelped sucking

the blood form the wound. Standing she picked up
the laundry pile and headed downstairs. Once he
was sure Anne was out of sight Arthur lifted the lid
and stroked the spinning top. Then removing it, he
pushed it to the back of the wardrobe until he
could put it back in the bunk.

"Come finish your maths Arthur." Anne shouted.

"Comin'" He replied. As he made his way down,
he sang to himself "*See Saw Margery Daw Anne will
have a disaster.*"

Chapter 6.

March 13th, 1957.

I

March rolled in on the farm, and with it the busiest time of the lambing season. The claws of winter had begun to retreat around the middle of February, with the last of the snow fall ending late January. The thaw which followed provided them with fresh spring water which ran through the Bradbury farm from the surrounding high lands and peat bogs which skirted the top of the shallow valley. The nights were for the most part still chilly, with a layer of frost in the exposed areas, but the days were warm, crisp, and clear. The harsh winter had served its job - clearing away the bugs, germs and other such things which flourished in the heat of the previous summer. The trees which had stood naked and defiant against the storms and snow now had a fresh covering of green. The grazing fields were lush and thick and the spring flowers which appeared every year to herald the coming summer were abundant in their spectacle.

Shep, as always, was beside his master's side, rounding the sheep and protecting them. Thomas had brought down the ewe's he felt were closest to giving birth. Though today was a typically warm spring day the weather this time of the year could

change almost hourly and the top fields which held
the sheep were exposed with very little in the way
of shade or a weather break big enough for the
entire flock. For now, the *sheep house* as Thomas
and Anne had come to call it, held around a dozen
lambs with their mothers and another five
expectant ewes.

It had been all hands-on deck for the Bradburys'
and George had been drafted in to help. As well as
the lambing, the farm also needed clearing after the
winter. The detritus which accumulated over the
winter months needed to be cleared. There was one
exception to this family mustering. Arthur had
become more reluctant to join in with the family in
any capacity and during the day he refused to do
his schoolwork. Initially Anne had sat over Arthur
to make sure it was completed, but as his
reluctance grew in proportion to her insistence
Anne lost the will to continue. Now she found
herself giving him a pile of books and walking
away. Often, she would hear him mumbling to
himself as she walked past a doorway or a room.
Sometimes she would stop, trying to listen to the
conversation, other times she would block it out
and pretend she hadn't heard anything. On the one
occasion Arthur had helped Thomas Anne had
taken advantage of him being out of the house and
sneaked a look in the box under his bed, but all she
found was the mechanical toy train. Unbeknownst
to any of them Arthur had put the repaired
spinning top back in the bunk, on top of the tallboy
next to the wash basin, where Jack instructed him
to. Thomas and Anne had no idea how they

should proceed. They had thoughts of bringing in the help Mr. Mason had suggested to them, but they were frightened that when Arthur would begin to tell this expert that Jack Bright was his father, a man who used to work on the farm, and who suddenly left, the truth of what happened that night would come out. There was another consideration too. Times were different, and to have a son who believes he's hearing the voice of a dead man would reflect on them as much as Arthur being a bastard. Anne was close to her limit. While George and Thomas worked outside, she alone was left inside with Arthur. She could see the changes in him. At the beginning of all of this he still looked like her son. A happy-go-lucky little boy who enjoyed family life and who wanted to be involved. She remembers leading up to his birthday how he seemed to be over his phase. But something changed on that August day in 1953, and whatever it was, her son was becoming less recognisable with each passing day.

Anne would often become angry and frustrated at Thomas for not seeing the change, for not taking his conversations with Jack seriously. There were days when Arthur would disappear for a few hours, only to come home dirty. She suspected that he was sneaking out at night, yet despite her best efforts she could never catch him doing so or find his bed empty. George had told her that Franks dog had gone missing, and that they had found a blood-stained pyjama top in the yard. When George had described it to her Anne recognised it as the top she couldn't find. She'd passed it off as coincidence, but as Arthur's demeanour continued to change, the thought of what he may have done to the dog kept niggling away at her. She'd asked George a few weeks later if they ever found the dog, but George confirmed they never did.

It would be the night of March 23rd when Anne would get the confirmation she needed. It would be a night she would not forget – ever. After the boys had gone to bed Thomas and Anne had stayed up for a few more hours. At around eleven, she poked the last of the fire out, switched of the lights and went to bed. As always Anne checked in on the boys' as she passed their bedroom. Seeing them asleep she made her way into bed and shortly after, fell asleep. She wasn't sure what time she heard the noise - Thomas had not allowed any watches or clocks back into the house. A creek on the stairs and the sound of a door on its dry hinges woke her from a light sleep. Anne climbed out of bed as quietly as she could. She had begun to keep her bedroom door open slightly. This was so she could hear any sounds, like the sounds which had woken her this night, but it was also so she could peek along the landing to the boys' bedroom without having to open the door, which was sure to make a sound that would alert Arthur. Anne peered through the crack in the door, but she could detect no movement. She turned back to Thomas, wondering whether she should wake him. She decided not to. Thomas was a level, placid man, but if she woke him in the early hours, he would be sure to simply walk into the boys' bedroom rather than try to catch Arthur in the act. And besides,

Thomas still wouldn't consider that Arthur had anything to do with the disappearance of Franks dog. As she stared into the darkness of the house, the sounds which she had, up until now, been oblivious to, came into focus. A bleating from the sheep house, then more and more joined the chorus. Anne moved to Thomas, now she would have to wake him. "Get up Thomas, summat's wrong in the sheep house."

Groggy, Thomas sat up listening. "Shit!" He said, leaping out of the bed and pulling on his clothes.

The ruckus Thomas and Anne were making woke George. He appeared bleary eyed, rubbing the sleep from them. "What's up Ma?"

Anne was now only focused on the increasing noise coming from the sheep house and didn't think to check if Arthur was in bed. Rather, she rushed past George - Thomas close behind. "Nothing, just the sheep, go back to bed."

Thomas pulled the door to the sheep house open and flicked the light switch and then stopped in his tracks. Inside, the ewe's bleated and every lamb lay slain. Their throats cut. Anne tried to follow Thomas in, but he stopped her. "Go back inside." He simply told her.

Anne stepped back outside and then turned to Thomas. "I'll go put the kettle on."

A noise distracted them both, the sound of something falling and landing in the soft muck which covered the damp farmyard. Anne looked over but couldn't see anything, then came the realisation that she hadn't checked on Arthur. As quickly as she could she made her way back across the farmyard. As she did, she noticed the yard brush lying on the floor. Anne figured she or Thomas must have knocked it over in their haste. She entered as swiftly as she could and made her way through the house to the boys' bedroom. She opened the door and stepped in, switching on the light. Arthur turned over in his bed, squinting in the light which now illuminated the room. Anne walked over to Arthur, clasping the sheets she pulled them back down to his knees. Arthur was indeed in his pyjamas. Anne pulled the covers back over him and turned to leave the room. George sat up "Is everything okay Ma?" He asked

"Go back to sleep George."

Switching the light out as she left Anne made her way back down to the kitchen and began to boil the kettle. It took Thomas an hour to remove and dispose of the carcasses. The ewe's continued to voice their anguish while he did what was needed. Shortly after the final lamb was removed a silence descended on the sheep house. As Thomas closed the door, he couldn't decide which was worse. This silence or the sorrowful cries. He entered the kitchen to find Anne pouring a cup of tea into his green tin mug. "What's happened Thomas?"

"Every lamb's slaughtered." Thomas sighed as he

spoke.

Anne thought for a moment. "Who do you think would do such a thing?"

"I've no idea, wife." He whispered in reply. Exhausted and troubled by what he'd seen.

"Could someone 'ave gotten onto the farm?" She asked, sipping her own tea.

"Could ave, I suppose." Thomas rubbed his hands across his bowed head.

"I wonder why Shep didn't bark?" Anne asked.

Then it dawned on Thomas. In the commotion and distracted by what he'd seen, he forgot about the dog. "Where is Shep?" Thomas stood. "Shep, here lad, here… Shep?"

Anne searched the house while Thomas went back outside. Dawn was just breaking over the North-eastern banks of the valley. They searched the farm for an hour. Eventually Thomas heard the whimpering of Shep. He found him with his front legs broken behind the workshop. Thomas picked him up, crying as he did. "Who could have done this lad?" He laid him in the back of the truck and then returned to the farmhouse to let Anne know he'd found him.

"Why is this happening?" She asked.

Thomas didn't answer her immediate concern. "I'm taking him to the vets, wife. Perhaps they'll be able to sort him. One way, or another."

Anne watched the Bedford truck make its way up the track. The sun was now low in the morning sky, bathing it in an orange glow. She decided that she would tell George that *men* had come onto the farm and had taken the lambs and that Shep had been hurt defending them. In some ways she guessed it was true.

It would be a little while longer before the boys would be up and George would be getting ready for another school day. As she made her way to the top stair, she noticed the boys' bedroom door was still open. *Must have forgotten to pull it closed* she thought to herself. She went to the door and placed her hand on the knob. Just as she was about to pull the door, she noticed one of Arthurs feet sticking out of the bed. He still had on his socks, and it was covered in muck. She stood, holding her breath. She entered the room slowly, the rising sun illuminating the house from behind her through the small window at the top of the stairs. Carefully, she placed a hand on the tip of the sock, where it had worked itself loose from his foot. It was damp. A shiver ran through her the instant she touched it. She knew immediately what this meant. It was Arthur who had attacked the lambs, and in all probability, Shep too. A rage rose up inside her. She wanted to drag him out of bed and do unspeakable things. Things she would not believe any mother would want to do to any child - let alone her own. But as she watched him sleep, whatever last feelings of hope or love she had for him slipped out of her. As far as Anne was concerned, he was no more her son than a stranger on a street. She felt no repulsion toward herself for feeling this way. Rather, a cold feeling of hatred swept over her. She would ignore her instincts to exact swift justice on him, she would wait until George was out of the house and Thomas had returned from the vets with Shep.

***

Arthur had lay awake after going to bed. As always, He'd change into his pyjamas and then gotten into bed. He waited until George was asleep and then until Thomas and Anne had come up the stairs - closing his eyes when she'd pushed open the door to check on them. Once the door was pulled most of the way back it would just be a matter of time before they would both be asleep. The voice guided him "They'll be asleep now son, time to do it." Arthur carefully pulled on his thick socks and slid out of bed. Then, he arranged his pillows into a form and size which resembled his own. Taking the time he needed – no hurrying was necessary – Arthur made his way onto the landing, and then slid the door back to where Anne had left it. He was halfway down the stairs when he stood on the wrong side. A creak, Arthur froze. He heard Anne's bed sheets rustle. Holding his breath, he waited to see if she would get out of bed. *"Lazy bitch won't get out - get on with it."* Jacks voice commanded. Arthur made his way through the house, the solid stone flagged floor making the egress easy. It was only the stairs which offered any real concern, and he'd learnt which stairs creaked and complained.

Entering the sheep house Arthur pulled out the sharp knife he'd taken from the kitchen a few weeks back. He'd watched Anne carefully as she'd prepared meals. She had her favourite knives and the one Arthur had found stuck at the back of the drawer wasn't one she'd used, and likely wouldn't miss. The attack on the lambs was quick and brutal. With Jack's voice willing him on, "Kill the little fuckers, show them bastards in there," Arthur slashed away. As he dropped the last dead animal, and washed the blood from himself, he heard the commotion of Thomas and Anne as they headed across the yard towards the sheep house. Scurrying, Arthur made his way to the back of the shed and slipped through a small lose board. As he did Shep approached him, growling. Arthur picked up a shovel which was leaning against the back of the building and swung it. Shep moved and then bit hard into Arthurs left leg. Arthur pulled back, the pain radiating through him. He swung again, this time across Sheps front legs. The dog yelped and fell to the ground. Arthur picked the stricken animal up and ran to the workshop. There he put the injured dog on the ground and pulled out the knife. Then he heard the sheep house door open and he saw Anne stepping out. Arthur pushed the knife back into his pocket and ran to the farmhouse while Anne was still talking with Thomas - her body half out the door but her attention fully distracted by Thomas. Just as he got to the kitchen door Arthur knocked a yard brush resting against the wall. He spun, trying to catch it, but missed. It landed with a splat in the muck just as he made it through the door.

He managed to get back upstairs and into bed without waking George who was exhausted from a day's work on the farm and had fallen asleep immediately. There he waited for Anne to come back inside - slowing his breathing and trying to distract himself from the pain of the dog bite. A few moments after pulling the sheets over him, he heard the kitchen door shut and then Anne moving around. He heard her coming up the stairs. He closed his eyes, and rolled onto his side, facing away from the accessible side of the bed. He could see the bedroom light come on through his tightly closed eyes. He turned to face her, forcing a sleep-ish squint against the light. He felt his sheets being pulled back and heard George ask what was wrong. Anne covered him over again and answered George. Then turning the light out, she went back downstairs. Smiling, he relaxed and closed his eyes. "Good lad, that'll fucking show em." The voice said, as he drifted off to sleep.

***

II

Thomas carried Shep frantically into the veterinarian's office. "Help!" he shouted as he carried the whimpering dog inside. Mr. Metcalfe, the local vet who worked with most of the farmers in the area rushed out to meet Thomas.

"What's happened Thomas?" He asked, taking Shep off of him.

"We've had some bastards attack the farm. They've killed every lamb and did this to Shep. I reckon he was trying to protect em." Thomas answered, still shaking with equal amounts of anger and dismay.

Mr. Metcalf lay Shep on the table. He checked the dog's heart and then looked into his eyes before pulling back the dog's lips. Thomas watched as the vet reached into Sheps mouth and pulled out a small chunk of what looked like meat. "Reckon he got one of em, this is flesh. He took a chuck out of someone." He threw the morsel into the bin, before turning his attention to the dog's legs. "Aye, they're broken alright."

"Can they be fixed?" Thomas asked.

"Aye, I can make him walk again, but he'll be no good as a sheep dog Thomas. He'll be nothing more than a pet." Mr Metcalf said, comforting the dog.

"He'll make a loyal pet. Do what you can for him, I need to get back to the farm."

"Come-by in a day or two. See how he's doing." Mr. Metcalf replied.

"Will do." Thomas replied, stroking Shep.

Before he left Mr. Metcalf grabbed Thomas's arm. "If you find out who did this, let me know. I'll help you batter the bastards." He whispered.

Thomas nodded and then headed out.

At home Anne had seen to George's breakfast. After leaving school three years ago, he now worked on the farm. Arthur was still in bed. It seemed to Anne that he rose later each day and it also seemed that that was in direct correlation to his decreasing enthusiasm for being a part of their family, or for completing the work sent home by the school on a Friday. She waited for Thomas to return from the vet while she cleared away George's breakfast pots and began the daily routine of cleaning. Around an hour later she heard the old Bedford truck pull into the workshop, followed shortly by Thomas entering the kitchen. Anne immediately put down the sweeping brush.

"What did the vet say?"

Thomas pulled off his boots. "Said he could fix him, but only as a pet - he'd be no good on the farm as a working dog."

Anne sat at the table and held Thomas's hand.

"Ave summat to tell ya."

"What's that, wife?"

"It was Arthur what done it, and Shep I'll bet."

Thomas pulled his hand away. "What makes you say such a thing?"

"When we came back to bed this morning, I checked the boys. I noticed Arthur was wearing socks in bed. They were damp Thomas and covered in muck."

"That doesn't mean owt, wife. He could have just left them on from the day."

"Remember George telling us of Franks dog going missing."

"Aye, what of it?"

"Well he said they found a blood-soaked pyjama top. When George described it, it's the same one that's gone missing. It was Arthurs."

"Where's the lad now?" Thomas asked, sternly.

"He's up in bed. I've left him there so we could talk."

"Go fetch him."

Anne stood and headed for the bottom of the stairway. At the bottom she shouted. "Arthur. Arthur, come down, me and your father need to have a talk with you."

In bed Arthur opened his eyes. He'd been awake since George had got up that morning but was biding his time before he went downstairs. The shout came again. "Arthur, do you hear me lad?"

Arthur spun around and sat on the edge of his bed, pulling off his damp - soiled socks. "Aye, I do, am coming." As he stood a sharp pain radiated from his left leg. Arthur winced. "Fuckin' dog." He stood, stretching his leg as he did, pushing the pain back.

"Don't tell those bastards anything son." Jack's voice once again came into Arthur's head as he made for the landing. "I won't dad, don't worry." He replied in a whisper.

As Arthur entered the kitchen Thomas stood from behind the table with Anne standing next to him. Arthur walked as best he could, trying to hide the pain and not limp, but the ache from Sheps bite made walking without any kind of a stagger impossible. Arthur pulled out a chair and sat. "What's up?" He asked, smiling between them.

"Your mother says you're responsible for the attack on the lambs that happened last night." Thomas said, firmly. His voice had a gravelly resonance about it.

"What attack?" Arthur replied.

"Give it up lad, I saw your socks when I went back to bed. Wet they were and covered in Muck." Anne scowled at him.

Arthur pushed his right leg out from under the table exposing a bare foot. "I'm not wearing any socks." He smiled at them.

Thomas moved around to Arthur and pulled him up from his seat. "Show me your leg." Arthur pulled up his pyjama legs. On his left leg was a deep wound. It was clearly an animal bite.

"What's that?" Anne asked.

"When I took Shep to the vet, he pulled a chuck of flesh out of his teeth. Said he'd bitten who'd been there."

A silence fell over the three of them. Arthur allowed his pyjamas to drop back down. Anne felt a sickening wave wash over her. The silence ended by Thomas. "Well lad, what have you got to say?"

Arthur looked directly at him. "It doesn't matter what I say. You've both made up your minds. But I didn't do it. I got this bite yesterday when I went down the station, some stray dog bit me."

Thomas yelled. "You're a bloody liar. Just admit it."

Anne immediately pulled on Thomas's arm, trying to calm him.

Arthur stood quickly, pushing the chair back a few feet across the stone floor. "What you going to do Thomas, break my arm this time? We all know how that'll end. You'll have another visit from the family welfare. This time I'll tell them what happened, about Jack and that you beat me. I have marks to show them."

Thomas stepped forward. "Why you little…"

Arthur cut him off. "Little what?" He turned to face Anne. "Bastard? Is that what you were going to call me." Arthur then picked up one of Thomas's boots. As hard as he could he hit himself across his left cheek with the sole. As soon as he did a red mark in the pattern of the tread appeared across his face. Arthur dropped the boot, smiling between them and then turning his back on them. Now clearly limping, he made his way back up the stairs.

Once he'd left the kitchen Anne turned to Thomas. "What we going to do with him?" Her voice shook.

Thomas looked back at her. "Honestly, wife I've no idea. There's something deeply wrong with that lad, and he'll only get worse. Once it's in em, that's it. If he were one of my animal's I know what I'd do."

"Aye, but he's not an animal. he's our son." Anne replied.

"Is he?" Thomas said, pulling his boots on, and walking out the door.

Anne felt those two words hit her hard. How could he say such a thing to her, knowing what had happened? As she watched Thomas making his way back outside, she felt an anger rise inside her. But this anger wasn't just for Arthur. Once the door was closed Anne made her way back toward the sink. As she did, she felt the air become cold, then she heard Jack's voice again. "Looks like Thomas is jealous of us." Anne gasped; her body tensed as adrenaline began rushing around her. In the fight or flight moment Anne clutched the sides of the sink and sobbed. Standing at the top of the stairs Arthur had heard Thomas's parting words, and on hearing Anne cry he smiled to himself while pushing his hand down and into his trousers.

III

July 1957.

The summer had been a poor one so far. Below average temperatures and above average rainfall meant that at least half of the crops had been spoilt. Add to that the loss of the lambs and income from the station, both Thomas and Anne were no longer sure of the farm's financial future, which now had to also provide George with an income. For now, they'd kept George out of the financial side of the business. There would be time enough to burden him with this. Besides George had begun to court a local girl from Thirstonfield village called Mavis. They didn't want to worry him about any possible future they may have together.

Mavis is the daughter of the local butcher. A slim

girl with shoulder length brown hair and a pleasant disposition. She, like many of the folk who grew up around these parts had little interest in matters outside of the local area. George had known Mavis growing up. They had often travelled to school on the same bus and sometimes sat in the same class – small rural schools often didn't split boys and girls for certain subjects. But there were those, like physical education and biology, which still required separation. Anne and Thomas had taken to her quickly, which was helped in no small part because they knew her parents Harry and Lucy very well.

Arthur had become even more distant from the family. He rarely sat with them at dinner, and hardly spoke to them, only doing so when it was unavoidable. Anne would often spot him sat on the old tree trunk at the end of the track talking to Jack. This was a truth she could no longer deny. Though she tried to, pretending that Arthur was talking to himself. But after hearing Jack speak directly into her, she could no longer dismiss it as the feeble mind of a troubled child. Arthur was about to turn ten, but already he was bigger than Anne and George, who had taken after her for stature. Only Thomas remained larger than Arthur, and she worried that wouldn't be for too much longer. The disappearance of the local pets had continued since the lambs had been slaughtered. Thomas had once confronted Arthur about this, but he denied it flatly and suggested that if he pursued it, knowledge of Anne's *fling* with Jack and the fact that he was their bastard child may come out. Thomas had no choice but to back down. If this came out now with the farm on the edge of bankruptcy it could send them over the edge.

He knew that once the local grocers believed that Anne had had a fling, and that the man she had it with then killed himself because of guilt it could ruin their reputation and that of the farm. He also knew that there would be accusations made because they'd lied that Arthur was their own child, and then Thomas would be seen by his peers as a man who couldn't be trusted and keep his woman from straying. Even if these facts were not true, that would matter little if Arthur's narrative were the one people heard first. He knew how people in these parts thought. If he tried to redress this lie with what had actually taken place, there would be a backlash for soiling the reputation of a man who fought for his country and is no longer alive to protect his name. He also knew that the local police would likely not get involved in tittle-tattle, so he couldn't count on them to back up his own truth and discredit the lies Arthur would spread.

For these reasons and others which made less sense Thomas decided that so long as Arthur no longer hurt the animals on the farm, he would turn a blind eye for as long as he could. Though this uneasy truce was never confirmed verbally, it seemed Arthur understood it, and for now at least, the farm animals seemed safe. As for Anne, he kept the reports of missing animals and nattering's from the village a secret from her. Most folks believed it was *roughens* coming in from Middlesbrough causing the trouble, and for now Thomas was happy it deflected their attention away. Since the events which had taken place, she had become withdrawn, as she had following Jack's attack. Thomas knew there wasn't much more her mind could cope with. The arrival of summer and Mavis had brightened her spirits, and he was pleased to see her smile again whenever George and Mavis were at the farmhouse. But he also hated that whenever Arthur was about. She would almost cower and avert her gaze in case she ever met his. For now, Thomas didn't know what to do or who to turn to.

It was towards the end of July when Arthur visited the station. The work to lift the track had taken British Railways longer than they thought it would. As for the station itself, it was now stripped of what could be lifted and re-used. The station house was empty, and already nature had begun to reclaim it. Inside small mammals and birds had built nests, and the ceilings were covered in cobwebs. Outside, the hanging baskets were overgrown with choking weeds, and the gravel driveway now looked more like the beginning of a wild forest track.

The track lifting was now entering its final phase. The workers were lifting the lines which ran through the Estdale tunnel. Once they were through that, they only had around two miles of track before they would abandon the rest. The tracks from that point on were old, and no longer serviceable. Had they not closed down the station and the route they would have needed to replace them. This was another consideration for closing the station now rather than letting the lease run its full term.

As a temperately warm sun beat down on his back Arthur followed the now empty trail until he reached the tunnel. Inside he could hear the sound of the equipment they were using and the men shouting commands over the bustle of the work. He began creeping inside the tunnel, keeping as close to the wall as he could. Around halfway in, the tunnel had a modest bend to the right as the topography followed the curve of the shallow valley. Arthur could now see the lights of the workmen and he could hear the sound of the diesel generators which provided them with power. Just at the point where the men were working, the wall had a man-sized cut in it. These were found every ten feet or so and were there for personnel to tuck into should they be working in the tunnel when a train came through. However, this cut out gave Arthur the perfect place to crouch down while the men worked, oblivious to the boy who now watched them from the darkness.

Arthur watched the men as they used the pneumatic tools to drill out the spikes which held the tracks in place. Close to him a short, older, fatter workman with thick unkempt dark-greying hair and a tangled mess of a beard struggled with such a drill. The vibrations made the unruly piece of equipment shudder and pulsate as he tried to keep it in place. Arthur noticed how close it often came to his feet. Only the steel track separated it from his soft leather work boots as it jostled around. Jack's voice came into his head, "Look at that fat bastard. Fuckin' doughball. We should teach him a lesson, stop the fat bastard from getting to the larder. We'd be doing him a favour. If he lost some weight, he might get a woman," Arthur felt a rush of adrenaline.

As the workman turned, attempting to keep the heavy drill in place, Arthur snuck out of the shadows and crept up behind him. Slowly, he placed his hands over the doughball's midriff and waited. His moment came seconds later. The drill skipped up. As the fat man fought to keep it in place Arthur grabbed him as hard as he could, shouting as he did. Instantly and instinctually, the fat man turned to see what, or who had grabbed him. As he did the pneumatic drill skipped the track. By the time the fat man realised what had happened, the drill was tearing through his leg. Before he had time to react to the shock of what was happening to him, his left foot was severed and his fibula and tibia shattered. Arthur retreated instantly to the cut out, disappearing back into the darkness. The screams of the man sounded to Arthur like the that of lambs and the ewe's as he'd slaughtered them. He felt a surge of growth in his developing male appendage. "Good lad, that'll teach the fat bastard," Jack's whisper of adulation filled Arthur with a warmth of acceptance and validation. One that he'd never felt in the company of Thomas and Anne. To Arthur, their praises always sounded like a mandatory compensation of George's - like they were sharing out sweets. If they praised George, then they had to praise him - *one for you one for him* - and those praises always sounded hollow and forced and were given begrudgingly.

The fat man's work colleagues were already tending to him. Turning the industrial lights around to illuminate his injuries. Arthur pulled as far back into the cut out as he could. After a few minutes he watched as the fat man, he now knew to be called Burt was carried, crying, and screaming out of the tunnel. Once cleared, the generators were cut, and the tunnel was plunged into pitch darkness. Arthur stepped out of his hiding place. He picked up a work torch he'd seen dropped in the chaos and switched it on. Laying in front of him was an assortment of hand tools. Arthur picked up a crowbar and swung it back and forth. He struck it against the damp brick wall. Sparks flew from the impact. Then something else caught his eye. With a clang he dropped the bar against the now dislodged track and made his way over to the object. There, on the ground, was the fat man's foot - still in its boot. Ripped from his leg just above the ankle bone, which protruded from the flaps of flesh and sinew. "Pick it up," The whisper said. "Pick it up…" Arthur bent forward and picked up the severed foot, holding it by the jutting bone. Unfastening the laces, he pulled the bloody stump from the boot, discarding it once the foot was free. The boot landed with a soft thud. Arthur squatted and placed the torch carefully on the ground. Then he held the foot in the narrow beam of light. Still holding the protruding bone with his left hand, he pulled off the blood-soaked sock and threw it away.

As Arthur made his way back out of the tunnel, he could hear the faint conversation of two men entering from the other – Middlesbrough - end. By the time they reached the accident area Arthur was out and clear of the tunnel. The two men began searching for the severed foot. Their flashlights danced around the darkness until one of the men shouted, "Found it." The second man moved to where the beam of the light pointed. In the shadow filled dim light he bent down and picked up the boot. Holding it up they realised with horror that it was empty. "What the bloody hell is this?" Asked the first man.

"Look, over there."

Placing the boot down he followed the beam of his counterpart until he saw the empty sock. "It's like someone has pulled the foot out." The second man whispered, looking around, following his narrow dim beam.

"Let's just get the fuck out. This place always has given me the willy's,"

The two men picked up the empty boot and sock and made their way back to the Middlesbrough end of the tunnel as quickly as they could. At the other end of the tunnel, Arthur, now bored of, and having no further use for the foot, simply tossed it to one side. He would never think of this moment again. Burt, however, would never work again, or recover mentally from the trauma of what happened that day.

At the farm Thomas was cleaning the pig sty. Since the slaughter of the Lambs he'd decided to sell the ewes for meat. Financially, he simply couldn't afford the cost of insemination without the income from the lambs. Even selling the ewes had meant they'd made a loss. The pigs were almost ready for sale to the local butcher, and with George now courting their daughter, Mavis, Thomas had felt somewhat obliged to knock down the price. *A family and friend discount,* as Harry had called it. As he cleared out the pigs and began to swill out the sty, he bumped into the door which led into Jack's former bunk. He turned to face the door. He felt a rage build inside of him of what that door represented. The place where he gave refuge to a man who would ultimately betray him. Thomas threw down the pitchfork. He marched out of the barn and into the farmhouse without removing his boots. Anne came in just as Thomas reached the dresser where she kept the key for the bunk. "Thomas!" She yelled when she saw the trail of dirt and detritus he'd left across the recently cleaned stone.

"Where's that bloody key?" Thomas demanded.

"What key? Take tha' boots off, you're dragging the yard through the kitchen." Anne scolded him.

"The key, the key to the bunk," Thomas insisted

again.

"Why, what do you want that for?"

"I'm gonna do what I shoulda done from the start. I'm going to rip the whole bloody thing down and burn every damn thing in there that belonged to that bastard, Bright."

Anne rushed to him and placed her hand on his arm just as his fingers found the key on top of the dresser. "No, please don't."

"Why not, wife?" Thomas asked, pulling the key down and slipping it into his pocket.

Anne began to cry. She sat in the nearby chair; her head bowed. "You wouldn't understand why if I told ya." She said, through broken breaths.

Thomas knelt in front of her. He gently placed his hands on her shoulders. "You can tell me owt, you know that. What is it, what's the matter?"

Anne wiped her face and looked at Thomas. "It's Jack. I can still hear him."

Thomas stood and took a step back. "Not this again, I thought you'd ave dropped this by now,"

"I know how it sounds. Like I should be in the looney bin, but I swear, I can." Anne pleaded with him.

"I suppose you can hear that spinning top as well?"

"No, I haven't heard that for a long time since,"

"Well, it's all hogwash, and I'll have no part of it, wife. I'll clear that damn bunk and then that'll be that!"

Thomas pulled away from Anne and headed back out the kitchen. Anne sat back in the chair, exhausted by everything since that November night. She wondered, what was it that she had done in this life, or a past life, that she should now pay such a huge price.

Thomas entered the bunk. It was exactly as he remembered it. His initial and only thought was to drag all of the belongings out into the yard and burn them. In his mind he would dance around the fire - celebrating the death and finally the clearing of that bastard. He would sing his name out loud, "Jack Bright is fucking dead, and all his shit is burning red," He would then celebrate the anniversary of this cleansing every year for the rest of his life. Of course, he would do that privately, within himself, no one would know why on that particular day of the year Thomas Bradbury, normally a man of polite restraint, would walk around with a smile on his face that nothing of man or indeed of God could remove. Then he saw it. The spinning top. Thomas stopped in his tracks. How could this be? He'd smashed it - hadn't he? Thomas took a step back, unsure, and unnerved. As he did the top began to slowly spin and as it did the tune began to play, *See Saw Margery Daw…*

Chapter 7.

May 5th ,1961.

I

It was a day of celebrations - spring had finally arrived. The trees were blossoming, and the air was filled with warmth from the sun and optimism as the country began to fully recover from the war. It was also the day George and Mavis were married. Friends, family, and villagers joined in the celebrations. Though rationing had officially ended in 1954, certain luxury items had still been hard to get a hold of. But as the country rolled over from the 50's there seemed to be a change of mood that was felt even in the rural areas, and Thirstonfield was no exception.

The service at the local parish church had been an idyllic one. The priest who had christened both George and Mavis now joined them in holy matrimony. Thomas and Anne sat proudly as they watched Father Crowley declare them man and wife, and George begin his own family life. Afterwards, there would be a small reception in the village hall, and then the happy couple would be off to Bridlington for a weeklong honeymoon.

Arthur had attended the service. Now at the age of 13, he was larger than all of them, including

Thomas. His temper and general demeanour had continued to spiral down. Unable to stop him, he had taken back the key to Jack's bunk and would now spend most of his days in there, playing with the spinning top while making up new endings to the nursery rhyme it seemed to endlessly play. Some nights he would sleep in the bed which was now damp, and mould ridden. Anne was now past the point of caring, "*If he wants to get pneumonia let him*," she had once said to Thomas. Following the accident at the Estdale tunnel, British Railways had erected fences that even Arthur could not get through. Once the last of the line was up, the fences were removed, which meant Arthur began to make regular visits once again to the station. Wildlife largely no longer inhabited the old station house, or the surrounding buildings. The ones who did stray on the land often met with a grizzly end at the hands of Arthur who would regularly pull out the curved Kirpan knife to hunt and kill anything he could find. Once his lust was satisfied, he would slip the knife back into the pit. The locals claimed that even the birds refused to fly over the *old place.* In their minds at least, it was a sure sign of something evil lurking. Thomas had employed the services of Yates & SONS, the local estate agent to sell the property, but so far, no interest had been shown.

Local farm animals and pets had continued to disappear - the locals had their own theory on that as well. Since the suicide of Jack Bright, things had begun to happen. Strange things which had no reasonable explanation. Apart from the birds and

other wildlife keeping clear of the Halt, there had
been reports of strange and ungodly noises from
the old station house at night. The head gossip of
the village, a large woman who went by the name
of Ethel, had said she'd seen a large man-shaped
apparition wondering around the village. The
locals, and the police, who she had reported it to in
a frenzy, simply placated Ethel and assured her
they would investigate it. Of course, they never
did. Ethel was known for her slight exaggerations
as well as her overactive imagination. Yet she
insisted on this particular tale of seeing this large
shimmering man walking in the direction of
Thirstonfield Halt.

Occasionally one of their own farm animals would
be found dismembered. Thomas continued to hold
the truce he'd forged in his mind; it was the only
way he could continue. It was either that, or he
would begin drinking – or worse. Though this was
a conversation he'd only ever had with himself. He
would tell George it was likely a fox or some *townie*
doing it for larks or a bet. *"Bloody Middlesbrough lot"*
He would call them.

As well as Arthur now being physically bigger than
any of them, he was also immensely strong for his
age, and Thomas was not getting any younger. The
years of hard work on the farm and constant
financial and family worry had also taken their toll
on both his physical and mental wellbeing. Thomas
knew he was a weaker man both physically and
psychologically, and the things he would have
found easy to do and deal with only a few short

years back, he simply couldn't handle anymore. Perhaps this realisation more than the things which proceeded it caused him the greatest sorrow when he was alone at night with his own thoughts. He'd also seen Anne age past her years. The constant fear she felt when Arthur was around as well as the absolute shame and sadness she felt for bearing such a wicked child had perhaps taken more from her than a dozen lifetimes working the land. Thomas felt his own regrets for not shielding her and giving her the life he'd promised her that summer day in July, all those years ago when they had wed.

After the reception, Thomas and Anne waved goodbye as George and Mavis headed away to Whitby in a car her father had hired - complete with driver. From there they would travel by train to Bridlington. Once the car had turned the corner Anne went back into the hall to fetch Arthur who had no interest in waving his brother off. Anne found him sat in the corner he'd occupied during the time they'd been there. In an ill-fitting suit – the only one the local rental shop had – he'd spent his time sipping the orange drink and plunging the spinning top, which he'd taken to carrying around with him once again. After that night in the bunk when it seemed to spin on its own, Thomas had not dared to interfere with it again, and Anne had long since become passive to Arthurs need for the top to be with him.

"Come on Arthur, it's time to head home." Anne spoke politely, afraid he would snap and cause a scene.

Arthur stopped pushing the plunger and looked up at her. "Ok Anne, I'm coming."

He stood. As he did Anne immediately took a step back. He half smiled at her fear of him. Arthur had stopped calling his parents mother and father, or Ma and Da as George mostly did a while back. This didn't bother either of them. Neither of them had any emotional connection with him. They only felt an obligation until he was old enough to tell him to leave and to never come back. They had decided to do this on his sixteenth birthday.

Once outside Anne and Arthur joined Thomas. They walked in silence to the car. The old Bedford truck had finally given up in the winter of 1960. The antifreeze mix hadn't been strong enough and during one particularly freezing night the water had frozen, cracking the block. The repair quotes Thomas had got made the repair uneconomical. He'd had no choice but to go to the bank and ask for a loan. With it he bought a new - pale blue, Land Rover. This was by far the newest and poshest thing they owned. It was only affordable because George helped with the repayments from his wages on the understanding that one day, it would be his. The journey home was, as always, one of quiet discussion between Thomas and Anne. Arthur sat in the back of the short three-door truck. In between they could hear the whispering of the nursery rhyme. At one-point Anne looked over to Thomas and smiled. He smiled back, yet both of their smiles were more about consolation of each other than they were about happiness. With George gone, albeit for only a week, Thomas knew he would now have to work the farm himself. Anne of course would continue with her duties inside the house and they would both have to deal with whatever came their way from Arthur. This last duty they each shared was one they continued to shield from George. And it was something they would also have to shield Mavis from when they returned, because they would eventually be moving onto the farm. The plan being that George and Mavis would ultimately take over from Thomas and Anne. And for Anne at least there were some days when she wished that day would come sooner than later. It seemed that because of Arthur, both Thomas and Anne kept secrets from each other. Secrets not of affairs or wishing to be without the other, but of a life without Arthur because somehow, someway, he would disappear without the ability to ever come back. They also shared another secret fantasy. It was one where Arthur had never been born and that Jack Bright had never come into their lives or at the very least not returned from the war.

After a journey which seemed to take longer than usual, they pulled up outside of the old farmhouse. Like everything on the farm – including themselves, it was beginning to look its age. The paint had cracked both inside and out. The stonework looked tired and worn and the windows were pitted from the relentless beating of the sun and the unyielding pounding of the winter. Anne had been fastidious in her routine and approach to cleanliness and hygiene. But the events since Arthur had been conceived, along with the continuous voice of Jack and the intermittent sound of the spinning top which only she could hear, as well as day to day stuff had drained from her the last of her desires to keep a clean home. She had known for some time that Mavis would begin to take over these responsibilities when they returned from their honeymoon, and so for the last year or so Anne had slipped back in her caring about what she now felt were trivial matters.

Thomas pulled the Land Rover into the workshop - the old Bedford now relegated to being parked around the side - outside with a tarp covering it. Anne and Arthur had made their way to the farmhouse. As Thomas pulled the workshop door shut, he heard the sound of a car pulling up. It was PC Dowding. Thomas waved as the car came to a halt. The constable climbed out. "Hello Mr. Bradbury," He said, pulling on his regulation hat. "Can we talk, inside?"

"Aye, we can." Thomas replied, leading the way across the yard and to the house.

PC Dowding followed Thomas inside. "Wife," Thomas called, "We have company."

Anne emerged from the pantry. "Constable," She said, respectively.

PC Dowding removed his hat and tilted his head in her direction. "Ma'am"

"Best come this way," Anne led PC Dowding into the living room. Once inside she closed the door. Thomas and Anne sat in their usual chairs - either side of the fireplace, while the constable sat on the settee. He looked up at the ceiling and pointed to it, "Will Arthur be able to hear us?" He asked softly.

"No, he'll not be interested in anything we're talking about." Anne replied.

"What is it, constable?" Thomas asked.

"We're still getting reports from the village of pets and animals going missing. Some say ridiculous things like it's the ghost of Jack Bright that's raging a retribution on the village. Others have a simpler view, that it's a young lad," He paused "Arthur to be precise."

Thomas and Anne looked between each other.

"Do you know where he goes when he's out of sight?" PC Dowding asked.

"Not always, what parent does? Perhaps if they'd kept him in school…" Anne snapped.

"As I understand it, they had good reason to expel Arthur." PC Dowding replied and then continued. "I'm aware of the accident – the injured arm, and that Arthur bit you Mrs. Bradbury."

Anne began to cry. She turned to Thomas, "I can't

do this anymore, I can't keep the pretence up everything's ok." She turned to PC Dowding "Take him away. If you think it's him that's done these things, best take him away, and lock him up,"

"Mrs. Bradbury, it's not as simple as that. We'd need proof."

Thomas leaned forward in his chair. "These people who say it's the ghost of Jack. Who are they?"

The constable turned to face him. "I can't tell you that Thomas, you know that. Besides it's all hogwash. Just idle gossip."

Thomas hesitated, and then continued. "Thing is, we would have thought that a while back. But I'm not so sure now."

PC Dowding studied him. "Pardon me?"

"We think," Thomas stopped and looked to Anne. She nodded, wiping her eyes clear. "We think Arthur is talking with the ghost of Jack. Somehow, he's corrupting Arthur, making him do things."

PC Dowding folded his notebook and pushed it back in his pocket - fastening the brass button. "You can't expect me to write that in a statement, can you?"

"It's true. I've seen it with my own eyes, and George has too." Anne pleaded.

"George?" PC Dowding replied.

"Yes, one-night George woke because he thought he heard Arthur talking with his father. But when he turned on the light, no one was in the room. George insists that Arthurs face had changed, and that it was the face of an older man. A man with a scar."

"Don't you mean their father?" PC Dowding asked.

"Pardon?" Anne asked.

"You said, his father - as in Arthur's father. Didn't you mean, their father - Thomas?" He said, pointing directly at Thomas.

Anne looked away from the Constable.

"You know what she meant," Thomas interposed.

"I'm not sure about ghosts of dead Jack and Arthur's face changing and such things. All I know is that people, good local people, are coming to me and telling me about their pets disappearing and other strange things. Now, I think all of these things can be explained, but with normal natural explanations and not supernatural nonsense." PC Dowding stood and replaced his hat. "We'll keep an eye out for Arthur, I would suggest you do the same. If we catch him, he will be arrested."

"Will do." Thomas replied. "I'll show you out."

PC Dowding turned to Anne. "Mrs. Bradbury."

"Constable." Anne replied.

PC Dowding followed Thomas through the house and out of the kitchen. The sun was beginning to go down, and the farmyard was cast in long shadows which it seemed were almost perceivably moving as the sun moved around the shallow hills. The Constable opened his car door, removing his hat and tossing it on the passenger seat. "We'll keep an eye open for Arthur, Thomas. Don't worry."

Thomas nodded and closed the car door once PC Dowding was inside. Thomas then turned and made his way back into the farmhouse. PC Dowding began to drive along the track, the soft yellow glow of its headlamps only partially illuminating it. Suddenly, Arthur stepped out in front of the car. The patrol car skidded through the thick muck to a stop, just a few feet from Arthurs legs. PC Dowding watched in the dimming day light and soft glow of the cars lights as Arthur slowly moved around the car. His gaze never deviating from the Constable as he did. A chill ran down PC Dowding. It was something that he'd not felt before. An unnerving sensation like something was telling him to get away from here, this farm and its land, and to never come back. PC Dowding shook it off. When he looked back, Arthur was gone.

Inside the living room Thomas had returned from seeing the Constable to his car. He'd already lit the fire and was sat back in his chair. Anne looked at him. "Well?"

Thomas thought for a second. "I don't know wife. I just don't know. Perhaps we should call Doc Brown back."

"I can't take any more Thomas, if summat isn't sorted it'll be me that's off to the mad-house. Mark my words!"

Arthur, now back in the house, stood at the top of the stairs - in the dark. He listened to Thomas and Anne's conversation. When Anne spoke of being all but broken, he smiled. Turning, he made his way back into his bedroom and whispered to himself, *"See Saw Margery Daw Anne will be gone ever after…"*

II

George and Mavis arrived home from their honeymoon. With the farmhouse being too small to accommodate the newlyweds, they had taken up the offer of Mavis's parents to live above their butcher shop in Thirstonfield. Discussions had taken place about moving Arthur out of the bedroom they had shared growing up, but George insisted that Arthur should not have to be squeezed into the small box room. Currently used and known as the *knick-knack room* it's where anything that was no longer useful and too good to be thrown out or isn't useful everyday ends up. Besides, it meant that George got to use the new

Land Rover for the commute, something the new driver revelled in the idea of.

They had been home for a couple of days when Thomas made the trek into Thirstonfield to collect them. The small flat above the shop was beginning to look like a home. Mavis, with the help of her mother had transformed the once empty two-bedroom property into a warm and cosseting home. Thomas pulled up outside of the shop and climbed out of the Land Rover. He entered the shop to find Mavis's father standing behind the counter.

"Ey up Thomas." Harry said, smiling whilst he pulled a large knife back and forth against a sharpening stone.

"Aye, how's things?" Thomas replied.

"Not bad… you?" Harry dragged the knife across the stone one last time before rinsing it under a tap.

"Can't complain too much."

"Seems the youngins had a nice time away." Harry said, pulling the knife through a slab of rump steak.

"Aye, though it's back to work now. That's why I'm here."

Harry sliced a large slab of steak off and placed it onto a piece of greased paper before he began to slice off another. "Go on up Thomas."

"Thanks, I will."

As Thomas stepped through the back of the shop, George and Mavis appeared at the top of the stairs. "Da, we're just coming." George said, as he hopped down the stairs. Thomas recognised the giddy excitement of a young couple fresh from their honeymoon.

"Mr. Bradbury," Mavis said, smiling as she passed by him.

Thomas followed them back through the shop. "Here you are Thomas. For you and Anne to enjoy." Harry placed the two slices of rump steak in his hands. Thomas looked down on them. It had been a long time since he'd enjoyed a steak.

"Many thanks Harry. These'll go down well with some fat chips."

"Just tell Anne, a few minutes each side in a red-hot pan, and then let them rest before you eat 'em."

"Aye, will do," Thomas nodded and smiled while thinking to himself that he wouldn't tell Anne how to cook the steaks.

Outside, Mavis and George were sat in the Land Rover with George excitedly waiting in the driving seat. In the Back Mavis sat with Shep. Thomas climbed in next to George and handed him the single metallic key. "There ya go, son."

Eagerly, George fired up the engine and pulled away. As the Land Rover trundled along the country lanes Thomas thought about what he was going to say to George. He wanted to tell him that it was his brother who had killed the lambs, and hurt Shep. He also felt that hiding Arthurs true heritage was a betrayal of George's trust. Thomas thought for a while longer. Then, pulling the small mirror over he peered in the back at Mavis and decided that this was not the time to do it.

George turned off the main road and onto the track which led down to the farm. The short-wheelbase Land Rover jumped and skipped over the rough ground. As he pulled up alongside the farmhouse Anne stepped outside. Thomas thought to himself that this was the first time he'd seen her smile since George's wedding day, and that brought on him the sadness of guilt.

"George, Mavis, you're home safe." Anne said through her smile.

"Ma, it were bloody great, a place the likes you've never seen." George announced as he hugged his mother.

"Mrs. Bradbury," Mavis said, smiling and nodding to Anne.

Anne grabbed hold of her and pulled her in, hugging her. "You can call me Anne, or Ma, should you wish Mavis. There's no need for surnames now, you're part of the family."

Mavis looked to George as she hugged Anne and smiled.

"That goes for me too Mavis. Call me Thomas, or Da, whichever you prefer," Thomas decided he should go along with Anne's example.

Anne, still with her arm around Mavis turned and led her into the farmhouse. "Come, we'll make a nice fresh pot of tea Mavis, while the men see to the truck.

Before George had a chance to question why his mother was leading away his new wife, Thomas shouted to him. "George, pull the Land Rover into the workshop while I open tha doors."

"But I'll be taking it back tonight." George replied, a little confused why he should be putting the truck away.

"None-the-less lad, just pull it in." Thomas said, walking towards the workshop.

George got back into the Land Rover and reversed it away from the farmhouse. Then, with the workshop doors open, he slowly drove it in.

"I'm not sure I see the point Da," George mumbled getting out.

"There isn't any point, but I needed you alone. It's Arthur." Thomas said, pulling the workshop doors closed with both of them still inside.

"Where is Arthur?" George asked.

"He's not here, he's down at the old station again. He seems to spend his days there." Thomas replied.

"Why?" George asked, leaning against the truck.

"There's something troubling that lad. Something that doesn't seem natural George."

He'd not heard his father this uneasy when he spoke. "How do you mean?" George asked. The sound of concern growing in his voice.

"It's his manner, the way he is. He hardly speaks to me or your mother, and when he does, he calls us by our names. He still carries that spinning top around too, whispers the tune to himself when he thinks we can't hear." Thomas took a deep breath; a look of foreboding came across his face. "At night, when he thinks I'm asleep, I can hear him on the landing. He stands outside our door, whispering that tune, making words up to change the ending. Sometimes…" Thomas stopped.

"Go on Da," George spoke softly.

"Sometimes, I can hear him pleasure himself as he sings it." A tear welled up in Thomas's eye. He sniffed hard, pulling back in his emotions, while wiping his cheek clear of the rogue tear.

Thomas wanted to carry on. The thoughts he had on the journey home came back to him, but he decided not to tell George that they believe it's Arthur who is hurting the local animals. Pets and livestock alike.

"What about the reports of the animals?" George

asked.

Thomas was taken by surprise. "Oh, as I've told you son, most probably the townies getting up to mischief,"

"Lucy mentioned some say it's the spirit of that Jack fella, the one who killed himself." George said.

"That's nonsense George, you know there's no such thing as ghosts and such."

"Aye, what I do know is that there isn't smoke without fire, and Lucy seemed fairly convinced of it."

Thomas thought for a while. Disguising his hesitation by checking something in the workshop. He too had heard the rumours and had initially dismissed them. But after the spinning top had started up in the bunk, and with the voices and sounds Anne had told him she'd heard, he was finding it harder to simply wave these rumours away. Besides, he'd told PC Dowding that he believed that Arthur was hearing the voice of Jack, so if he truly did believe that, was is that much of a leap to believe that Jack could somehow, in some way manifest himself and cause physical harm. George brought his thoughts back.

"Well, do you think it could be Arthur, or the ghost of Jack?"

"No, son, I don't. One more thing though before we go inside. Let's keep all of this away from Mavis. The poor lass doesn't need to know what's gone

on, and nor does the likes of Ethel need more tripe
to gossip about. Now, Let's go have tea, the wives
will be wondering where we are."

"Ok, Da."

George followed Thomas from the workshop and
into the farmhouse.

Anne placed a fresh pot of the mashing tea down
on the table, covering it in a thick woollen cosy. She
placed out three mugs and Thomas's green tin
mug. Then, with the warm welcoming smile she
had worn just a few minutes previously gone, she
sat. As Thomas and George entered, Anne reached
across to the tea pot.

"Let me Anne." Mavis stood and pulled the cosy
off the pot. Starting with Thomas she poured the
fresh tea into each of their cups, followed by a
splash of fresh milk.

"So, what were you two boys talking about out
there?" Mavis asked, smiling as she poured the last
of the fresh milk.

"Oh, Da was just bringing me up to speed on the
farm and such." George answered, looking down at
the floor.

Mavis smiled at George. "Oh, nothing exciting
then…"

III

The year, as it seems they always do, moved along at a brisk pace. May passed into June and then July and with them came the searing heat of summer. As August finally gave way to September, the cooler temperatures and shorter days brought relief to Thomas and George. This year had been especially hard. Thomas was now visibly able to do less work. George noticed he was weaker and tiring quicker than before. In the home Mavis had taken the burden of work from Anne. The only room Anne had insisted that only she would continue to clean was Arthur's room. Mavis hadn't asked why this was the case, but secretly she was pleased this rule existed. It was clear for anyone to see that on the rare occasions Arthur was in the house, both Anne and Thomas were wary of him, and it was also clear to see why. There had been no August birthday festivities this year. Thomas and Anne decided that they would no longer celebrate the date that this stranger amongst them was born. This hadn't sat well with George, who still believed there was good in Arthur – somewhere. But regardless of his protests, no party or acknowledgement was given.

Arthurs demeanour had become dark. He rarely said a word to any of them when he entered the house, and his size continued to increase. Now well over six-foot tall with a build to match he was an intimidating figure. His hair had become unkept, long and had begun to curl under at the ends. His fringe now covered most of his face. Every so often they would get a glimpse of his eyes and like the rest of him they seemed dark and troubled. He'd taken to wearing black clothes only, and a long coat he'd found in the bunk amongst Jack's old belongings. When Thomas insisted that he remove it Arthur simply ignored him. For the most part Arthur now confined himself to his room when he was home, and as for the rest of the time he spent it between the old station and Jack's bunk house.

Thomas had received some interest in the property and the land, but always turned away anyone who become what Anne called *seriously interested*. This was partly because he was worried what Arthur would do if he sold the land, and partly because he worried what Jack would do. This second worry was his largest concern. Not only because the thoughts which flooded his imagination when he dared to consider the ramifications, were in themselves terrifying, but also that he now accepted that such things existed without any hesitancy. For the last few weeks, at least, an uneasy truce seemed to have fallen over the house. But all that changed the night the storm rolled in.

George and Mavis had left - the day was all but done. Thomas had watched as the Land Rover made its way up the track and turned onto the road. Its lights shining against the ever-encroaching darkness of the coming night. Thomas had made his way back to the workshop to lock it, this would be his last job of the day. Soon, he thought to himself, he would be inside, eating his tea and looking forward to putting his feet up. In the distance he heard the first rumble of thunder. He looked up - dark clouds were gathering above the farm. Even in the dimming of the day he could make out the swirling violent storm clouds as they amassed themselves above. He pulled his coat tighter and shivered against the breeze which seemed to come out of nowhere. Then he noticed the light in the bunk house shining through the cracks in the slats of the wooden wall. He knew this meant that Arthur was home. He sighed and checked the workshop door as the first flash of lightning lit the sky across the farm and over the eastern hills. Thomas knew this would be a bad storm. It was coming in from the east coast, the same direction the storm had that night - some fifteen years previous.

Anne was preparing Thomas's tea when he entered. The rain began just as Thomas had made it inside. He pulled off his coat and boots and placed them by the door. The kitchen lit up as another lightning flash lit the heavens. Seconds later thunder rumbled somewhere in the distance. But with each flash, the thunder followed sooner. Anne looked to Thomas who smiled, trying to reassure her.

"Is Arthur in that bunk?" She asked, putting his dinner down in front of him

"Aye, he is, wife."

Another flash, and another heavy crack of thunder. It was getting closer.

"This'll be as bad a storm as that night Thomas." Anne said. The fear palpable in her voice.

"Jacks gone Anne. There's nothing to fear, I promise."

A flash of lightning lit the farmhouse as if the sun itself was inside with them. The thunder followed instantly. The air vibrated around them and the sound seemed to find its way into their souls. It was as if their bodies pulsed in harmony with the thunder from the inside. Then the door burst open, and as another strike of lightning lit the farmyard Arthur stood silhouetted in the open door. Thomas and Anne froze. Rain poured in behind Arthur. The long black coat hung heavily from him.

"Get in lad!" Thomas shouted against the storm.

Arthur stepped inside the kitchen and swung the door closed behind him. His hair, wet through, clung to his face. He looked between Anne and Thomas. Then he began to sob and collapsed on the floor. On seeing this something in Anne switched over. In an instant she went from the heavy resentment she felt towards him, to wanting to protect him. She rushed to him, kneeling, she cradled him and tried to calm him. "There, there, it's just a storm." Arthur didn't respond, he continued to sob like a fearful child.

As the storm continued Anne had managed to take

Arthur through to the living room. There in front of the roaring fire, she wrapped towels around him and dried him. For now, all Anne saw in front of her was the little boy she thought was gone forever. Thomas had already called Doc Brown and was waiting for him in the kitchen. After what seemed like too long a wait Thomas saw the Doctors car pull up. Immediately, Thomas opened the kitchen door. Moments later the doctor ran inside. The few seconds he'd taken getting out of his car and to the farmhouse was enough to soak him almost to his skin. As more lightning flashed closely followed by the thunder, Thomas led Doc Brown through to the living room. There he found Arthur curled up with Anne. Even in this pose, he could see how large Arthur now was.

"What's up Arthur?" Doc Brown asked him.

"He's frightened of the storm," Anne replied.

"Has he said that?" Doc Brown asked.

"No, but I can tell."

Doc Brown pulled open his bag and took out a syringe. "This is a mild sedative; it'll help him sleep." He knelt next to Arthur and injected it into his arm. "He'll feel better in a few moments."

As Doc Brown closed his bag another volley of thunder shook the house. Then Arthur spoke. "I'm not frightened of the storm."

Anne pulled back a little. "What?" She whispered to him.

Arthur sat up. No longer curled up like the frightened small boy. "I'm not frightened of the storm. I hate the storm."

"Why do you hate the storm?" Doc Brown asked.

Arthur turned to Thomas as he stood to his full height. Pointing directly at him he spoke. "Because it was during a storm like this when he tried to shoot my father."

Doc Brown looked between Anne and Thomas, "What? what is he talking about?" Then he turned to Arthur. "Thomas is your father, what do you mean he tried to shoot himself?"

Arthur's head bowed down. Under the locks of damp clinging hair, he began to smile. Then he glared at Thomas and began to sing. *"See Saw Margery Daw Thomas is not my real father. See Saw Margery Daw Thomas is not my real father…"*

Thomas yelled at him. "Stop it! Stop it you evil bastard!"

Another bolt of lightning lit the room followed instantly by a violent crack of thunder. As it did Arthur screamed louder, *"See Saw Margery Daw Thomas should go ever-after."*

Anne pleaded with Arthur to stop, but he kept singing, louder and louder *"SEE SAW MARGERY DAW THOMAS AND ANNE."* He stopped. Outside the storm had died down.

In the silence Thomas, Anne and Doc Brown

looked between each other unsure of what to do.
Then they heard a soft whistle of wind. The eye of
the storm had passed over. The rain began again,
tapping on the window as the wind blew up to its
previous strength. Arthur moved over to the
fireplace. He looked firstly at Anne and then to
Thomas. Then he sang, *"See Saw Margery Daw…"*
As he did his voice changed as he continued, and
Thomas and Anne recognised immediately. It was
Jack's. *"You two should have finished me when you had
the chance!"*

Arthur turned towards the fireplace. He reached in,
pulling out a burning log, he flung it across the
room. Immediately, the curtains it landed against
burst into flames, followed by the carpet.

"GET OUT!" Thomas shouted to Anne and Doc
Brown.

They fled through the house, outside and into the
storm which was raging again. Once outside and
safe Doc Brown opened his car door. Bending
inside the open car he opened his bag and pulled
out another dose of the sedative. This time he
doubled it. Moments later Arthur came out. He
stood in the doorway – his arms raised up as
lightning flashed and thunder boomed around
them. Behind him, they could see the flames
passing from the living room and through into the
kitchen.

"Grab him," Doc Brown shouted against the storm.

Without hesitation Thomas struck Arthur across

the face. Off balance, Arthur stumbled back. He turned to face Thomas, his fists clenching. As he did, Shep grabbed the back of Arthurs leg, sinking his teeth into the soft muscle as far in as his jaws would allow. Arthur screamed in pain, and turned, trying to break the dogs grip. Thomas seized his chance. He grabbed him around the waist and using what weight and strength he had he pulled Arthur down. Shep released his bite as Doc Brown straddled across him while Arthur threw punches wildly and without aim. As one of them made contact with Thomas, Doc Brown managed to get the syringe into Arthurs leg. He pushed down on the plunger, emptying the vial completely. Within seconds Arthur passed out. Thomas, cut above his eye from the landed punch, stood. On the floor, in the muck of the farmyard, lay Arthur. A few yards behind him, the farmhouse burned.

"Give me a hand, help me lift him into the back seat." Doc Brown shouted.

Thomas and Doc Brown struggled to lift Arthur into the back of his car. Eventually, they slid his unconscious body far enough in to close the door.

"I should get him to the police station. I don't know how long he'll be out for." Doc Brown shouted as he pushed the car door closed against the force of the wind. Then, pointing at the barn he yelled. "What about the barn, and the animals. Do you need to stay here?"

"It's too far away, besides it's too wet for the fire to jump, it'll not catch in this weather. They'll be fine." Thomas shouted his reply.

Doc Brown handed Thomas the car key. "Ok, then you drive, I'll sit in the back, ready with another dose in case Arthur comes around."

"Ok," Thomas replied.

As he spoke the burning house groaned. Then with a crash, the roof above the living room collapsed in on itself. Anne screamed. Thomas held her, gently pulling her towards the Doctors car, "We need to go." Anne slid across the front seat in silence. Thomas turned to Shep, "Come on boy." The aging dog climbed in next to Anne.

The drive to Thirstonfield Village was one of silence save for the noise of the wind and rain which continued to assault the car. Eventually, they reached the police station. Thomas turned to Anne, "Stay here, I'll go get some help."

After a few moments Thomas emerged with two police officers. With their help Thomas and Doc Brown managed to drag the still unconscious Arthur into a cell.

"Don't worry Thomas, we'll keep him here." The duty sergeant said, as he turned the key on the cell door, which locked with a reassuring clunk.

Thomas nodded. "Thank you."

Doc Brown turned to Thomas. "You and Anne stay with me tonight. We'll sort a room out at the guest house tomorrow until you get the house fixed up."

"What will they do with Arthur?" Thomas asked.

"I'll come back tomorrow and have him sectioned; he'll end up in St Lukes."

"He won't be coming home then?" Thomas asked, nervously.

"No Thomas. Not after what I've witnessed tonight. He'll be locked up."

Thomas felt a weight lift from him.

The following morning Anne and Thomas returned to the farm with George and Mavis. The journey back was a difficult one, but not a silent one. Anne and Thomas had decided that they would tell George and Mavis the truth about what had happened the previous night. They also finally told George that it was in fact Arthur who had hurt the animals. Thomas then confirmed what George had heard - and what he'd earlier denied. That Arthur was in fact hearing the voice of the man who'd committed suicide. But Thomas stopped short of telling him that Arthur was this man's biological son – for now.

Eventually, the Land Rover turned off the road and onto the track. After the previous night's torrential rain, the track was nothing more than a riverbed of soft mud. The four-wheel drive slipped its way down to the farmhouse. When they arrived, they saw the full extent of the damage. The rear of the house was gone. Only the front half, which included the kitchen and Thomas and Anne's bedroom remained. "Dear God." George whispered. He switched off the truck and they climbed out. Shep jumped out, making his way passed them, keen to ensure no more threats remained. Inside herself Anne felt something fracture at the sight before her. She had reached her breaking point. Thomas held her hand. He had no idea what she was feeling at this moment, and that she had just lost the last of her strength and will to carry on. George pushed the door open.

They entered through the open kitchen door. Inside, the kitchen itself was largely untouched. The only notable damage had been caused by the rain which had found its way in. George began to climb the staircase. At the top, his parents' room was undamaged. But the room he'd once shared with Arthur, along with the bathroom and *nick-knack* room were gone - collapsed into what was the living room. From where the entrance to the bedroom once was George could see down into the burnt-out shell and out across the farm and to the hills. He sighed heavily.

"What's it like up there?" Mavis shouted from downstairs.

George looked down. "Bleak."

In the kitchen Anne had made a fresh pot of tea. Sitting at the table she poured out four cups. As she took her first sip Thomas came in.

"How's the animals" Anne asked.

"They're all fine, thankfully." Thomas replied, picking up his green tin mug and taking a sip.

"What do we do now?" Anne asked.

"We have no choice, wife. We rebuild it. We 'ave to."

"Do we?" Anne replied. Her voice more sorrowful than Thomas had ever heard it.

"Aye, we do. Arthur's gone now. Doc Brown says he'll be locked up for good, we can rebuild and live here with George and Mavis."

"What about us?" George said, entering the room.

"I was telling your mother you two can move in when it's rebuilt. You can make it how you want." Thomas said, forcing a smile.

Chapter 8.

August 8th, 1964.

I

Arthur had remained in St Lukes mental hospital Middlesbrough since the incident three years previous. Since his incarceration his mental health had deteriorated further, while his size and strength had increased to a point where they no longer had the option but to keep him restrained in a strait jacket for the wellbeing of the staff when he wasn't confined to his cell. His aggression was not only uninhibited, but he had no pattern of when his temper would break. Toilet and bathing routines were only possible using a strong sedative. In two days, it would be Arthurs seventeenth birthday. As with the previous few, neither Thomas or Anne had any intentions of celebrating this date, and neither had they visited Arthur since he was committed.

The farmhouse was now fully rebuilt and modernised. The only original items which survived the fire were the range oven, the long solid oak dining table and Anne's family crucifix which remained above the kitchen door. Much of the modernisation came from George and Mavis, including a television set which sat proudly where the radiogram once had. Shep, who had helped them that night take Arthur down, was now an old boy of eleven. With grey hairs on his legs and around his chin, he spent most of his days lying in the sun, either asleep or watching the hustle and bustle of the farm – when the weather allowed.

Mavis had now fully taken over the duties of running the farmhouse, whilst George carried the heavy work of the farm. Anne, who's health both physically and mentally had continued to decline, now spent most of her time sat in the living room, either reading, watching the TV, or knitting. Some habits never go away. Thomas had seen the light slowly extinguish from her eyes in the months before the fire. It would take him a few more months to fully realise that whatever small amount of life force she did have, had been lost the morning they returned to the burnt-out shell. Thomas had tried to re-engage with Anne, but all his efforts proved to be fruitless. She had become frail, weak, and withdrawn. She'd all but stopped eating, only doing so when absolutely necessary, and she had no interest in the comings and goings of daily life. The energy she once seemed to have in spare amounts was gone. She would take to her bed around five or six, even earlier in the winter months, and not come down again until after nine the following morning. Thomas felt he had lost his wife, and while outside working, alone in his own thoughts, he would remember how they used to be. For all intents and purpose, he was mourning her loss.

This loss, and the way it had affected Thomas had been noticed and discussed by George and Mavis, who themselves felt a sadness for them both. But more than that George also felt a responsibility for them. He'd seen at an early age what Arthur was like, and because of his own fear he'd kept that to himself. While working he would often wonder if things would have been different if he'd stood up to his little brother, and maybe told his parents of Arthur's behaviour when their backs were turned. It was for these thoughts that George had continued to visit Arthur in St Lukes. He made these visits because he needed the reconciliation to be able to move on, but also because he still believed that Arthur had the potential for good and that he could be redeemed. These visits had been against the wishes of Thomas, who felt worried that keeping a connection with Arthur would somehow keep not only Arthurs connection with them, but also that of Jack's.

At the end of another long day, Thomas and George headed inside to clean up for tea. Mavis had prepared their dinner while Anne sat at the table. As they began to eat George brought up the subject of Arthurs birthday.

"I was thinking of visiting Arthur on his birthday. The last time I was there, they told me I could take him out for a few hours, with it being his birthday." George said, in as natural way as he could.

"What do you mean out, you mean here?" Anne's

response had a worried tone about it.

"No, Ma. Not here, just a run around in the truck. Let him see the outside. He'd be in his jacket and there'd be an orderly with me. Probably Keith. He's the only one Arthur seems to settle with."

"You can do what you want George. But you keep him away from here. Now, we'll have no more talk of that… person in this house. It's upsetting your mother." Thomas snarled his response to George.

George returned to eating his tea. Once they'd finished, Anne stood and made her way back into the living room whilst Mavis cleared away the pots. Thomas pulled George to one side. "Now listen lad, what you do is your business until it affects me and your mother and mentioning that name does that more than I like."

"Aye, I know Da, I'm sorry for bringing it up at the table. I won't talk about him again when Ma's around." George replied.

Later that evening they were all sat in the living room. Unusually for Anne, she had stayed up past her usual time, though with no clocks or watches to be found in the house, or indeed on the farm, her usual time was normally once the men had finished their work for the day, and dinner had been served, consumed and cleared away. Thomas was reading the paper, while Mavis and George were sat watching the TV, waiting for one of their favourite shows – *The Third Man*. Anne was knitting a new jumper for Thomas and George, ready for when the weather would once again change. As the show began, Anne put her knitting away. Then, turning to George she placed a hand gently on his arm. Thomas looked over to her, and then to Mavis and George.

"It was his sixth birthday when it all began." Anne whispered.

"What Ma?" George replied, taken back by his mother's sudden impulse to talk. Mavis reached over and turned off the TV. The black and white picture slowly dissolved into a dot before it disappeared.

"Arthur, he was five when he started hearing that voice. The one who told him to do things. But it was his sixth birthday when he turned evil."

George looked to his father. "Da?"

"Anne, what are you talking about?" Thomas asked.

Anne ignored him. Her gaze, while directed to George, seemed to pass through him. Her eyes were wide. "It was that voice what told my little boy to pleasure himself, I found him at it. It took away his innocence."

Mavis turned to George. "George?" Her tone was one of concern for Anne.

Anne continued. "It was that voice what told him to hurt the animals, to do the things the constable told us about. Your friend's dog and such." Then

Anne turned to Thomas, her face became red. The melancholic tone of her voice changed to one of anger. "It was you who brought that monster into our lives. It was you!" She pointed a bony index finger at him. Stabbing it through the air.

A shiver ran through Thomas. He had to stop Anne before she blurted out who the monster was and what he'd done. A thousand thoughts flooded Thomas. He wasn't able to deal with such things anymore. He simply didn't have the strength he once did.

George stood. "Ma stop talking like this. It's no one's fault. Especially not Da's."

Anne looked back to George. "Oh son. Dear, dear son. What have I done to you?"

Upset George left the room, unable to see his mother in such a state. As he pulled the door closed behind him Anne turned to Mavis and continued. "You see it was him, that monster that he brought onto the farm and into our lives that caused all this."

"What do you mean Anne, what monster?" Mavis asked.

Thomas stood and tried to pull Anne from her chair. "Come on, wife. I think you've passed your bedtime."

Anne pulled her arm away. "Get off me, it was you, you! You brought Jack Bright onto this farm and he raped me, he raped me," Anne's anger turned to sorrow, and she broke down in tears. "That bastard son of ours came to be because of you! It's my fault, it was always my fault. We should have killed him before he was born."

Thomas turned to Mavis who sat motionless. Her gaze moved from Anne to Thomas. Tears welled up in her eyes. "Is it true Thomas?" She asked quietly.

Thomas sighed heavily. He began to cry. "Please don't tell anyone. This is a secret we've carried since the night it happened, George can't find out, please don't tell him."

Mavis had no idea how to respond. She'd known Thomas for as long as she'd known George. She'd grown up with Thomas visiting her father's shop with meat. He'd always been typical of a farmer from these parts. A strong, powerful, and principled man. But now, to see him reduced in stature and to tears by this confession was just heart-shattering to her. Mavis stood and hugged Thomas. "I promise, I won't." Then she turned to Anne who had once again sat back in her chair and begun to knit. "Anne, should we get you to bed now? It's been a long day."

Anne gazed up at her. It seemed to both Mavis and Thomas that she had no recollection of what had just happened and the things she'd said. "Yes dear," Came the reply. "It's late and I'm tired."

Mavis helped Anne from the chair. She turned to Thomas, "Don't worry, I won't tell anyone, especially George." Then she smiled at Thomas and took Anne out of the room. Thomas sank back into his chair. All he could do now was hope that Mavis would keep the Bradbury family secret to herself.

In the kitchen George paced up and down. He felt he needed to do something, but what? He felt that the responsibility of running the family was now his. He of course acknowledged that Thomas was still head of the household and family, but he also understood that his father was a weakened man compared to what he once was. Then turning, his gaze came upon the crucifix which had hung above the door since the house was built. Like the table and range oven, it too had survived the fire. Anne had put it down to divine intervention – no one had argued with her summation. George felt a sensation come over him. It was a clarity of what he felt he could do to save Arthur, and by extension the family. Making sure that the kitchen door was closed, he picked up the receiver of the wall mounted phone. Then he dialled one of the few numbers written on the small directory within the circular dialler. It rang – then it answered.

"Hello?" Came the softly spoken voice.

"Father, Crowley?" George replied.

"Yes, it is, who is this?"

"George, George Bradbury."

"Ah, hello George. It's nice to hear from you. How's your mother and father?"

"That's why I'm calling, Father. They're not so good, especially Ma. I wonder, could I call over tomorrow? I need to talk with you about something."

"Yes, I'll be free after one."

"Thank you, father. I'll see you then."

George entered the living room to find Thomas and Mavis. "Has Ma gone up to bed?" He asked.

"Yes, I've settled her in for the night." Mavis replied, smiling warmly at him.

"Why do you visit Arthur?" Thomas asked.

"Because he's my brother Da, and I still think he can be saved."

"What do you mean saved? Saved from what?"

"Oh, nothing... Just an expression is all." George replied.

Thomas accepted his son's response with a fatherly nod and smile and yet he felt that he was still concealing something that perhaps George had not meant to let slip. Even so, he decided not to push the point, especially after George had come so close to learning the truth.

II

August 9th

At a few minutes past one George entered the church hall. "Father Crowley?"

"George, how are you? Lovely to see you." Father Terrance Crowley announced as he entered through the vestry door. "Please, follow me, we'll go sit in the parlour, it's more comfortable than this drafty old hall."

George smiled nervously and followed Father Crowley. Inside the parlour, two large old leather chairs sat either side of a fireplace. A large table sat under the window and the walls were clad with ornate dark wood panelling. Illuminated only by a single ceiling lamp the room was dark, yet it felt safe and cosy. Father Crowley pointed to one of the chairs. "Please George, sit."

George did as he was asked. Father Crowley sat opposite him. "So, tell me why you're here."

George took in a deep breath. "It's about Arthur."

"How is he George? Always struck me as a troubled young man that one. Not at all like you."

"That's why I'm here. I want to ask you something, but I'm not sure how to." George mumbled his words, trying hard to use what Anne would call *Queens English* rather than his native Yorkshire dialect.

Father Crowley sat back. "Relax George. Tell me."

"Do you believe someone can be taken over by evil?" George asked.

The priest thought for a moment. "If I say I believe in God, which of course I do, and his power to redeem sinners and those who have fallen and been seduced by evil, then yes, I would also have to believe in the evil spirit which seeks to corrupt." The priest then hesitated and then continued. "Why do you ask? Do you believe this to be the case with Arthur?"

George took in a deep breath. "Aye, I do." The Queens English didn't last very long.

"And when did you begin to think this George?"

"When I got back from my honeymoon, my Ma and Da told me what Arthur had done. And that he'd began to hear the voice of someone. Ma says it's this voice that told him to," George stopped, he was uncomfortable. Gathering his strength, he continued. "Ma said this voice told him to play with himself and hurt animals."

"I heard what had happened at the farm George and that he's now in St Lukes..."

"There's more, Father." George interrupted him.

"Tell me, son."

"When I was a boy, we shared a room. One night he woke me up by talking with someone he called his father. I swear on everything I hold dear, Father, when he looked at me, his face was different. It was an old man."

Father Crowley sat forward. "Tell me more."

George felt a change in the room. It seemed this last piece of information had peaked the priest's interest. "It was an older man. A man with a scar down his face. What do you make of it?"

Father Crowley drew a deep breath through his teeth. "I've come across this before. A few years ago, shortly after the war, I completed my training at the Vatican City. There, I shadowed a priest who carried out exorcisms. What you've described, the change in behaviour, the change in appearance and what I've heard in the village matches what I saw back then. If this is a possession, I'd hoped that I would never again have to see it or deal with it."

George's mind stumbled for the logic. A fog descended over his thoughts. "What do you mean, Father? Are you saying you think Arthur needs an… exorcism?"

"I don't know. I'd need to meet him, face to face. Only then would I know. Tell me George, when did this start?"

"Not sure, when he was young. Why, does that matter?"

"It may do, can you get him out of St Lukes?"

George sat forward. "It's his birthday tomorrow, Father. They may let him out for that."

"Then we don't have a lot of time George. I need to see him."

"Before you do, what does it involve? The exorcism." George asked, hesitantly.

Father Crowley rubbed his hands around themselves. "Firstly, I will implore God to forgive Arthur his sins. This is important, because once he's forgiven it will make driving the evil out much easier. Then, I will demand that the evil spirit leaves Arthur and that once departed it never returns. But I must warn you..."

"Of what" George whispered.

Father Crowley leant forward. He began speaking in a solemn tone. "An exorcism can be a violent and terrifying thing. Once seen, you will never be able to unsee it. The possessed can and often do change their physical appearance. They will use whatever deeds they can to resist. Arthur may appear to you as his younger self - a boy, a scared little boy." Father Crowley stopped.

"What is it?" George asked.

"I should prepare you, and as we don't have much time, I will tell you what to expect. But first, some tea." Father Crowley lifted a small brass bell from the table next to his chair. He shook it gently.

From another room George heard the voice of an older sounding woman. "Yes, Father."

"Some tea for myself and my guest Mrs. Doyle."

"Coming right up."

Father Crowley turned back to George. "It's getting a little nippy." He leant forward and pulled a newspaper from a brass bucket next to the open fire. Lighting it, he threw it on the freshly stacked pile of logs. Within a few minutes the fire was burning, and George could feel its warmth. After a few more moments of innate conversation Mrs. Doyle wheeled in a tea trolley - made up of a brass frame with three wooden trays. "There you go, Father." She said, placing the trolley in between the two chairs. Father Crowley smiled and gave her a slight nod.

After she had left the room, pulling the door closed behind her, Father Crowley poured out two cups of tea. Outside, clouds had rolled over the day, making the parlour even more cosy and cossetting. After taking a long drink Father Crowley cleared his throat.

"An exorcism has six parts to it. Firstly, I will feel the evil presence. This, unfortunately, I can do quickly. Even when I don't want to feel it. Then, the evil spirit will play a game of pretence. It will try to make out that it is Arthur. My role now is to break this, to force the demon to reveal itself." Father Crowley took another sip, while George sat listening. He continued. "Soon after these two steps, we will reach the *breakpoint*, this is the moment the demon - the evil spirit, will no longer be able to continue with its pretence. This is when the demon will panic. It will become violent and abusive. It will begin to speak of itself and then Arthur as a third person."

George took a long drink. His mind scrambled at what he was hearing. Was this really going to happen - is it real? He had a strong compulsion to walk out. To just leave Arthur in the asylum, do what his mother and father had done. But these conflictions soon disappeared.

Father Crowley continued. "Next George, you will hear the demons real voice. This will be distressing to you. You cannot unhear this voice. It will stay with you forever, but I must silence the demons voice for the exorcism to continue and be successful. As the demon loses its voice you feel a tremendous pressure as the demon collides with the will of the Kingdom, Gods Kingdom. Then and only then can I demand the expulsion in the supreme triumph of God."

"How will we know, Father?" George asked, in a whisper.

"All the feelings of pressure and of an evil presence will be gone George. Don't worry, we'll know."

"Do these always work?" The reluctance to ask this question was palpable to Father Crowley.

He sighed, and then answered. "No George, they

don't. And I've seen people lose their lives as the demon has left them. Do you still wish for me to meet with Arthur?"

"Yes." George replied.

"Then we'd better go see him."

George stood and placed his empty cup on the trolley. As he turned to leave Father Crowley asked one more question. "This man, the voice he hears. Do you know who he is?"

"It was the man who killed himself at the Halt. He was a farm hand when I was a young boy, but I can't remember his name…" George hesitated and thought back through his memories. "John, Joe, Jack something with a J, I think. Why, does that help?"

"Perhaps." Father Crowley answered.

"I'll fetch the car and wait for you outside." George said, leaving the parlour.

In the long shadows of the cooling day George sat in the Land Rover waiting for the priest to appear. After a few minutes Father Crowley came out of the church and climbed in next to him. Smiling, he whispered. "Let's go George."

They arrived at St Lukes around an hour later. George hadn't spoken any further of demonic possession or the possible exorcism. But his mind had scrambled to understand what he'd just heard and why he had sought this line of inquiry. As the truck came to a stop, part of him once again wanted to abandon what they were about to do, even if this was just a visit. St Lukes was an imposing old building. First built in 1898, it was a square, red bricked structure with a central clock tower and slim, tall windows. Father Crowley followed George into the building. As they entered Father Crowley noticed a plaque on the wall dedicating it to, *Charles Henry Howell.* They were met at the reception desk by a young female orderly wearing a white tunic. "Hi George." She said, smiling.

"This is Father Crowley; he's come with me to visit Arthur."

The young orderly looked the priest up and down. "That's fine George. You know the way. Once you're at the door just knock. I think Keith is on duty today."

George nodded and led Father Crowley through the bland corridors. After a fairly short walk they reached a heavy, strong looking door. Father Crowley wondered to himself if this was to stop those on the inside getting out, or the other way around. George pushed the buzzer. A short while later the door clanked and opened. "Mr. Bradbury, here to see Arthur?" The large orderly asked. Father Crowley noticed his name badge, it read Keith.

"Aye," George turned to the priest who standing next to him. "This is Father Crowley, he's here to see him with me."

"He's in his cell. Had a bit of trouble from him again while he was on the commode." Keith announced, closing the heavy door behind them as they stepped through.

"Was he not in his jacket?" George asked.

"Aye, he was, but even wearing that he can be a handful. We've taken it off for now. If you want to go in, we'll need to put it back on. Oh, he stripped off again. For some reason he always does."

"Aye, thanks, I'll let you know if we want to be in." George replied.

"As you wish. Here we are," Keith stopped outside of Arthur's cell. Placed centrally in the door was a large window. "I'll just be down there should you want me, Mr. Bradbury."

George nodded before he approached the glass. Inside the padded cell Arthur sat naked in the opposite corner, his legs sprawled out in front of him. Between them, the spinning top – which George had brought in soon after Arthur had been committed. George was taken back at his increased size. It had been a few weeks since his last visit, but even so, the difference was obvious. Though he was sat upright against the padded wall it was easy to gauge that Arthur must be closer to seven feet tall than six. His bare physique displayed the muscle mass under his skin. And though Arthur was clean, his hair had become even more unkempt. It hung around his shoulders and over his face - only his mouth was visible. They had tried to cut his hair previously but had to abandon their attempts. George watched his brother with a sadness he wished no one should experience. A thought which often came to him did once more. Perhaps, it would be better for Arthur to be dead than live like this. He pushed it away and tapped on the reinforced glass. Arthur looked up. Seeing his brother, he smiled through the strands of thick brown hair. Then with his left-hand Arthur pushed the plunger down. As the spinning top began, and the tune played Arthur began to sing along. As he did, he grabbed his erect cock with his right hand and began frantically masturbating. George felt his heart sink. He stepped back, "Have a look Father Crowley, tell me what you think." George said.

The priest replaced George at the window. Seeing this new figure seemed to both excite and agitate Arthur. He stood, still frantically pulling at himself and then walked towards the door. As he did, he ejaculated into his left hand. Then, smiling at the priest, he flung his semen at the glass. When Father Crowley flinched, Arthur screamed in delight and at the top of his voice he began to sing. *"See Saw Margery Daw, the priest shall feast on my pole milk,"*

"Now you've seen him, and from what I told you, what do you think?" George asked.

Father Crowley stood away from the door. "I think we should at least try George."

George nodded. "Where should we do it?"

"Does he have a connection to anywhere in

particular?"

"Aye, growing up he'd spend all his time down at the old Halt." George answered.

"Then that's where we should try."

"I'll make the arrangements."

George turned back to the window. A tear welled up as he watched Arthur smear his semen over the window, while still singing the nursery rhyme. "See you tomorrow little brother." George said as he turned and walked away.

III

August 10th

Since closing, the station had soon fallen into disrepair. George stood on the platform and looked around at the old place. The once proud Station Master's house was a forlorn shadow of how he remembered it growing up. Once the station had closed George, like his mother and father had not returned, save for the one time when Thomas had met with the local estate agent a few years back. Their sign still hung from the wall, but even that was being attacked by the ivy which had begun to creep along the walls and platform. The old station clock showed the time the power was finally turned off; 1.20 pm. It symbolised to George, the stations time of death.

After a few minutes wait, he saw the priest's car turn off the road and pull up at the gate at the top of the single lane road which once led to the car park. George walked up to meet him. "Father Crowley, you'll have to climb over the gate, I wasn't able to find the key, and I didn't want to ask Da," George shouted to him as the priest approached the gate.

Waving his acknowledgement Father Crowley climbed over. "What time are you expecting him?" He asked George.

"I told them mid-day; it must be around that."

Father Crowley checked his watch. "Three minutes to! Very good George."

George smiled, but his nerves were building inside.

"How did you persuade them to bring Arthur over?"

"I asked them. Said it was his birthday, and it would be a nice treat for him to come to a place he loves, and used to play at when he was a kid." George drew a breath. "They went along with it."

As he spoke a white van with the words, *St Lukes Hospital,* pulled up alongside the priest's car. Keith and another orderly George hadn't seen before, climbed out.

"This is a weird place to come Mr. Bradbury."
Keith said as he approached the gate, resting his
arms on top of it.

"As I said, it was his favourite place as a kid. He'd
often come here." George replied, smiling.

"Takes all sorts. We'll go get him out." Keith
replied, smiling between George and Father
Crowley. He turned to the other orderly. "Give us a
hand." The other man, who was larger than Keith,
and yet sill considerably smaller than Arthur
nodded and headed around the back of the van.
George remained on the other side of the gate, but
he could hear the conversation on this warm, still,
August day.

"C'mon Arthur. We've a surprise for your
birthday…" Keith said, as he helped Arthur out,
wrapped in his strait jacket. As they emerged from
the back of the van, and Arthur recognised where
he was, and that George was waiting for him he
began to smile. They approached the gate.

"So, how do we get over this?" Keith asked.

George swallowed hard, his nerves at their limit. "I
can take him from here; I'd like to walk him down
ma-self."

Keith looked at the other orderly and then back to
George. "Mr. Bradbury, if something were to
happen to you, or he got away, I'd be in for it."

Father Crowley approached Keith from his side of the gate. "Son, it will be fine. You're here," He turned pointing at the station only a few hundred yards down the track. "And we'll only be there, we can shout if we need you, and besides, he's in his strait jacket, what could he possibly do?"

Keith rolled his lips while he thought for a second. "Ok, but only a few minutes - as it's his birthday."

"Thank you," George said to Keith before turning his attentions to Arthur. "C'mon Arthur, we're going down to the station, it's your birthday."

Arthur Looked at George and then back to Keith. Clearly, he was unsure of what was happening.

"It's ok Arthur, you can go. But just for a while." Keith reassured him.

Arthur turned back to George and smiled again. Then, with what seemed no difficulty at all, and in only two steps Arthur climbed over the gate. Keith looked to the other orderly, who returned a look of *Holy crap!*

George took hold of Arthurs strait jacket and led him down to the platform. The sun was high in the blue sky. Only the infrequent wisps of soft thin cloud broke the deep blue above their heads. The ground underfoot was crisp, dried out by the summer sun and lack of seasonal rain. Arthur could feel the heat of the sun on his face, and the warm air which flowed across his face - which did so only by his own movement. There was no breeze today. It seemed that the planet had stopped spinning, and nothing, not the air, or even the long thin grass moved. Around them, everything seemed silent and perfectly still. And the closer they got to the station, the quieter it became. At the top of the track, by the gate, the sounds of crickets and birds were plentiful. But here, on the platform where they now stood, there was no sound of nature. Arthur slowly sniffed in the fresh summer air until his lungs reached their limit. Instantly, the dank smelling air he was used to in his confinement was forgotten. He raised his head to the sun - his eyes closed. Pursing his lips, he let the air escape as slowly as it had entered.

George looked back up to the gate. Keith and the other orderly were sat against the van, enjoying their own time in the sun. But more importantly for the reason of being here, they were facing away from them. "We should go inside." Father Crowley suggested.

George nodded. Checking the orderlies once more, he pulled the brass key from his pocket. He inserted it, and then with a clunk, it turned, and the doors jolted open. George guided Arthur inside followed by Father Crowley who pulled the doors closed behind him. Then he turned to George.

"Before I begin, are you sure this is what you want?"

George looked at Arthur. "Yes, Father… I want my

little brother back."

Inside, The Victorian décor was still visible, though damp and mould had begun to mask it. The station master's house was a grand affair, high ceilings with elaborate cornices and central roses exhibited an attention to detail and craftsmanship. The bulky metal radiators stood proudly against the encroachment of nature. They stood in the central hallway. To their left, through another set of double doors was the waiting room, and to their right, the ticket office.

"Where should we go?" George asked.

"Here is fine," Father Crowley replied, placing his bag on the floor, and pulling it open. As Father Crowley donned his Surplice and Purple Stole, Arthur stood, silent and motionless, looking around at the lost grandeur of the building. He turned to George. Looking down on him he smiled. George smiled back, "Don't worry brother, this is to help you."

As he spoke, Arthur's smile was replaced with a look of confusion.

Chapter 9.

The Exorcism.

I

George pulled a forgotten chair over, and gently coerced Arthur into it. Then, he pulled out a length of rope from under his shirt and wrapped it around his brother, fastening it behind him. Arthur watched him do it. Then gently, he turned to George "Why are you tying me to a chair, brother?" His words were soft and carried a tone of disquiet he'd not heard from Arthur – ever.

"Don't worry Arthur. I won't let anything happen to you." George said, reciprocating his brother's soft tone.

Arthur didn't reply verbally. Rather, he smiled and continued to look around the interior. Though the sun outside was strong and brought with it the heat of summer, inside it was dark. The ornate windows were streaked with the dirt and detritus of seasons past, blocking out any warmth and light. George shivered, a realisation of just how cold it was in here suddenly came to him.

Now in his traditional robes Father Crowley reached into his bag and pulled out a small ornamental bottle. He handed it to George. "This is blessed holy water, don't drop it." George nodded his recognition. Father Crowley reached into his bag and pulled out a final item - a crucifix. It was a large opulent crucifix, and it seemed to George that it would indeed be the crucifix of a priest. Father Crowley turned to George and nodded his intent to begin. "Stand ready with the vile of holy water, and when called upon, do not hesitate George." George swallowed hard and clutched the delicate bottle firmly.

Father Crowley then approached Arthur whose head was now bowed. Even sitting, his head was level with that of the priest. Raising the crucifix, he began. "All in the Name of Jesus Christ, our God and Lord, strengthened by the intercession of the Immaculate Virgin Mary, Mother of God, of Blessed Michael the Archangel, of the Blessed Apostles Peter and Paul and all the Saints and powerful in the Holy authority of our ministry, we confidently undertake to repulse the attacks and deceits of the Devil. God arises; his enemies are scattered and those who hate him flee before him. As smoke is driven away, so are they driven; as wax melts before the fire, so the wicked perish at the presence of God." Father Crowley drew a breath, and then continued. "Behold the cross of the Lord, flee bands of enemies, the lion of the tribe of Juda, the offspring of David, hath conquered." He turned to George. "Now George, splash him with the water."

George flicked the bottle toward Arthur. A spray of water landed on him. Father Crowley and George waited for a reaction.

In the absolute quiet of the old building a chuckle began. A deep menacing laugh. It began slowly and quietly and in step with Arthurs shoulders which moved up and down. Father Crowley began his prayers again.

"May thy mercy, lord, descend upon us," His voice became raised.

Then Arthur raised his head. He stared between George and the priest. "Is this why you brought me here, brother. To this place because you believed you would have me weakened? And on my birthday. Tut, tut, tut... brother."

"Don't listen to it George, remember what I told you." Father Crowley said, pushing George behind him.

Arthur turned his attention to the priest. "Is that the best you can do, priest. A fuckin' prayer, and bunch of shitless, worthless, cock-sucking words?" Arthur's voice deepened. "As if you're pure enough of heart and sinless enough to perform this party trick."

"Don't listen George, remember what I told you." Father Crowley shouted, waving the crucifix in front of Arthur.

Arthur turned to George. "That's right brother! Don't listen to me. Don't listen to me when I tell you what the priest thinks about when he's alone at night with his own thoughts."

George looked to Father Crowley, and then back to Arthur. "Stop it Arthur, Father Crowley said you'd say things, I'll not believe anything you say."

Arthur laughed and then continued. "Should you tell him priest, or shall I tell him? Who you think of at night when you're alone - in bed?"

George turned to face Father Crowley. "What's he talking about, Father."

"Nothing George, it's all part of his defence, to deflect us, make us fight amongst ourselves, we must stay focused."

Arthur laughed again. His voice seemed to split. "At least I'm honest, brother. Not like your priest – a fuckin' liar…"

"No, these are lies, you're trying to deflect me, like the Father said you would, whatever you have to tell me is a lie Arthur."

"Is it, at least when I pleasure myself, it's only a song, a nursery rhyme." Arthur said, grinning while he looked at Father Crowley.

"A Childs song, none-the-less." Father Crowley scolded Arthur.

Arthur laughed. "At least I don't covet my neighbour's wife, hey priest?"

George turned to Father Crowley again. "What's he talking about, Father, tell me."

Arthur turned to George. "You want to know brother?" He laughed again.

George put the vile of holy water down and grabbed Arthur. "Tell me, stop fukin' teasing me!"

Father Crowley shouted, "George, no! step back, pick up the holy water, remember what I told you."

George was no longer listening to Father Crowley. He held Arthur's strait jacket and was shaking him with all of his mite. "Tell me Brother, tell me what you know."

Arthur stopped laughing and looked George dead in the eye. "When your priest goes to bed at night, and his hand slips under the covers, it's Mavis he thinks of. He wants to fuck your wife brother. Fuck her hard and good, just like you can't." Arthur began laughing again. This time it was a guttural laugh. From out of nowhere a wind picked up inside the station house. Years of dust and debris swirled around them as the wind and the noise which came with it increased exponentially.

George let go of Arthur and stepped back. Then he turned to Father Crowley. "Is this true?" He shouted against the wind.

Father Crowley looked at George. "Remember what I told you, the tricks, the deceit."

"Is it true?" George shouted, insisting that Father Crowley gave him an answer - one way or another.

"George, we must stay united, we must stay focused!"

As George focused on Father Crowley, all became silent and the wind stopped as suddenly as it had begun. Then George heard Arthur as he was when he was a boy. George turned. Somehow Arthur's chair had turned, and he now sat with his back to them.

"George, brother, is that you? I'm scared, help me, I can't move, I'm tied to this chair."

George moved closer. It was Arthur as he remembered him when he was six or seven. George crept up behind him.

"George, it's a trap, don't get any closer." Father Crowley insisted. But George ignored him.

"Brother, help me, brother." Young Arthur pleaded softly again.

George reached his little brother and moved around the side of him. His head was bowed - George could only see the top of his head. "I'm here Arthur. Don't worry."

As George drew level Arthur snapped his head around. It was the face George had seen that night, all those years ago. Arthur's voice changed again, and the small frightened boy was gone. "He wants to fuck your wife! He wants to fuck your wife…" Arthur repeated over and over again.

"NO!" George shouted as the shock of that sinister

face sent him scurrying backwards. His feet caught on an old electrical cable, discarded when British Railways moved out. George fell, landing heavily on his left arm.

Father Crowley moved forward, picking up the bottle of holy water, he sprinkled Arthur. His scream resonated around the empty building. Holding the crucifix up Father Crowley began again. "We drive you from us, whoever you may be, unclean spirits. All Satanic powers, all infernal invaders, all wicked legions. In the name and by the power of our lord, Jesus Christ."

Arthur twisted in his seat, the voice that Father Crowley had warned George about began to come through. Father Crowley continued, he splashed more holy water on Arthur. George, still half sat, half crumpled in the corner watched as Arthur thrashed in the chair.

"Most cunning serpent, you shall no more dare to deceive the human race, persecute the Church, torment God's elect and sift them as wheat." Another splash of holy water, another cry of anguish from the voice which now completely replaced Arthur's.

Father Crowley turned to George. "It's working George, we're at the breakpoint, the demon is almost defeated. I must continue to drive it out for good."

As he spoke the wind began again. Father Crowley continued to pray. "God the Father commands you.

God the son commands you. God the Holy Ghost commands you."

As Father Crowley raised the crucifix again, the rope conceded to Arthur's continual twisting and thrashing. George scrambled to his feet, but it seemed to him that the next few moments happened in slow motion. As George regained his footing Arthur was already towering above Father Crowley. George watched as he ran towards them as the strait jacket gave way and Arthurs right arm became free. He grabbed the priest around the throat and lifted him off of the ground. Then with his left arm free he grabbed the crucifix. As he did a blinding white light emanated from it. In the intense, searing pain now radiating through Arthurs left hand, he let go of both the crucifix and Father Crowley. By the time the priest hit the floor, gasping for breath George was with him. He helped him to his feet and then turning, they ran from the station house. Outside George turned to Father Crowley. "Run, get the orderlies down here as quick as you can."

Father Crowley didn't hesitate. As he made his escape George turned and headed back inside. Arthur stood in the middle of the empty room. His strait jacket in tatters. His arms were by his side and his fists clenched.

"You shouldn't have done that, brother." Arthur said. His voice once again a mixture. "You almost had me… almost. Next time bring better rope."

George didn't move or respond. His only plan was

to wait for the orderlies.

"What now, cat got your tongue, brother?" Arthur took a step closer.

George took a step back.

At the gate, Father Crowley placed his left hand on the post as he attempted to climb over, then he realised he still had the crucifix in his hand. He stopped and looked at it. There, where Arthur had grabbed it was an imprint of his hand. Burnt into the silver. Father Crowley watched as the silver crucifix tarnished before his eyes. Immediately, he dropped it in the long grass by the gate. He knew, it would be forever cursed and whoever should carry it, would also carry what that print was attached to. He thought for second. Should he be the one to dispose of it, but he knew he wouldn't be. For all his experience, and good intention Father Crowley was not a brave man. His thoughts drifted back to that day in the Vatican and the exorcism he'd witnessed. A young girl of twelve - tied to a bed deep under the city. In the clouds of mist which began to swirl around his mind, his nightmares returned as he once again saw her disfigured body twisting and writhing on the bed. This image along with her mottled complexion and cries of anguish were burnt into his memory. The feelings of repulsion and fear came flooding back to him. He'd lied to George. He had worked with an exorcist while completing his training, but it had frightened and marked him for life. He believed today that he would be up against nothing more than a feeble-minded simpleton. He never in his wildest nightmares believed he would ever encounter a demon, an evil spirit, or that it would almost cost him his life. Not here, not in a sleepy village lost amongst the rolling hills and shallow valleys of the North Yorkshire Moors. Father Crowley clenched his eyes tightly together to chase out the image. He looked at the cross, half covered by the long weeds and grass which slowly engulfed the gate post. Without a second more thought, he climbed the gate and shouted the orderlies. "Help, help, he's escaped his jacket, you must get down there." As the orderlies rushed past him, over the gate and down towards the station house. He climbed into his car. As he started it, he thought to himself, *I will call George tomorrow and tell him to never speak of this, or what Arthur said.* This last part was especially important. Not least because it was true.

In the station house George watched as Arthur moved closer. Now only a few feet away George knew that if Arthur rushed him, he would have no time to react.

"I'm going now, brother. Don't try and stop me. I'm going away, but I may come back. Pay that wife of yours a visit. That's if your priest doesn't first."

The rage in George was now at a tipping point. He wanted to attack Arthur. Hit him so hard, maybe even kill him. But he knew any attack by him would be futile. As Arthur walked towards him, the doors burst open. It was Keith and the other orderly.

"Arthur, stay there, don't make this difficult." Keith shouted.

Arthur hesitated. Conditioned to obeying the orderlies without hesitation gave enough time for both of them to rush him. While the larger orderly grabbed Arthur, distracting him, Keith emptied a full vile of sedative into his arm. Within seconds Arthur's eyes rolled back, and he collapsed to the floor in a cloud of dust. Keith turned to his oppo. "Go get the other jacket and the trolley. I'm not dragging his arse up the hill." As the orderly left, he turned to George.

"This - here, this bringing him down on your own. It didn't happen, none of it. Ok?"

George sighed heavily. "Thank you."

"Aye, all well an' good. Maybe best if you don't visit for a while. Until he calms down, he'll be pissed when he wakes up."

George watched as they placed the unconscious Arthur into another strait jacket and then bundled him onto the trolley. As they left George spoke. "How did he brake out of the strait jacket? I thought no one could've."

Keith chuckled a little. "Your brother could break out of anything. I've not seen anyone this strong. It's why we always have a spare on hand and a shit load of sedative. What I've given him, it'd kill the likes of you and I."

Once they had Arthur out George locked the doors.
Then, he followed them up the hill and watched as
the white van set off. He noticed Father Crowley's
car was gone. George thought about going to see
him but decided that he would call him tomorrow.
For now, he would head home. And never speak of
what happened.

II

The next few weeks and months were a blur to
George. What he'd witnessed would change him
for life. He would no longer be the smiling
congenial man he'd grown up to be. Like his
mother he became withdrawn, sullen, and short
with people. George told Mavis what he'd done.
That he'd attempted an exorcism with Father
Crowley and that it had gone terribly wrong. He
decided not to tell her of Arthurs allegations.
Rather, he convinced himself that it was Arthur
trying to disrupt the exorcism. And because he'd
settled that in his mind, he also decided not to
confront Father Crowley about it. In fact, he hadn't
spoken to the priest since that day. Father Crowley
had called once but George refused to take the call,
and the priest didn't call again.

He had visited Arthur one last time a few weeks

after the event. Since returning from the Halt on his birthday trip out, the staff reported to George that he has worsened. The drugs which normally kept him sedate enough to clean and feed no longer had any effect on him. They were now considering electric shock treatment. He was constantly kept in a strait jacket and in the most secure part of the building. When George had visited, he'd heard Arthur singing the nursery rhyme. Again, the words were changed, but this time they spoke of killing. Though George couldn't make out the name. He hadn't made his presence known to Arthur. He simply stood outside the door and watched him while Arthur played with the spinning top with his back to the door. After this visit, and as far as George was concerned, he no longer had a brother. This last visit would also be his last report to Thomas and Mavis. Though they had disowned Arthur following the fire George always felt duty bound to let them know how he was. Their response was always one of uninterest.

Anne's health continued to deteriorate. George, Mavis, and Thomas now feared the worst for her. She was frail and aged beyond her years. Thomas once confided in George that he felt it was only a matter of time and that Anne no longer wished to live the life forced upon her by circumstance and bad luck. George knew deep down his father was right. They were all expecting this soon, though each of them expected it privately.

Chapter 10.

October 17th, 1967.

I

The call had come early on a typically autumnal afternoon. The spring – especially April -had been a kind season for the farm and the following summer had been the right type of warm. The farm was once again flourishing, and George and Thomas found themselves preparing once again for the change of seasons. The hours of light were becoming shorter and while the days were still pleasantly warm, the nights brought with them the early frost which was the precursor to the coming ice of winter.

Mavis had taken the call while she prepared a fresh chicken pie with mashed potato and the days picked veg for dinner. Anne, as usual, sat at the table with a cup of tea. Once she'd received and digested the news the call had brought, Mavis left the kitchen in search of George and Thomas. Mavis thought it best not to tell Anne herself. She found George in the workshop changing the antifreeze and coolant in the Land Rover – the lesson had been learned with the Bedford. On hearing what Mavis had to say, George went in search for Thomas. He found him in the higher fields, mending the stone wall which bounded their farm from the public bridleway which skirted it around the southern valley. Gathered, they headed back to the farmhouse to tell Anne collectively. She took the news much worse than any of them thought she would. Arthur is dead. "How?" Was all Anne could muster. Her lips trembled as she asked

"The electric shock treatment, Ma." George answered, softly. He continued. "He wouldn't 'ave felt a thing, it was instant."

Anne stood and turned to Mavis. "I need to lay down."

Mavis helped Anne to bed. In the kitchen George and Thomas spoke softly.

"Do you think he would've felt anything, Da?" George asked. His previous statement was only for his mother's comfort. He imagined the pain would have been intense.

"Aye, you ever stuck your finger in a socket?" Thomas said.

"Fair point." George replied.

After a momentary silence, Thomas turned to George. "So, what do they do with the body?"

"I expect they'll want us to bury him. Have a service and such." George replied.

"Aye well, we'll not be doing that! Not for him."

George sighed and took a second to collect his thoughts. "He is family, Da. I know what he's done and what he became - me more than most. But he is still my brother."

Thomas thought. "Well, he can be buried here, on the farm, in the woodland outback. That land is no good, it'll be quite fitting because he wasn't any good either."

George didn't respond. He took the small win. At least his brother's body wouldn't be burnt and tossed away on the breeze. "I'll make the arrangements tomorrow."

"Keep it from your mother. She doesn't need to know what's happening to him. If she thought he was on the land, it'd finish her."

"Will do." George said as he stood. He headed for the door and pulled on his boots and jacket. "I'll go finish the Landy. Then once we're sorted in the morning, I'll head over to the hospital and arrange to pick him up."

"You could just call em George. That's why we got the damn thing, wasn't it? To make life easier."

"Aye, I could. But not this time. Not for this, Da."

Thomas nodded in agreement as George turned and left the kitchen. As he did Mavis entered.

"Was that George heading out?" Mavis asked.

"Aye, love. He's gone to finish the truck. How is

she?" Thomas asked, pointing above him with his eyes.

"She's asleep. I didn't think it would hit that hard. She hasn't seen him for the last few years."

"True, but maybe she's glad it's all over now." Thomas stood, pulling his jacket over him. "Anyway, I've to get that wall finished while there's some light left."

"Don't be too long, dinner will be ready soon. Tell George on your way out." Mavis said as Thomas pulled the door open.

"Will do." Thomas smiled, nodded, and then stepped outside.

In the afternoon air he could feel the temperature dropping almost by the minute. He walked over to the workshop figuring that by the time he got to the top field there wouldn't be enough daylight left to do any meaningful work. *It can wait till morning* he thought to himself as he entered. Inside the dimly lit but warm workshop George was just topping up the last of the coolant. "You got the mixture right George?" Thomas asked, dipping his finger into the top of the radiator before tasting the mixture. "Aye, nice and sweet, reckon that'll be fine."

George smiled. "That stuff will kill ya, Da." He scoffed.

"Not that small amount. Besides, what won't...?"

George moved around to the cab of the Land Rover and started the truck. Moving back to the open engine bay he began squeezing the top hosepipe. After a few air bubbles cleared he fastened the cap and dropped the bonnet. "That'll do her till next year."

George leant in and switched off the engine. A quiet fell over the workshop as the autumn night drew in. Mist began to roll in over the hills and across the farmyard. George and Thomas walked out of the workshop, each pulling the two wooden doors shut. George locked it, then flicked a heavy weatherproof switch. Immediately, the farmyard was bathed in a warm-soft glow. "Dinner's up soon, son." Thomas said, rubbing his hands against the dampness which now encroached around them.

"Sounds good, Da."

They walked through the thickening mist back to the farmhouse. Inside Mavis served up their meal. Anne's absence was noticeable and had become more frequent. As usual, and after washing and clearing away the dinner pots, Mavis would take Anne's dinner up to her bedroom with a glass of water. A few minutes later, Mavis joined her husband and father-in-law in the living room. A fire roared against the cold damp night outside. Shep laid in front of it. The old dog, now confined to the house, was more grey than black and white. He sighed and twitched in his deep sleep. "Shep's chasing them rabbits again," Thomas smirked, his feet atop a foot stool in front of the fire.

"Did Ma eat her tea love?" George asked Mavis.

"Some of it, mostly the veg." Mavis replied, turning her gaze for a second away from the TV. "What time are you going through to the hospital tomorrow?" Mavis returned a question to George.

"Once I've given Da a hand to get the farm up."

"I can manage for a day son. You get over there, and then back. I'll need more help later in the afternoon." Thomas replied, twitching his feet – which were becoming too toastie.

"Ya sure, Da?"

"Aye, son. Get it sorted, then it's done." Thomas gave in and pulled his feet away from the fire while Shep continued to dream of his days as a younger dog. "'I've now idea how he stands the heat."

Mavis smiled, still holding her attention on the TV.

Outside, the mist had become a heavy fog. Between the farmhouse and barn, it lingered – thick, floating ominously in the air. Swirls of minute water droplets hung in the air as the slow breeze which had brought the fog over the hills wafted between the buildings. The soft glow of the yard lights illuminated this dance, highlighting the patterns the thick clouds made. Inside the barn, the pigs and chickens huddled together for warmth. Across the moors, past the Halt and as far as the village of Thirstonfield, the fog now enveloped everything.

II

Early the next morning George pulled up to St Lukes Hospital and switched off the truck. The fog which seemed to swallow everything the previous night was still with them. The breeze which had brought it in from the east coast had now gone. George entered and approached the reception desk. An older woman he'd not met before smiled at him while she closed a brown folder. "Can I help?"

"I'm Mr. Bradbury - George, I've come to see about fetching my brother." George hesitated; his words didn't seem to want to come out. "He died here yesterday."

The older woman's face turned from, *welcoming smile* to *I'm so sorry to hear of your loss.* "I'm sorry to hear that. What was his name?" She asked, her face still holding the correct expression.

"Arthur Bradbury."

"Please take a seat, I won't be long, dear."

George turned to see a small armada of neatly placed chairs – every one of them was empty. He approached the closest chair and sat. Immediately, he realised this seat wasn't a good choice – it was too close to the door, but the older woman was now back at her desk and George felt too self-conscious to begin moving for no apparent reason.

After a short while of fighting within himself to move, an elderly man approached wearing what George could clearly see was an expensive suit under a white coat. He held out his hand. "I'm Dr. Williams. Please come with me." He said smoothly, while shaking George's hand with just the right amount of grip. George followed him into his office. Inside, Dr. Williams sat behind a large desk. Placed neatly on it was a few more of the brown folders and a desk lamp with a brass stand and neck topped with a dark-green glass shade.

"Can I see him. Arthur, can I see him?" George asked.

"Of course, Mr. Bradbury. First, I just need you to sign the release forms. Then, we can make arrangements for the funeral home to collect him."

George scribbled his name on the piece of neatly printed paper, Dr. Williams had placed in front of him. Then he gently spun it around and slid it back over the desk. Dr. Williams smiled and slipped it inside one of the brown folders.

"Which funeral home will be collecting your brother?" Dr. Williams Asked.

George shuffled in his seat a little. "I'm taking him. We're burying him at home. On the farm like…"

Dr. Williams sat back in his seat. "Your choice, of course." He breathed heavily and then stood. "Come through, I'll take you to him."

George followed him once again. After walking

through a few corridors, it seemed to George were hidden behind the walls the visitors usually see, they arrived at a room shielded by double doors with a panel of rippled glass in each. Above them it read, *Morgue.* George breathed heavily as Dr. Williams pushed the doors open. Inside George could see a wall of metal doors. In the middle of the room above a drain was a large metal table. Above it was a large movable light. On the table was a body covered in a white sheet. George guessed by its size, that this was Arthur. Dr. Williams approached the table. George readied himself against what he thought he may see. "I must warn you his injuries were significant"

"I'm ready." George replied. Even though he knew he was anything but ready.

The sheet was pulled back. "Here he is."

Arthur's hair around his temples was burnt – as was the skin. Black crispy flesh spread down both sides of his face to his lower jaw and across to his eyes, which themselves were burnt along with the eye lids. As George looked down at him, it seemed to him that Arthur was staring back through chard-black eyes. It was the same with the flesh around his ears and over his scalp. The hair which hadn't burnt was thin and looked crispy, as if a strong breeze would snap it. George pulled back, gasping, desperately trying to hold onto the contents of his stomach.

"What happened?" George whispered once he'd steadied himself.

"The sedatives were no longer working. So, we decided to try electric shock therapy. At first it had no effect, so we increased the amount and duration."

"Until it killed him?" George asked. A little firmer this time.

"No. That's the strange thing. The dose which killed him was less than we'd been using. But that's not all." Dr. Williams hesitated and then continued. "Just before this dose was given, the orderly heard Arthur shout something."

***

October 16th

Arthur was led into the room where they carried out the electroconvulsive therapy. Sedated and in his straight jacket he was put into the chair and strapped in. The orderly then placed the electrodes over his temples and placed a small leather bite into his mouth. As the orderly moved behind a screen and switched on the apparatus, Arthur sat motionless. A tear formed in his left eye. Arthur had brief moments of clarity. Small interludes when the fog which had enveloped his mind since he'd first heard the voice of Jack seemed to disappear. It was in these moments the memories of everything he's done flooded over him. And like the wave of those memories, the tsunami of regret and pain that came with it was too much to bear. This was one of those moments. As the first hit came Arthur screamed through the pain, biting down hard on the small leather bite between his teeth. The charge stopped and Arthur relaxed. His body no longer convulsing. Then he heard Jacks voice. *"I'll come back soon, son."* As soon as he heard his voice Arthur felt an emptiness inside him. He felt vulnerable and weak and he felt frightened. He wrestled his tongue around the bite, managing to get it free. As the orderly placed a hand on the control panel and flicked the switch Arthur spat it out and shouted. "Don't leave me Jack…" The surge of electricity came as he shouted the name - Jack. His jaws instantly clamped shut, severing his tongue which slid down the back of his throat. The intense pain sent white hot surges through his mind. He could see nothing but exploding patterns of light for the briefest of seconds before complete blackness took away his vision. In that instant the smell of his own burning flesh overcame any other sensation. In the final moments, he was once again an innocent small child. He remembered his own birth, the warmth of his mother's love and joy he felt as a baby being coddled. Then, he felt it all slip away as he gasped for air as the pain intensified. For Arthur there was no light. No warmth or feelings of euphoria. As his brain shut down and the memories of his childhood left him, only utter blackness and despair waited for him. In the final nanoseconds before his brain finally died, he felt a resentment for everything and everyone. Especially the one who called himself his father. The one who left him here on this table to die in the worst way he could imagine. The one who called himself, Jack.

In the glimmering of his dying brain - as the last of the neurons fired, he promised he would have his revenge on them all. Then, exactly two seconds after he had shouted the words, "Don't leave me Jack." Arthur died.

***

 "What… what did he shout?" George asked. Now with his back to Arthur.

"They heard him say Jack come back, or something like that. Does that name mean anything to you?"

George thought for a second. "No, at least not in connection with Arthur."

"There was another thing. They claim, as he said it, the lights in the room intensified for a brief second. I have no idea what to make of it. The dose which killed him was a large dose. Too much for me, or you. But Arthur had previously had much higher doses, and it hadn't affected him in anyway." Dr. Williams pulled the sheet back over him. "When do you want to take him?"

George thought for a moment. He would need to have his mother out of the house. "Day after tomorrow? My father will come with me, give me a hand."

"I'll have him ready." Dr. Williams replied.

As George turned to leave, Dr. Williams moved over to a cupboard and pulled out the spinning top. "What do you want to do with this?"

George took it off him. "I'll take it home."

Dr. Williams turned off the lights as they left. As the doors swung closed George took one last look at his brother, laid in the darkened room. As he did, a shiver ran down his spine. George returned to the farm after a drive of silent reflection. As he pulled into the workshop Thomas followed him in. "So?" Thomas said after George had turned off the engine, but before he got out of the Land Rover.

"We're to collect him the day after tomorrow. I'll get Mavis to take Ma out for the day. Maybe a shopping trip to Middlesbrough or Whitby." As George climbed out, he pulled the spinning top off the passenger seat. Thomas saw it and stepped away.

"What's that here for?" Thomas snapped.

"I didn't know what else to do with it Da. I'm just going to put it where he found it. Then we can forget about the bloody thing."

Thomas didn't answer verbally. He simply shrugged and walked out of the workshop. Just before he headed out, he shouted back to George "I'll be up in the field. I'll need a hand later." The sight of the spinning top had unsettled him. He wanted to smash it to pieces. But he didn't dare to. Like George, he believed the best thing to do was to place it back in the bunk and forget about it.

"Ok." George shouted after him. Then he walked over to the barn and to the bunk. Reaching up, he pulled the key off an old cupboard and unlocked the door. He pushed the door open and stepped inside. The air was damp and smelt moist in the cooling autumn day. George placed the spinning top on top of the tall-boy next to the water basin and jug. He looked around. Mould continued to claim the bedding and clothes which were left folded neatly. George couldn't understand why the farm hand, whose name he still couldn't remember, had left such personal belongings. He looked over to the photo of a woman he assumed was a relative, or a lover. Shrugging, he pulled the door closed while swearing to himself that he would never again step foot in this place. With a turn of the key, he locked it and placed the key back atop the cupboard. After exiting the barn, he made his way up to the top field and helped Thomas to finish rebuilding the fallen wall.

Later that night, after they'd eaten and cleared away, and Anne was once again in her bed, George, Mavis, and Thomas discussed their plan to bury Arthur in the woods out back. The land they believed would be ideal was located behind the farm. It was an uphill woodland of around five or six acres - no one had ever bothered to measure it - which had no use either for grazing or for growing. Its single biggest benefit was the fact that it protected the farmyard and house from flooding when they had heavy rainfall or thawing from heavy snowfall. The woodland was a great natural barrier and was far enough on their property that no one would wonder through it. After some time of discussion, the plan was set. George and Thomas would drop Anne and Mavis off in Thirstonfield. It was agreed by all that Anne would not go to Middlesbrough. The place was too crowded for her as was Whitby. Once there, Thomas and George would then go pick up Arthur, take his body back to the farm and bury him before returning for Mavis and Anne. With everyone happy, Mavis turned on the TV and while Shep once again dreamed of being a young pup, George, Thomas, and Mavis watched Z-Cars.

The day after tomorrow soon arrived. With Anne and Mavis in the village, George and Thomas headed off to St Lukes Hospital. The journey seemed to take longer than it usually would.

"What state was he in?" Thomas asked as the blue Land Rover made its way from the small twisting country roads to the wider roads of the town.

"Not good, Da. He was badly burnt." George replied, concentrating on the town traffic. "I'll never get used to these town roads."

"Did they say how it happened?" Thomas asked, wating for the right moment.

"He said the dose of electricity they gave him was lower than usual. But he said as they hit the button, the lights in the room flickered and then Arthur said summat strange."

"Aye, what were that?"

"Summat like…" George thought for a few seconds. "Don't go Jack, or don't leave. Summat like that."

Thomas took a breath. *Should I answer…?* He thought to himself. "Funny the things we'd say when getting electric passed through us, I reckon." Thomas fumbled his answer. Even he wasn't sure of that subterfuge.

"That name Jack. It keeps coming up. Why would Arthur know it? What's it to do with him?" George asked as he pulled into the car park at St Lukes Hospital.

"God only knows, and he'll not tell us." Thomas dismissed George's question. Then quickly climbed out.

Inside the hospital George and Thomas were guided through to the morgue. Inside the room - on a metal trolley - a large wooden crate held the body of Arthur.

"Would you need a hand to load him?" The orderly asked.

"Aye. Do we need to bring the truck 'round back?" Thomas asked in reply.

The orderly thought for a second. "We can manage him if we go through the back way."

George looked to Thomas. Both shrugged to each

other and then turned to the orderly. "Can we get on with it then?" George said.

The orderly pulled the trolley around. "After you…" He said.

After what seemed like an impossible task was completed, the crate was loaded into the back of the Land Rover. With what they believed to be Arthurs feet sticking out the back - held in only by the rope which secured the half-closed tailgate in place, they were ready to drive home. "careful!" Thomas said as George pulled out of the car park.

III

The track through the woodland was narrow, steep, and badly rutted. George was experienced at guiding the Land Rover over this terrain. He would, when he was able, drive through the woodland to make sure no one was camping, and that no animals from the farm, or local pets had found their way in and become lost. Eventually, around halfway along the track and around a mile or so from the farmyard and house George brought the truck to a stop. He looked out of his window to a patch of clear ground. He pointed to it. "That should do it Da."

Thomas looked across him. "Aye, reckon it will.

Let's get this over with."

George switched off the engine and they both climbed out. Unfastening the rope Thomas grabbed a hold of the crate and pulled it as hard as he was able. It slid out and crashed to the soft muddy floor. George looked over to his father with a questioning look. Thomas shrugged, "He's not gonna feel it, son."

George sighed and along with Thomas they dragged the crate over the rough ground to the spot they'd chosen. As the first shovel broke ground on the spot that would become Arthurs grave, a silence fell over the woodland. George looked around as the sudden quiet became obvious to him. "Hear that?" He asked Thomas.

"What?" Thomas asked, halting his digging.

"Everything's gone quiet…"

"Let's just get this done and get out." Thomas said. His fretted tone was more apparent to George than the silence which now surrounded them.

After around half an hour of digging they dragged the crate over to the hole and as carefully as they could, dropped it inside. It took another fifteen minutes to fill the hole back in. Sweating, covered in damp mud and aching more than they had in a long while, Thomas and George made their way back to the truck. "We should get cleaned up, then pick up Ma and. Mavis." George said as he turned the key. Thomas nodded as the truck pulled away.

They had agreed to meet in the local pub, *The Kings Head.* Thomas and George parked up outside a short while later. Washed and changed they made their way inside to find Mavis and Anne sat at a table near the open fire. Outside the sun was already below the highest trees, and the cold air which accompanied the night was making itself known. "Should we have a treat, and eat here before we head home?" George asked.

Thomas thought for a while. He couldn't remember the last time they had a meal out. Sure, when George married, they had food and such, but it always seemed to be a special occasion. "Aye, go on then. What do you think, wife?" He said, asking Anne directly.

Anne looked between them. "I think that would be nice." She replied, her voice meekly projecting the words only enough, so they were just about audible.

"It's settled then. I'll get us some drinks, and the menus." George said, standing.

As George headed to the bar Anne turned to Thomas. "Is Arthur going to join us?"

Thomas looked to Mavis. He felt a cold run through him. He'd known for some while that his dear wife was not well. The stress of the last twenty years was more than most could carry. Add to that the guilt she had once confessed to him for bringing Arthur into the world, he was surprised in many ways that she was still with him. Surprised and grateful. Even though their marriage was not what either had hoped it would be since that night, at least he still had her by his side.

"No Anne, Arthur won't be joining us tonight." Mavis replied.

Thomas looked over to Mavis and smiled his acknowledgment.

"Is he away at work?" Anne asked.

"Yes, that's right. He's gone for a while now, we're not sure when he'll be back." Mavis said as reassuringly as she could.

"He's in the army, remember? He'll be away for a long time." Thomas added, not really thinking about any possible implications to the lie.

Anne, content with the answer turned away from Anne and Thomas and stared into the fire, warming her hands as she did.

After the meal they headed home through the dark night. The headlamps of the Land Rover only partially illuminating the road ahead. Eventually, they reached the farm. George parked close to the door. They entered the kitchen. "Brew, anyone?" Mavis asked.

"Aye," Replied both George and Thomas. Anne looked between them smiling, "I'm off to bed. Make sure to leave a cup out for Arthur."

George looked over to Mavis, she shook her head

and smiled, then she turned to Anne. "I will, don't worry. You head up, I'll be there soon." As Anne left the kitchen, Mavis turned to George. I'll explain in a bit."

Thomas pulled off his jacket and made his way through to the living room. The small table lamp was already lit. In front of the fire lay Shep. Thomas could see the moment he looked at him that the old dog had died. Comfortable and warm, and in his sleep. Thomas smiled at the dog. Leaning down, he stroked him. "Goodnight lad." He whispered. At that moment George entered.

"Is he still in front of that fire Da?" George asked.

Thomas turned to George and smiled. "He's gone, son."

In a corner of the workshop, under the heavy tarp Thomas had covered it with all those years ago, the hands on the grandfather clock began to move. Moving faster than they would do to keep accuracy, they moved as if they were catching up with time itself. Then, as they reached precisely 9.30 pm – the time it was – they stopped, and the clock chimed a single strike.

Chapter 11.

The Hauntings.

October 28th, 1967.

6 am.

<u>Mavis.</u>

The day began much like every other day. Mavis climbed slowly out of bed while fighting every instinct she had to remain in it. The October mornings were cold. The only way to beat back the autumn morning was to light the fires in the living room and the kitchen. In the dead of winter, they would sometimes leave the fires burning when they went to bed, but it wasn't quite cold enough for that - not yet anyway though Mavis knew those days were fast approaching. Mavis also knew she had to make a start on breakfast before Thomas and George went out to work on the farm. Then, she would see to Anne who always stayed in bed until the men were out of the house. She needed the house to be peaceful before she would come down. This routine had set in almost immediately after they returned to the house following the fire. Anne's decline could be road mapped from that event with almost military accuracy. As Mavis stoked the fire in the living room, where Anne would soon take her place for the day, it dawned on her again that this was pretty much her life now.

The bacon sizzled in the large cast-iron pan while the kettle – hung over an open flame - began to whistle its own morning tune. As Mavis added the eggs and turned over the black-pudding, Thomas and George entered the kitchen. "Morning Mavis," Thomas said.

"Morning Thomas." She replied without turning to face him.

Thomas and George then began talking to each other. Mavis could hear their voices but the conversation to her was, for the most part, indistinct mumblings. Mavis lifted two large dinner plates from out of the oven where they'd been placed to warm through, *"No good putting warm food on cold plates,"* Anne had once told her when she first started to help out around the house. Bacon, eggs, black-pudding, and fried bread was slid onto each plate. She placed them in front of Thomas and George who both nodded and said *"Thanks."* while Mavis poured out the mashed tea. Four cups, one each for the men, one for her, and one for Anne which she would take up to her now.

Mavis climbed the stairs and entered Anne's bedroom. There she found her mother-in-law laid in bed. The thick winter sheets pulled up around her. Mavis moved over to her. Placing the cup of tea down on the side table, she gently placed her hand on Anne's shoulder and moved it back and forth. "Anne, wake up, it's time for your morning tea." Mavis whispered.

Anne opened her eyes. "Arthur, is that you?"

Mavis pulled back her hand. "No Anne it's Mavis. I've brought you your tea."

Slowly Anne sat up. Turning she took the tea from the side table and took a sip. "Thank you dear, I'll be down soon." As she spoke, they both heard the kitchen door slam.

"That'll be the boys going out to work Anne. Come down when you're ready." Mavis said, smiling at her.

Anne smiled and with her eyes she followed Mavis as she left. Just before Mavis walked out of the bedroom, Anne spoke. "Arthur is back from the war you know."

Mavis stopped and turned. "Arthur?"

"Yes, I can hear him when he speaks to me. He's back from the war. He's a hero you know." Anne said, smiling and then taking another sip.

Mavis stood still in the doorway. She had no idea how to play this. Should she go along with this fantasy and put it down to Anne's mental demise - something they all knew was happening but didn't speak of. This was mainly due to Thomas's reluctance to acknowledge it. Or, should she confront Anne and insist that Arthur isn't here. She took a moment, but before she thought herself through to a conclusion Anne said something else.

"Can you hear the children, dear?"

A chill ran down Mavis. "Children?"

"Yes, just like George and Arthur when they would sing that lovely nursery rhyme."

Mavis made her decision. "That's lovely, yes I can hear them…" She decided to play along and speak to George about it tonight. Sure, Mavis was married into this family and was running the home while looking after Anne, but she was George's mother. He could deal with this. Mavis smiled. "You finish your tea Anne and get yourself dressed. I'll be back up when I've cleared away breakfast."

"Yes, ok dear." Anne said, taking another sip. As Mavis made her way down the stairs, she heard Anne singing. *"See Saw Margery Daw…"*

Mavis came into the kitchen to find the back door wide open. A stiff cold breeze blew in, trying its best to extinguish the fire. Swearing under her breath Mavis closed the door – locking it. "That'll teach them when they want to be in." She said in an angry whisper. She headed over to the table. Picking up the dirty plates, mugs, and utensils, she walked over to the sink and dropped them in the hot soapy water. As usual, there were no leftovers or scraps of food which needed to be cleared first. While they soaked, Mavis then made her way into the living room to check on the fire. She knew Anne would likely be down soon. Mavis fluffed up the large blanket which Anne kept over the back of her chair. She would use this to cover her legs while she knitted or watched whatever was on the TV. Mavis then cleared away yesterday's newspapers and picked up an empty glass she guessed had been left by Thomas. "It's a bloody good job I hadn't washed-up yet…" Mavis scowled as she turned, happy with the room, and headed back through to the kitchen. Placing the glass in the sink, she made her way back up the stairs to retrieve Anne's cup and to make sure she was getting out of bed. After collecting it, she made her way back down. This routine was draining in so many ways, not least because of its monotony.

As she made her way into the kitchen, Mavis stopped. On the table she saw the dinner plates, cutlery, and mugs. They were wet and covered in soap. It was as if someone had simply lifted them out of the sink and placed them back exactly where Thomas and George had left them. A stiff breeze brought her attention back to the door, which was wide open. A thought flashed through her mind. Had Anne come down, placed out the pots and then walked out of the kitchen. It was warm enough outside with a coat on, but the rain was coming down hard. She knew Thomas and George were in the fields today and not in the yard. If Anne had walked out, they may not see her. Mavis put the glass on the table and rushed to the door. "Anne!" She shouted, "Anne!"

"Yes dear?" A soft voice behind her.

Mavis spun around. Anne was standing in the

doorway which led up the stairs. Still in her dressing gown. Mavis pointed to the table and the wet pots. "Did you do this Anne?"

Anne moved her gaze over to the table. Then she looked back to Mavis. "You shouldn't put wet pots on the table dear. You'll ruin the varnish. Let's get them in the sink."

Mavis stood dumbfounded for a few seconds. *What the hell is going on?* She thought to herself as she watched Anne move the pots back into the hot soapy water. Snapping back, she repeated the question. "Did you move the pots Anne?"

Anne stopped halfway across the kitchen with Thomas's glass in her hand. "Yes dear. I'm putting them in the sink for you."

"No, before that. Did you take them out of the sink and put 'em them on the table?" Mavis asked. Her tone becoming more frustration than reasonable.

"When, dear?" Anne asked, placing the glass in the sink.

"A few minutes ago."

"I've just come down the stairs. What a silly thing to ask." Anne replied.

A stiff breeze blew in again accompanied by a splattering of rain. Anne moved over to the door. "We should close that door." She said, pushing it shut.

Mavis moved closer. "I did close the door. And I put the pots in the sink. Then I went to check on the living room and when I came back…"

Anne cut across her. "Oh, don't worry Mavis, it's just the boys having fun, that's all."

Mavis felt sick to her stomach. She moved over to Anne. "Come on let's get you settled in the living room. See what's on the TV, shall we?"

Anne smiled and allowed Mavis to guide her through the room. She settled into her chair, and Mavis pulled her blanket across her knees. Then, she switched on the TV. The hazy green blob in the middle of the screen expanded into *Grandstand* on BBC 1. "There you go, the sport is on. I'll bring you in the lovely cup of tea." Mavis said, tucking the blanket corners in.

"Yes. We'll watch this." Anne replied.

"I haven't time to watch it with you." Mavis said, standing and then continuing. "But I'll bring you a cup of tea and a slice of toast."

Anne looked up to her. "Oh, silly. I meant me and Arthur."

Mavis took a deep breath as a shot of adrenaline rushed through her. She nodded to Anne and headed back for the kitchen.

George and Thomas.

George woke at his usual time. Outside it was dark, though the first cracks of sunlight were beginning to make themselves known. Mavis stirred and cuddled into him. "Morning," She said - still mostly asleep. He kissed her on the forehead and returned the verbal greeting as he climbed out of bed and made his way to the bathroom. By the time he'd washed, pulled on his clothes for the day and brushed his teeth – a routine he'd had since being a boy - and returned to the bedroom, Mavis was already out of bed and making her way downstairs. George sat on the end of the bed and pulled his feet into his slippers. Then, wiggling his toes he stood and stretched. As he did Thomas came out of his bedroom. George watched his father walk to the bathroom. It was obvious to him that he was getting slower and it was becoming harder for him with each year that passed by.

He remembered that Thomas would always be the first to rise and always the last to go to bed. Now, as the years had taken their toll on him, he could see the struggle it was for him to continue this. On a night, it was George who now locked up. The duty of the last person to go to bed was to ensure the house was secure. His father would often go up before Mavis and always complaining of his aches and pains. He sighed and realised this would probably be the last year he was helping his father on the farm. From next year it would be very much the case that his father would be helping him. The sound of the frying pan and the accompanying smell brought him back from his melancholy realisations. Thomas appeared from the bathroom. Looking down the narrow hallway he smiled at George who was now standing in the doorway to his bedroom. "Smells good." Thomas said, going back into his bedroom. George smiled and made his way down the stairs. Before he reached the bottom Thomas began to follow him down. They entered the kitchen to find Mavis standing at the range cooking their breakfast. "Morning." Thomas said as he and George sat at the table. "Morning Thomas." Mavis replied to him, without turning around.

Thomas turned to George. "So, lad, what's the jobs for today?"

George thought for a second. "I've to finish sorting out in the workshop Da. The Landy is getting squeezed out by all the rubbish that keeps getting piled up. Before long she'll not fit in, and I don't want her sat outside over the winter. I've a feeling it's going to be a bad one this year."

Mavis placed their breakfasts down in front of them and then poured out four cups of tea. George and Thomas both smiled and said, "*Thanks.*" As they picked up their knives and forks and began eating. George noticed Mavis carrying a cup of tea out of the kitchen, and up the stairs. Then he turned to Thomas. "What you doin' today?"

Thomas chewed a mixture of bacon and black

pudding, before swallowing it down with a gulp of sweet tea from his green tin mug. "I'm going to sort the barn out. There's a few holes in the back wall need fixing before the weather changes."

With their breakfasts eaten, and with Mavis still upstairs seeing to Anne, George and Thomas stood, pulled on their boots and jackets, and headed out the door. "Thanks for breakfast." George said, knowing she wouldn't hear him, but he just felt better for saying it. He pulled the door closed with more strength than he normally would making it slam. Whispering an apology to no one in particular, he headed for the workshop while Thomas made his way to the barn.

At the entrance to the workshop George pulled open the double doors. Squeezing his way passed the Land Rover, he climbed into it and pulled it out of the workshop. Once parked where he needed it, he got out and walked by it tapping the front wing. "You'll have plenty of room tonight girl." Once back inside George stood for a moment and took a look at the years' worth of junk which had piled up. He scratched his head. *What the bloody hell do I do with all this?"* He asked himself. After taking a few seconds to decide whether he wanted to continue, or give in before he started, he sighed and grabbed the closest box. *"Better get on with it."*

After a couple of hours of pulling boxes and old pieces of burnt items and furniture which had been dumped in the workshop following the fire, George could finally see the back wall and Thomas's office.

George smiled when he saw the partitioned room for the first time in a few years. Whilst he hadn't forgotten it was there, it had slipped to the back of his conscious. George pushed the ill-fitting door open and stepped inside. The room, which he hadn't been in since his late teenage years was just as he remembered. Even the foisty smell was still evident. It was a mixture of spare parts, oil, and grease from the tractor, and general long forgotten crap. As well as the historical paperwork from a time when Thomas would keep accurate records. In the corner he noticed an odd shaped object covered in a sheet. Instinctively he wanted to look at it but decided that could wait for another day when he had more time. Taking one last look, George smiled at the old office, and then stepped back out, pulling the door shut. For the time being it could stay in this mess. Besides, it was kind of an historical time capsule. A living memory from his youth and he wasn't quite ready to lose that just yet. George moved over to the back wall. Against a metal workbench, tucked in a corner he spotted a tall object covered in a dull green tarp. George moved over to it. He didn't recognise what it could be. Carefully, he lifted a loose corner of the tarp and began to pull it. Slowly, the grandfather clock was revealed. As the tarp fell to the ground in an explosion of dust, George could see the brass pendulum swinging back and forth and as it did, he could hear the seconds tick tock. George stepped back and gasped.

Around the back of the barn Thomas had begun the job of plugging the holes in the wooden structure.

The rot had set in where the wood slats met the ground. Only in the warmest parts of the summer was the ground around the back of the barn dry. It was shielded from any direct sunlight and so for most of the year it was perpetually damp. Thomas made his way along the rear wall, cutting out the rotten wood and piecing it with fresh off cuts. After a couple of hours, he reached the section of the barn which separated into the bunk house. Thomas stopped. The slats here were worse than most of those he'd already replaced but he felt a reluctance to continue. This bunk – which he would dare not tear down – represented everything which had gone wrong with his life since that night, now some twenty years ago. The conflict inside him was simple. If he didn't replace the slats the rot would spread, eventually contaminating the fresh wood he'd put in today. If he did replace the slats, the rot would be stopped for a good few years, but in his mind, he'd be somehow doing something good for the bastard that used to live in this place. He could feel his anger rising. It was the thoughts and memories which brought him to this dark place for the most part. But what really hurt Thomas was the betrayal he felt towards Jack Bright. He'd given this man a roof over his head. A job and food. He'd also given him the benefit of doubt on more than one occasions and welcomed him to his family. And yet, after doing all of this out of the goodness of his heart, he betrayed him in the worst possible way.

Thomas threw down his tools. He would no longer be cowed into keeping this shrine to the man who destroyed his life. He marched inside the barn just as the rain began to fall. Pulling the key off the top of the cupboard. He unlocked the door and stepped inside ready to smash the place into oblivion and burn every possession. As Thomas stood, his fists clenched, he saw a movement in the corner of his eye. Slowly, he turned his head and watched as the plunger of the spinning top began to press down.

George turned and ran from the workshop towards the barn. He remembered his father telling him he'd gotten rid of all the clocks and watches because they were distraction. The rain was falling hard as he splashed his way across the yard. As he ran past the house, he noticed the open door. His instinct of course was to close it, but it would have to wait. George entered the barn to find Thomas standing in the open doorway of the bunk, staring at the spinning top. "Da!" George shouted. Thomas turned.

"What's up, what ya doing in here?" George asked.

Thomas stepped back through the doorway into the barn, pulling the bunk door closed behind him. He turned the key and slid it back on top of the cupboard. "Nothing, son. Why are you running in here all flustered?" Thomas struggled to make sense of his words before he spoke them, but he could tell there was something which was disturbing George.

George stopped, getting his breath back, he questioned Thomas again. "Why were you in there? You weren't going to do summat daft, were you?"

Thomas thought for a second. He decided not to tell George about the plunger. "No, just checking for rotten wood, son." He took a breath. "Besides, what's up with you running over?"

"I've summat to show you." George turned and began walking back towards the workshop. Thomas followed him.

Inside the bunk, the plunger stopped and then released itself. As it did the top began to spin, and the tune began to play.

Thomas followed George into the workshop. As they passed the house George noticed the door was now closed. *Perhaps Mavis was airing the kitchen*, he thought to himself. Inside the workshop George stopped in front of the clock. Thomas stood next to him.

"Thought you'd got rid of all the clocks?" George asked his father.

Thomas walked to it and placed a hand on it. "I forgot all about this thing." He whispered and then continued. "It's still going!"

"It wasn't until I pulled the tarp off it." George said, now standing closer, "What should we do with it?" He asked, softly.

Thomas looked at George. "Only one thing to do." He took a hold of the tarp and pulled it over the old clock. Then, he grabbed an old length of rope and tied it around the tarp. "It'll not fall off again."

"Aye, but how's it still going, Da" George asked.

Thomas gave the rope one last tug. "It doesn't matter how. It'll stop soon enough. Now, finish up here, and get this place sorted. We've still to get all this trammel over to the old shed so you can keep your precious *Landy* warm at night." Thomas said, half smiling at George.

George returned the gesture. After another few hours of them both working, the workshop job was completed. The rubbish, or *trammel*, had been moved to the old shed which had been long since abandoned when the new barn had been built just before George was born. With the Land Rover unloaded, George drove it back over to the workshop and pulled it inside. As he did, he smiled at his small victory - there was now more than enough room.

Thomas put away the tools he'd used to repair the barn. He fed the pigs and chickens and then made his way back over to the house with George.

<u>Anne.</u>

Anne woke when Thomas came back in from the bedroom. Thomas leant over her and kissed her softly, "Morning, wife." He said. Anne smiled and kissed him back. She could smell the breakfast Mavis was cooking. It smelt nice, but she was no longer able to eat first thing. A cup of tea would suffice – as it usually did. She watched as Thomas left the room. Anne slid a little further under the covers and closed her eyes. As she lay listening to the muted sounds of her family enjoying their breakfast, she heard a soft voice. "Ma, I'm back." Anne recognised the voice instantly. It was a voice which she believed to be Arthur's.

"Hi son," She whispered in reply and then continued. "Are you here?"

"Yes, Ma. I'm home from the war now. I've got a medal, Ma I'm a hero. Are you proud of me?" Arthur's voice whispered.

"Oh, that's lovely Arthur. Your father will be so proud of you." Anne said, smiling – her eyes still closed.

"No! You mustn't tell Thomas. This is a secret for us." Arthur's voice said.

Anne then heard the floorboard next to her bed squeak. Then she heard a voice.

"Anne, wake up, it's time for your morning tea."

Anne opened her eyes. "Arthur, is that you?"

Mavis pulled back her hand. "No Anne it's Mavis. I've brought you your tea."

Slowly Anne sat up. Turning, she took the tea from the side table and took a sip. "Thank you dear, I'll be down soon." As she spoke, they both heard the kitchen door slam.

"That'll be the boys going out to work Anne. Come down when you're ready." Mavis said, smiling at her.

Anne smiled and with her eyes she followed Mavis as she left. Just before Mavis walked out of the bedroom Anne spoke. "Arthur is back from the war you know."

Mavis stopped and turned. "Arthur?"

"Yes, I can hear him when he speaks to me. He's back from the war. He's a hero you know." Anne said, smiling and then taking another sip. "Can you hear the children, dear?"

"Children?" Mavis asked.

"Yes, just like George and Arthur when they would sing that lovely nursery rhyme."

 "That's lovely, yes I can hear them…" Mavis smiled. "You finish your tea Anne and get yourself dressed. I'll be back up when I've cleared away breakfast."

"Yes, ok dear." Anne said, taking another sip. As Mavis left the room Anne took another sip and then began singing *"See Saw Margery Daw…"*

As she did Arthur's voice came back. This time it sounded angry. "Why did you tell her that?"

Anne placed her cup down. "Shouldn't I have told her?"

"No Ma. I told you, this is our secret. Now I don't know if you should see me..." Arthur's voice said, this time sounding sad.

"Please Arthur. Don't do that, I promise I'll not tell anyone again." Anne pleaded.

"Ok, Ma. I'll see you later." Arthur's voice said.

Anne smiled to herself. "Thank you, son."

After around fifteen minutes, and as she finished her tea Mavis came back into the bedroom and picked up her empty cup. "Come on Anne. Get yourself dressed."

"I'll be down soon." Anne replied.

"Is Arthur still talking to you?" Mavis asked, as she turned to leave.

Anne smiled. "No, it was just a dream."

A few minutes later Anne made her way downstairs. When she walked into the kitchen, she saw Mavis standing by the open door, shouting for her.

"Yes dear?" Anne answered softly.

Mavis spun around, pointing to the table and the wet pots. "Did you do this Anne?"

Anne moved her gaze over to the table. Then she

looked back to Mavis. "You shouldn't put wet pots on the table dear. You'll ruin the varnish. Let's get them in the sink."

"Did you move the pots Anne?" Mavis snapped.

Anne picked up a glass form the table. "Yes, dear. I'm putting them in the sink for you."

"No, before that. Did you take them out of the sink and put them on the table?" Mavis asked. Her tone becoming more frustration than reasonable.

"When, dear?" Anne asked, placing the glass in the sink.

"A few minutes ago."

"I've just come down the stairs. What a silly thing to ask." Anne replied.

A stiff breeze blew in again accompanied by a splattering of rain. Anne moved over to the door. "We should close that door." She said, pushing it shut.

"I did close the door. And I put the pots in the sink. Then I went to check on the living room and when I came back…"

Anne cut across her. "Oh, don't worry Mavis, it's just the boys having fun, that's all."

"Come on let's get you settled in the living room. See what's on the TV, shall we?" Mavis said.

Anne smiled and allowed Mavis to guide her

through the room. She settled into her chair, and Mavis pulled her blanket across her knees. Then, she switched on the TV. "There you go, the sport is on. I'll bring you in the lovely cup of tea when I'm ahead of the work." Mavis said, tucking the blanket corners in.

"Yes. We'll watch this." Anne replied.

"I haven't time to watch it with you, but I'll bring you a cup of tea and a slice of toast."

Anne looked up to her. "Oh, silly. I meant me and Arthur."

Anne heard Mavis leave the room. Turning her attention back to the TV, she watched as the horses lined up at Cheltenham.

II

8 pm.

Outside it was dark. A Mist had once again encroached from the east coast enveloping the farm and the shallow valley it sat in, in a dank iridescent cloud. The cold and damp it brought was the kind of damp which seemed to penetrate into your bones and would take hours in front of the fire to force out. Inside the farmhouse, dinner was over.

The kitchen now sat in darkness. The washed dinner pots dried on the draining board and only the light of the fire and the glow of the range provided any resistance to the blackness inside the room. In the living room, George, Mavis, and Thomas sat watching, *The Val Doonican Show*. The fire again, keeping the cold outside.

***

Upstairs Anne was in bed. The small table light kept the bedroom illuminated enough to navigate. Anne slept in a shallow sleep. Her exhaustion came quickly towards the end of any day and usually just after dinner. Tonight, it had been around six o'clock. As she breathed slowly and almost silently, a shadow materialised by the side of her bed. Anne instinctively woke, aware of something but not sure what. She struggled to focus in the dim light. "Thomas?" She said through a sleepy croaking voice.

"Ma, it's me, it's Arthur." The soft voice of what Anne believed to be Arthur whispered in reply. The soft shape beside her bed swirled and twisted.

Anne began to fully wake, excited that her son was here. "Arthur, you came back, just like you said." She moved to where she thought she could see him. Leaning out of the bed, she put out her hand, but she felt no resistance as her hand moved through the dark room. "Arthur?" She asked.

"Follow me, Ma." Arthur's voice said.

"Where?" Anne asked.

"Do you want to see me, or should I leave?" Arthur's voice snapped a little.

"No, please don't go Arthur. I'll come to you. Where are you?" Anne pleaded.

"Follow my voice. But don't let the others see you or know. If you do, I'll leave, and I won't come back." Arthur's voice said.

Anne hastily pulled on her dressing gown and stepped as quietly as she could. She moved down the stairs and past the semi-closed living room door. Inside she could hear the TV playing, and the muffled chattering of her family. "Where are you?" Anne whispered as she entered the kitchen,

In the far corner she saw the shadow waft through the closed door. The whisper came in a soft wave. "Outside."

Anne pulled her gown together and then made her way across the dark kitchen to the door. Silently, she turned the key and pulled the door open. Stepping outside into the mist, she pulled it shut.

***

Inside the living room Mavis cocked her head. She turned towards the door. "Did you hear something?"

"Nope." Thomas answered.

George, still watching the TV simply shook his head. Mavis put down the magazine she was reading. "It'll just be the wind." George said.

"Aye, you're probably right." Mavis said, picking up her magazine.

***

In the mist Anne continued to follow the voice. "Over here, Ma," It said softly, with a childlike tone. Anne walked through the farmyard and past the barn. Under her bare feet, the thick muck of the yard squelched between her toes. Anne wiped her face clear of the water droplets which now gathered on her. The ambient light of the moon allowed her to make her way slowly. The terrain changed as she left the yard. Gone was the soft muck carpet of the yard. Now, she was walking on stone. Focused on following the voice, she ignored the pain this new ground brought. Eventually, she reached the gate which led to the woodland. She stopped. "Arthur?" She asked.

"This way, Ma." The voice replied.

Anne pushed open the gate and stepped into the thick woodland.

***

In the living room Thomas was falling asleep in front of the fire. Mavis had finished flicking through her magazine while George was waiting for the Saturday Thriller to start on BBC 1. Mavis sighed, "Fancy a cuppa?" She asked and continued. "I'll check on Anne, while I'm up."

George thought for a second. "Maybe in ten minutes, love." He answered.

Mavis pulled another magazine out of the wire-curved stand next to the settee, "Ok, I'll check on her then."

***

Outside, in the dark woodland, Anne reached an open piece of land nestled in between the trees and next to a rutted track. She stopped. When she did, she could immediately feel the cold which had penetrated her since leaving the house. She shivered rapidly pulling her hands up and down her arms. "Arthur?" She asked. There was only silence. "Arthur?" She asked again. Again, no response came. Anne suddenly realised she wasn't sure where she was, or how to get home. She had never wondered into the woodland – there had been no point. As a young mother, she was too busy running the house and seeing to children. After the fire, she lost interest in everything. She felt a panic rise inside her as well as the cold mist which now seemed to penetrate every pour of her skin. Panicking, she turned around on the spot. "Help!" She shouted. Then she heard a voice. But this wasn't Arthur's voice.

***

After about another half hour Mavis asked George again. "Cuppa?"

George looked over to Thomas who was now snoring deeply. "Aye, I will now."

Mavis stood and made her way to the kitchen. She filled the kettle with water and then placed it over the range. While the kettle warmed, she went upstairs to check on Anne. When she stepped inside the bedroom, she found it empty. Mavis turned and headed for the bathroom. Knocking gently on the door, she called for Anne. When no response came, she pushed the door open. The bathroom was empty. That feeling of dread she'd felt earlier that day when she thought Anne had wondered out of the house came back. She ran down the stairs and into the living room. "George, Thomas!" She shouted.

"What the hell is it?" George snapped.

Thomas came around from his deep slumber. "What the bloody hell is going on?"

"It's Anne. She's not in the house!" Mavis said. Her panic was evident.

***

Anne moved backward, away from the direction she felt the voice came from. It came again. "Hello Anne." She now recognised the voice instantly as it changed from the voice she'd heard throughout the day – believing it to be Arthur's - into one she would never forget. It was Jack's.

"What do you want Jack?" Anne shouted. The tone of her voice gave away her fear.

"I want you all to suffer. You put my son in that fuckin' home and they killed him." Jack's voice shouted at her. As it did, a wind picked up. The woodland debris began swirling around her.

***

Mavis stayed home in case Anne returned. Thomas and George hurriedly got dressed and rushed out into the damp night. Switching on their torches they began to scan the farmyard first. The beams shone left and right like the beams of a warships search light. When they couldn't find her here, they split up. George ran up the track which led to the main road while Thomas looked around the back of the outbuildings and inside the barn. The door to the bunk was locked. Thomas felt on top of the cupboard, the key was still there. He sighed. *At least she hadn't gone in there.* He reassured himself. As he came out, he came across George. "Any joy?" He asked, his heart thumping through his chest.

"No, Da." He replied, sniffing heavily.

Thomas became upset, he was out of ideas. George could see how his father was feeling. "We'll find her, Da. Let's check further out." George comforted him.

"Where?" Thomas asked.

"Let's go around back." George said, pointing his torch in the direction of the woodland.

"She wouldn't have gone this way George." Thomas argued.

George caught something in the beam of his torch as he pointed where he thought they should go. "What's that?" He knelt down. In the beam of the light, he could make out her footsteps in the thick muck. "This way Da." George and Thomas began to follow the footsteps silently. They eventually reached the gate to the woodland - it was open. "Bloody hell, I hope she hasn't gone in there." Thomas whispered. They shone their torches ahead. In the darkness of the woodland the light penetrated only a few feet in front of them. Where trees and other natural obstructions prevented the light from going any further dark shadows gave the monsters of their imagination a place for ambush. Thomas pushed through the darkness, "Anne! Anne!"

***

Anne, now shivering violently with the cold and fear, began to sob. "Leave me alone, you've done enough. Now leave me…"

Within the tornado of detritus which now engulfed her an apparition began to appear. Anne instantly recognised it. "No, no, no" She pleaded.

"Do you know what your husband and son did with my boy's remains?" Jack's apparition asked.

Through her tears Anne replied. "Nothing, the hospital buried him."

The laugh that followed was pure evil. "Look down Anne."

Anne did as she was told. The tornado began to strip away the earth beneath her. The crate became visible and Anne realised with horror what this was. "No!" She shouted, but the tornado continued. As the air continued to swirl violently around her, a piece of crate tore off revealing Arthur's decomposing face. Anne could see the burns he'd suffered even in his decaying state. Anne's mind and body released the feelings of guilt and anxiety she'd carried for the last thirteen years. Her screams were audible even over the sound of the tornado which continued to twist around only her. Then her heart stopped, and Anne fell to the ground. As she did, the apparition and tornado vanished. The detritus which had been swept up now fluttered down around her. Anne fell on top of Arthur's crate. Her last thoughts were of how she'd wronged him.

III

9.30 pm.

Inside the workshop the rope around the tarp untwisted and fell to the ground followed by the tarp. Then the grandfather clock chimed. Inside the kitchen Mavis paced up and down waiting for Anne or at least for news from George and Thomas. Up the stairs she heard a knock. Her heart lifted. She was sure it was Anne – who else could it be? She ran up the narrow staircase and into their bedroom. "Anne?" She shouted ahead of herself. As she entered the bedroom it was empty. Another bump came, this time in the bathroom. Mavis made her way quickly in. The room was empty. Another bump – it came from her bedroom. This was the only room that was left. Mavis moved cautiously into the room and flicked on the light. In the corner a dark shape stood motionless. Mavis stood, unsure of what it was she was looking at. She moved further in, slowly. Lifting a pillow from the bed while staring at this unmoving shadow which seemed to be of full form, she threw the pillow at it. The pillow went through the apparition and hit the wall. As it did, the apparition moved with speed she didn't believe towards her. Before she could react, it shrouded her. Mavis screamed and waved her arms, punching out at anything, yet hitting nothing. Then the voice came. An otherworldly voice, and in it Mavis could hear the menace and evil. "Move me… move me…" It repeated over and over. Mavis ran from the room and down the stairs. In the kitchen, she panicked. She had no idea where to go or what to do. The voice came again, "Move me…move me…."

Mavis yelled. "I don't know what you mean."

"Move me… move me…" The apparition appeared in the doorway.

Mavis felt her bladder empty as she knelt by the kitchen table, her tears running freely. As her mouth curled, she pleaded through her crying "I don't know what you mean."

Thomas pushed ahead of George through the woodland. After what seemed like hours, and with his lungs bursting and his legs buckling, Thomas came upon Anne's body. George heard the cries of anguish from his father before he reached him. When he did Thomas was cradling his dead mother. Thomas's light shone where it had landed, straight into the open crate of Arthur. George fell to his knees and held onto both his parents.

Thomas laid Anne carefully back down, but to the side of where he'd found her. Then he covered over Arthur's face with lose dirt.

"She found him George." Thomas said, wiping away the tears. "She found him, and it killed her. The shock…"

George took hold of his father's arm and pulled him to his feet. "Come on Da, we need to go get the truck. We can't carry her back."

"I can't leave her George." Thomas said.

"Da, you can't stay here, it's freezing cold. We'll come straight back."

Thomas agreed reluctantly. Picking up their torches, they made their way back out of the woodland, leaving Anne where she lay.

When George and Thomas got back to the farmhouse, they entered to let Mavis know what had happened to Anne. Inside they found Mavis hiding under the kitchen table – sobbing. George rushed over to her, "What is it?"

Mavis looked up at George. Upon seeing him, she rushed from under the table and hugged him. "I think Arthur was here."

George pulled back a little. "What do you mean Arthur was here?"

"I heard his voice and saw… something." Mavis said, through her distress.

"What did he say?" Thomas said, calmly.

"He said the same thing over again. He just said, *move me.*"

George turned to Thomas. "We should move him, Da. Especially after…" He stopped.

"What is it?" Mavis asked, drying her eyes.

"We found Ma. She was on Arthur's grave."
George said.

Mavis looked past them. "Where is she, is she
okay?"

Thomas took a breath, "She's dead Mavis. She died
on his grave. She found him."

Mavis sank into a chair and began to cry. "We need
to go move her, love." George said, placing a
loving hand on her.

Mavis nodded. "It's fine. Please don't be too long."

"Put the kettle on. By the time you've made a brew,
we'll be back." George said.

George and Thomas made their way to the
workshop. When they pulled open the double
doors, they each noticed the grandfather clock. In
his grief-stricken anger, Thomas picked up a
pickaxe and repeatedly brought it down on the
clock. With Thomas exhausted and the clock laying
in a smashed pile, Thomas dropped the axe and
climbed into the truck. "Let's go." He said.

11 pm.

The Land Rover was parked back in the workshop. In the back wrapped up as respectfully as they could, lay Anne. They would take her body to the doctor's first thing tomorrow. With a cup of tea in each of their hands, Mavis, George, and Thomas sat at the kitchen table in silence. Still in a state of shock at each of their own experiences during that day, they were individually pleased that this day was almost at an end and they could put it out of its misery. As George took a deep sip of tea, he turned to Mavis.

"When I passed the house this morning, the door was wide open. It were raining hard, were you looking for summat?"

Mavis looked to George. "No, I came down to find it open, twice. I thought it was…" She paused. "I thought it was Anne." But she was upstairs."

"Did tha see anything else?" Thomas asked.

"The pots. I put them in the sink after you'd left, but when I came down, they were back on the table. Why?"

Thomas looked between them. "When I went into the bunk earlier, I was going to rip the place down." He stopped.

"Go on, Da" George said.

"But that bloody spinning top started up again. What the hell is going on? What do we do to bring an end to all this?" Thomas asked.

Mavis thought for a moment. "This is what we do. We move Arthur's body away from the house. He needs to be entombed, somewhere. We stay away from that damned bunk house. We don't go in it – ever. And whatever happens to us financially. We never-ever sell the Halt. Let's hope that over time, it's forgotten about."

George looked to Thomas. Then they both looked towards Mavis and nodded their agreement.

Epilogue.

Shep had been buried in a corner of the top field where he'd worked as a sheep dog before Arthur had attacked him. This field – Thomas always said – was Shep's favourite place on the farm. From here you could see down into the distant yard and across to the house, and east, right across the shallow valley, almost to the coast. In the summer it was a sun trap where the dog would bask, and in the winter the wall gave protection against the worst of the wind, rain, and snow. Thomas knew Shep would be happy here and just to make sure, Thomas constructed a small kennel with the left-over stones. *"That'll do him nicely."* Thomas had said, placing the last stone.

After that night, George and Thomas had moved Arthur's body. They wouldn't tell anyone, including Mavis where it was. All they would say was that *"It was sealed up for good."* They were sure no one would ever come across it again. Thomas himself had died peacefully at home two years following that day in October 1967. He'd often said that Anne visited him and that she had finally found peace. On his death bed he'd confided in George that Arthur was the son of Jack Bright. It was to be a secret which he must now carry on. Before, and following Thomas's death, they had received offers for the Halt but both Thomas and George had agreed never to sell it. The villages never spoke of it, and it seemed it had faded away into local folk law. A tale some would tell to frighten themselves around a campfire. George, for the most part kept himself confined to the farm. The events he'd witnessed had changed him. Mavis had been the constant in his life. On more than one occasion, when he was sure he was alone, George had confessed to himself that she had saved his life more than once.

July 2015.

On one particularly hot summer afternoon George was in the kitchen with Mavis. The old Land Rover Thomas had bought new, was parked outside. Sat between his legs was his faithful sheepdog. As he took a sip from the old beaten up green tin mug, the phone rang. "Bloody hell! Who could this be?" George said, as he struggled to lift himself from his seat.

Mavis watched as he took the call. "Aye, what of it. No, it's not. I don't care how much - I'm not interested." George put down the receiver. He turned to Mavis

"Who was that?" She asked.

George sat back in the old seat. Sighing as he did with the pain. "One of those *yuppie types* called himself, Paul Sullivan. Says he wants to buy the Halt. Said he'd pay anything. I told him we're not interested."

Mavis thought for a second. "George, it's been quiet now for years, and we need the money…"

THE END.

Afterword.

Written by Steven Ellington.

Those who have read the first book to this prequel entitled Thirstonfield Halt may recall I wrote a foreword and epilogue exploring a number of important spiritual subjects relevant to the subject matter within the storyline. In the foreword I explained the fundamental difference between a ghost, which is nothing more than an apparition, and a spirit, the continued living consciousness of an individual that has departed the physical body. In the epilogue I explored the concept of Universal Energy, the building block of all that exists and the very foundation on which all spiritual teachings are based. In this book due to the subject matter covered within the events of the story line I wanted to concentrate on two particularly important spiritual subjects. The first is "Psychic Attack" and the second is "Possession".

A "Psychic Attack" happens when a spirit of an immoral nature deliberately attacks the individual by concentrating purely on the individuals negative character imperfections. Whether the negative character imperfections are fear, greed, anger, impatience, jealously, lust, control, or low self-esteem to name just a few, such spirits are very capable of first recognising and then manipulating the individual's negative flaws within their character.

The victim then reveals these intensified negative character imperfections through their personality finding it almost impossible to control or contain them. Although not "Possession", the intrusion of "Psychic Attack" can still have a dramatic detrimental effect on the lives of everyday normal people. The symptoms of "Psychic Attack" vary, however victims usually become generally despondent and disheartened and begin to view life from a very negative and pessimistic perspective. Victims feel their whole approach and attitude to life becomes subdued without a logical understanding as to why, creating emotional instability as the confused victim tries in vain to understand exactly what is happening.

Anyone is prone to "Psychic Attack" but generally "Psychic Attack" only effects those who have a highly sensitive nature, those who are intuitive, and those who are either consciously or naturally evolving in a spiritual sense. This is because once you broaden your horizons beyond the conventional constraints of the five physical senses, you naturally expand the conscious levels and are therefore receptive to the higher spiritual realms of the universe. Those however who have narrow or closed minds are firmly grounded within the dimension of sold matter and therefore only ever experience what the five physical senses relay, denying themselves the humbling experience of universal connection as well as inadvertently protecting themselves from "Psychic Attack".

Once again, this phenomenon highlights the importance of protection, such protection however in the event of personal spiritual development can only be gained once you develop responsibly in a spiritual development class supervised by an experienced spiritualist medium. Not only will you learn how to protect yourself using very effective visualisation techniques, protective prayers and mantras, you will also rightfully earn the commanding protection of highly evolved spirits who reside in the eternal Kingdom of God. Self-protection therefore is a vitally important teaching and practice, offering ongoing protection from the contact and influence of negative ill-natured spirits that reside in the lower darker spirit dimensions.

But however negative, dark or malevolent a spirit may be, the one thing they all have in common is the absolute dread and fear of high benevolent energy vibrations that represent the will, ways and light of God. If you therefore act positively in all you think say and do, respect the world in which you live, express heartfelt love and compassion unconditionally, you are representing the very energies of God. You will consequently not attract nor be affected by such controlling negative spirits, you will simply appear far too strong, appear far too powerful, and they will move on seeking weaker more vulnerable less protected individuals.

In very serious cases which are thankfully exceedingly rare, evil demonic spirits have been known too forcefully violate a person's body, this is known commonly as "Possession".
The symptoms of "Possession" are many and varied and generally happen to those who have a

broad negative outlook on life, those who lack faith inner strength and are weak minded. Those who practice satanic rituals and worship demonic spirit's and mercilessly the young, including children and in particularly those who are experiencing adolescent years.

During "Possession" victims can alter physically, especially in the facial area, they may suffer internal pain, experience fainting spells, fits, or convulsions as well as severe vomiting. The victim from time to time will experience a noticeable change in the vocal cords which may become unusually deep and gruff, including the use of foul abusive language. The fear of religious symbols and sacred artefact's is also quite common. The "Possessed" normally experience the symptoms of a severe panic attack when confronted by anything representing the higher realms of God, especially positive benevolent energy such as love and compassion.

Those individuals who are spiritually evolved will also pose a threat, their high energy vibrations causing the victims great discomfort and anxiety. An evil demonic spirit will show no mercy to those who it possesses, their body is simply a tool it chooses to control and use in order to spread malicious negative intent. Very often the victim feels nothing unusual and will find it almost impossible to differentiate between their own reality and the influence of the evil demonic entity. Those individuals with whom the victim is closely associated however will see a disturbing transformation, experiencing alarming changes in personality and behaviour, as well as their woeful troubled attitude too life in general. The two most common cures for "Possession" are repeated exorcisms and visits to holy sites or shrines, in time this will help eventually dislodge the evil demonic entity from the body. The difficulty however in removing such demon spirits and the key to a successful exorcism is making the victim aware that their current disposition no way reflects their true personality or normal manner. As well as making the victim aware that the positive benevolent energies of God, such as love, peace and joy are very much absent from their current discontented existence.

The word "Exorcism" is from the Greek word "Exorkismos" meaning "binding by oath" and is a series of prayers statements gestures and appeals during which an experienced priest would ask God to free a possessed victim from a demonic spirit. Commands are also used in the name of the Father, Son and Holy Ghost with the assistance of the cross amulets and holy water. During an exorcism, the priest works through a number of key stages in which firstly the priest must become aware of the demonic spirit's presence as well as demon's identity. The priest then entices and encourages the demon to speak through their victim before the priest locks into battle with the demon attempting to dominate the proceedings in the name of God. Finally, during the expulsion stage, the demonic spirit leaves the victim in the supreme triumph of God, often leaving the priest exhausted and the victim with no or little memory of exactly what has happened.

Whilst the priest is locked in battle with the dark demon spirit during the exorcism to expel it from the victim's body, at the same time the victim is also locked in battle fighting for the self-acknowledgement that something very wrong and evil is present within them. This self-acknowledgement is vital, because it is only through this acceptance by the victim that the evil demonic spirit is present within that it begins to gradually dislodge from the body. Once this seed is planted and begins to take root in the mind of the victim, along with the holy commands of the priest in the name of God, only then does the fight back truly begin. Because only then does the evil demonic spirit begin to feel rejection, and rejection by the victim as well as by the priest in the name of the Father, Son and Holy Ghost is the key to a successful exorcism.

Once the demonic spirit has left the formally possessed victim, the physiological void must be filled as quickly as possible with the divine benevolent energies of God. Once again with the help of sacred prayers and appropriate scripture readings asking for the protection of God's intense light. It is also vital the victim mindfully encompass as soon as possible the positive energies of God in all they think say and do. Only then will the evil demonic spirit be cast from the body and banished forever.

A word of warning however, throughout the exorcism process evil demonic spirits will fight back at every conceivable moment, and upon leaving the victim's body, will almost certainly strike out in one last act of defiance against the authority of God. This normally involves the throwing of an inanimate object, the intention to injure those in the vicinity representing the higher realms of God. Although the forced violation of the body or "Possession" is thankfully rare, "Psychic Attack" the detrimental influence of a negative spirit on the personality of an unwary individual surprisingly, is not so rare. "Psychic Attack" and "Possession" are both the direct assault on individuals by negative and sometimes demonic spirits. Those who have strayed from God or have no trust, faith or belief in the universal governance of God are without doubt most at risk from the harmful influence of dark negative spirits.

Believe it or not in some cases dark negative spirits can be lured and invited by those who believe to be playing nothing more than an innocent fun party game.
I have over the years investigated a number of cases where normal people's lives have been seriously disturbed and sometimes violently disrupted because they have played a certain game in complete innocence, that so-called game is called an "Ouija Board". So, after helping numerous people over the years get their lives back to some normality after experiencing very dark malevolent spirit activity in their homes immediately after dabbling with an "Ouija Board" let me give you some very important information and advice concerning this wrongly perceived amusing pastime.

The name "Ouija" comes from the French and German meanings for "Yes", "Oui and Ja", the word "yes" of course denoting the desired response when using the board to confirm the presence of a spirit. Originating from ancient China since the time of Confucius around 500 BC, it was also used around the same time by the Greek mathematician Pythagoras at his extraordinary school of 300 acolytes in Croton, southern Italy. There are many types of "Ouija Boards" made from many different types of materials. The board design is generally either circular or rectangular and consists of the letters of the alphabet, the numbers "1" to "9" and the words "Yes" and "No" written around its circumference. The user or users of the board then lightly touch the pointer commonly called the "Planchette" a French word meaning "Little Plank" a small piece of rigid material such as wood or plastic with a pencil or pen held secure through its centre, and guided by spirit the pointer moves around the board spelling names words and answering questions with a "Yes" or "No".

The "Ouija Board" was initially used by the Victorians as a parlour game before becoming extremely popular in the sixties once Parker Brothers of America released it as a board game in 1966, selling two million of them the following year, outselling the popular board game Monopoly. In more recent times the "Ouija Board" has being generally withdrawn from retail outlets because of the stigma attached to its purpose, and the risk posed to the unsuspecting users, which after all is to conjure up spirit activity and attempt spirit communication. The problem with "Ouija Boards" is the users have little control as too what spirit manifests and little or no protection once a spirit appears. Used extensively as entertainment, a game it certainly is not, if a séance is to be attempted using an "Ouija Board", it is absolutely vital there is an experienced spiritualist medium present at all times in order to control the proceedings and protect all those present. Over the years many people have suffered numerous psychological problems caused by negative and malevolent spirits tormenting the minds of naive individuals attempting séances, trying a little unorthodox amusing entertainment.

Genuine psychic ability like all gifts can be used in a positive way or a negative way. If you have such psychic abilities you must never try to harness powers, other than your own inner gift, which must be used for positive use only. Never try to summon a spirit with the use of candles or with such devices as "Ouija Boards" and never try to hold a séance. Remember talking out loud in a gentle and loving way to a departed much-loved relative is quite different than trying to invoke a spirit by way of demonstrating your own psychic ability either positively or negatively. Mediumship is not a game; it is a very responsible practice and should only be attempted in a controlled situation with the assistance of an experienced spiritualist medium at all times.

I have known developing self-taught mediums driven to the point of insanity thinking they can control and manipulate spirits, you simply cannot, you may inadvertently summon a spirit in which you have no control or protection. So, if you want a simple golden rule regarding the use of "Ouija Boards" here it is, "Leave well alone".

Steven Ellington.

Spiritualist Medium.

Other titles available:

M.E. Ellington.

The Martialis Incident
Devolution of a Species
Tomorrow's Flight (Coming 2020)
Thirstonfield Halt – A Haunting Beyond Time
(Coming 2020)

Steven Ellington.

Thirstonfield Halt – A Haunting Beyond Time
(Coming 2020)
Developing Your Spiritual Potential